BORROWED TIME

BOOK 2 - MISSING

Infinity Books

DÄNNA WILBERG

For the children

ACKNOWLEDGMENTS

Borrowed Time 2 – Missing is based on facts, half-truths, and mostly fiction. When I began writing the book, I was on a Mediterranean cruise. I knew where I was going with the story, but something was missing. Literally! That's when the universe handed me a gem. The real-life Lewis Howard and his wife were seated at our dinner table. When Lewis began to tell me about his near-death experience, I knew the story was meant to be written, and he was the missing element I was looking for. And although I took some liberty with his account of what happened to him, the majority of what I wrote is true. Thank you, Lewis Howard, you are forever etched in my heart.

Another aspect of this book that is true to my heart is the subject matter. Human trafficking is *real*. I witnessed first hand the seduction of young girls near the train station in Cologne, Germany. My experience was not an isolated incident—it happens in your backyard, and all over the world. I would like to express my gratitude to my traveling partner, Beatrice Gregory, for being my sounding board and voice of reason when the incident broke my heart.

My gratitude to undercover agent Andrew (who remains anonymous), not only for answering my questions about human trafficking in Sacramento, California, one of the hottest trafficking spots in the United States, but for risking his life every day to eradicate crime where he can, and for rescues he has performed with his team. I also want to thank the fabulous author, Robin Burcell, for agreeing to be a character in my book. I am grateful to my friends, Noreen and Linda, who supply me with information to investigate, and psychic friend, Linda Schooler, for listening to me ramble and for her unwavering support.

Before I thank my writing community, I would like to thank my readers. Your support, reviews, feedback, and compliments have meant the world to me. *I write for you.* Special thanks to Nancy St. Germain for waiting patiently for this release!

To my critique group, Tarra, Michele, Linda, June, Cathy, Cheri, your support and suggestions have been more valuable than you know. To the El Dorado Writers Guild, thank you for your excellent feedback. I thrive on your expertise.

I am truly grateful to my talented cover artist, Karen Ann Phillips. You rock girl! To Tarra Thomas, my editor and formatter, thank you for putting up with my last-minute changes and all my "was's." I am also grateful to my talented author friend, Terry Shepherd, for whipping up extraordinary trailers and promos for my books at the drop of a hat. You kill it, my friend. I am blessed to have all of you, wonderful people in my life!

As always, I'd like to thank my family for their love and support. They are my joy, and the fuel that keeps me going. Special thanks to my sister, Kathy Partipilo, for being my tough and loving critic.

Lastly, I'd like to thank my late Mother for encouraging me to write and for being *my* angel.

FEAR

"I still get frightened." Suzanne Cash folded her hands in her lap. "You know—when the visions start." She'd never imagined herself in therapy, although, it wasn't as if her life hadn't warranted a little help. Her marriage was the perfect example of dysfunction...but she wasn't there to fix what was permanently broken. She was there to understand what happened to her, and learn to cope. She was tired of being afraid.

Manila folder and pen in hand, therapist Grace Simms sat forward, closing the gap between them. "You've been through a lot. One can only imagine—" she said, her tone gentle. "You were shot, left for dead, kidnapped, assaulted, drugged...I mean, seriously, Suzanne—how could you *not* be affected by what has happened to you?" Grace exhaled. "The mind has limits. Post-traumatic stress syndrome is the result of a traumatic experience. You can say it's our bodies auto-response to mental injury."

"Are you saying PTSD is causing my visions?"

"I don't know how you were able to communicate with your dead fiancé, or how you were able to lead police to a serial killer—all I can do is offer you an explanation of how your mind has responded to your experience." Grace leaned back, opening the space, allowing Suzanne to process her assessment. "How are you sleeping?"

"I'm having lucid dreams. They're eerie like the visions, but not as gruesome. Feels like the calm before the storm." Suzanne's gaze dropped to her lap. "Like something is about to happen. I just don't–" Her eyes lifted to meet Grace's. "There's a girl…"

"A girl? Can you tell me about her?"

"I wish I could. The word "missing" keeps popping up in my head like bread in a toaster." She pulled on a loose tendril of chestnut hair and twisted it around her finger. "But what does it mean? Am I *missing* something? Is the girl *missing*? Detective Metzger hasn't mentioned anything to me–I don't know what to think."

"I'm sure you'll figure it out in due time." Grace jotted a few words on her pad. "How are things going with Metzger?"

"He's well."

"Are you still seeing each other?"

"Not really–I mean, we talk. I'm not ready."

"You're following your gut–good for you. It's easy to jump into a relationship for the wrong reasons."

"I'd be lucky to have a man like Sam in my life…" She paused; her lips slid into an upward curve. "…when it's time."

"Speaking of time, this is a good place for us to stop." Grace put her pen aside, closed the manilla folder, and rose. "Would you like to make another appointment?"

"I'll call you. I appreciate your advice, Grace, but right now I'm caught between regaining my sanity and otherworldly stuff."

"I can help with your sanity," she placed a hand on Suzanne's shoulder, guiding her to the door. "Not so sure about the psychic experiences, but that doesn't mean I can't listen."

Suzanne smiled. "I have a friend to help with the psychic stuff, but she too has her limits."

Grace returned the smile. "I'm here if you need me."

That night, Suzanne teetered on the edge of sleep in her 1940s Victorian style house. Beside her bed, a clock ticked, a floorboard creaked, a cool breeze came through an open window. Downstairs, directly below her bedroom, water shushed through copper pipes; the refrigerator hummed; ice plunked into a plastic container. Outside, quail babbled in the shrubs, owls hooted in the trees, a train whistle wailed a lonely cry.

One sound no longer heard in the nightly chorus was Ben's snoring. Admittedly, she didn't miss him, or his snoring...their divorce was almost final. *Hallelujah.*

She hugged herself, shielding her heart. Her thoughts shifted to Sam, the man who cared enough to walk through hell for her. The man whose touch made her shiver. The man she wished she could commit to.

Maybe one day. That's all she could offer. At this stage in her life, she had become a student. Her quest to understand what happened to her the night she was shot, thrown into a pool, and left to die, weighed heavy on her mind. Jack, her first love, had held her head above water, saved her life...but few believed her. *Who could blame them?* Jack had died in Iraq fifteen years prior. The only person to provide answers about her experience was psychic, Linda Schooler.

Left with a superpower she didn't want did little for Suzanne's temperament. Anger, fear, heartbreak consumed her like a burning house. *How do they do it, the psychics of the world? How do they shut off the barrage of injustices bombarding their souls without warning?* And then there was the million-dollar question: *How long will this go on?* Perhaps Grace Simms was right. Perhaps she should focus on getting mentally healthy before tackling the unknown. *But how?*

She sank into a deep sleep.

In her dream, she walked down a dark, empty street, her surroundings unfamiliar. Her breath quickened.

Fear gripped her hard. She ducked into an alcove of a small shop, closed due to the late hour, and waited.

Across the street, a door opened. Out came a stunning young woman dressed in a charcoal wool mini, the kind leggy girls wore with ease. Thick burgundy locks, tipped in caramel and gold escaped her red beret. Like molten lava, her hair sluiced down the back of her red leather battle jacket, and burst into flames under the streetlamp. Black boots clicked on cobblestones as she disappeared into the night.

Suzanne noted the door from which the woman came; bottle green, trimmed in ornate swirls. A brass number "6" divided two beveled glass panes. She spied the woman now in the distance. *What does it all mean?* Her answer came soon enough when a man stepped out from the shadows. He too had his eyes on the prize.

Suddenly, a gust of wind disrupted Suzanne's dream state. She sucked air into her lungs, and pulled the covers tight around her shivering body. Light sneaked between lids still sticky with sleep. 6 a.m.? How could that be? It was just–*dark*.

She felt stiff.

She closed her eyes, letting her fatigue pull her down. This time there was no girl. No man. No dream. Just sleep.

～

FUN

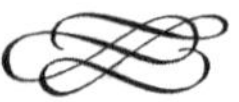

Audra Metzger boarded a plane to Vienna.

Day one of her three-week holiday before stepping into the role of Au Pair to Marie-Élise and Alan-Pierre Duveaux, the children of prominent art dealers. The twenty-five-year-old had left Munich five years prior to pursue her love of the arts. Budapest proved to be a great place to lose oneself in a gypsy nouveau-riche lifestyle, one she felt born to live. Her long, flowing tresses now shocked with chunks of burgundy, crimson, and caramel reflected her need to feel rebellious. Imagining her stoic parent's reaction to her new look brought her joy. She knew they'd hate it, but would refrain from commenting. They'd save their commentary for Sam.

She and her brother Samson hadn't communicated in months. Good ol' Sam. No matter what he did, or didn't do, he'd always remain the golden child. He chose a different path. So be it. She denied missing him terribly by filling the void with friends, school, and the occasional "mistake." She was older now, wiser. It was *her* time to shine.

Audra managed a small suitcase through the bustle of excited travelers and navigated her way to the S-Bahn platform. The S-7 train, due to arrive in twelve minutes, would take her to LandstraBe where she would get on U-Bahn 3 and head for Karlsplatz.

Nearby, a handsome man looked her way with interest. When he suddenly retreated, she summoned his sapphire gaze to return, and he responded. She wondered his age. *Older?* Hard to tell, his shoulder length hair and gemstone eyes reminded her of a fallen angel. *Or a rock star.*

When the train arrived, she lost sight of the handsome man. So, she thought.

"Is this seat taken?"

The intensity of his stare almost made her giggle. "You're American?"

"Yes, I am." He settled in the seat beside her.

"My brother lives in California," she said, shyly.

"How nice. I know California well. Where does your brother live? We may know—"

"You wouldn't know my brother. Unless you broke the law, or something."

"I see. No chance, then. Do you live there as well?"

"Me? No, I'm from Munich. My brother watched "Dirty Harry" one too many times."

"Who?"

"Exactly. Not someone I care to talk about."

"What brings you to Vienna?"

"Holiday—I rented a flat in the museum district."

His eyes brightened. "Me too. I am anxious to see the Klimt exhibit at the Belvedere Palace."

"I'm sure you'll enjoy the display." Suddenly, she found herself blushing, sitting next to this handsome man who shared her appreciation for art.

"I'd enjoy it more if you would accompany me," he said. "Is that possible?"

The train came to a stop. She rose and picked up her small valise. She tilted her head and smiled. "We can meet at the south gate tomorrow, say one o'clock?"

"I'll be there!"

Audra hurried off the train. Before the doors closed behind her, she turned to wave and say, *"Auf Wiedersehen,"* but the man was gone.

She descended the station's dank stairwell to make her connection to the purple line. She planned to meet Britta, an old classmate, at the Karlspaltz Café. She moved gingerly in dainty heels, avoiding the hand rail. The air reeked of stale cigarette smoke and cheap cologne. She could've opted for a clean, well-lit station, but this one provided the perfect route. The further down she went, the more indistinguishable sounds became. She didn't hear the footfall tracking her course.

When she reached the U-2 platform for the purple line to Karlsplatz, she checked the schedule board. A nine-minute wait. *Perfect.* Enough time to text Bruno, her flat-mate in Budapest. Bruno worried if she didn't check in. Sometimes she wondered if his concern was a guise for knowing where she was at all times. She knew Bruno liked to feed his sexual appetite while she was away. They had an understanding, his small hips did not belong in her jeans, skirts, dresses or panties! His love interests and playmates were not allowed on her pull-out sofa, and he was to empty the trash before she arrived home. She dearly loved Bruno, but steered clear of his wild escapades and wouldn't tolerate remnants from one of his romps.

Her fingers quickly worked the keys:

Made it to hotel, meeting Britta for a Cappuccino. Behave. XOXO

A response came within seconds:

Behave? I am not you my friend! LOL! XOXO

Audra sighed. *Yes, I live like a nun. But all that may change…*she thought about the stranger on the train. She didn't expect him to keep his word and meet her at the Belvedere, then again, a *girl can hope.*

. . .

The man standing on the Schottenring platform had no intention of going that direction. Once the train arrived for Karlsplatz, he would dart across the platform, grab a car close to hers. He loved the game. *Cat and mouse.* The glee filled moment prompted him to laugh out loud. *Not yet. Be cool, man, be cool.*

When Audra pushed through the heavy wooden door to the café, Britta rose, pounced on her friend like a playful puppy, and squealed, "Auuudraaaa!"

Audra hugged her friend tight. "I can't believe it, how long has it been?"

"Too long! Come, sit. I ordered Cappuccino's and strudel."

Audra slid into a red leather booth trimmed in hand-carved wood. Britta slid across from her and leaned forward, her heavy breasts resting on the wooden table. "Your hair! I love it! It's *gooood.*" Her thick accent made "good" sound weighty and important, delicious and decadent, all at the same time.

The server brought a tray with two cups topped in foamy hearts, and a small platter of strudel dusted with powdered sugar. Audra perused the selection.

"Apple, peach, and custard, all my favorites."

"How was the train?" Britta leaned back allowing

the server to place the drinks and small pastry plates on the table.

"Interesting," she replied, catching the server sneaking peeks of Britta's bosom. "Not as interesting as your breasts are to this young man." The server dropped a spoon, retrieved it, and scurried away, red faced.

The girl's covered their mouths, suppressing a fit of giggles. Britta sipped her cappuccino, and nearly choked. "Audra, you naughty-good girl, how I have missed you."

Audra squeezed Britta's hand. "I missed *you*."

"Tell me about the train. I adore the train. So many handsome men."

"You read my mind. I met this man from America. Quite handsome. I like his fashion. And his eyes." Audra bit into a pastry and moaned.

"And you gave him your number?"

"No."

"*Blödmann!*"

Audra pretended to be shocked by her friends insult at first, but then her lips spread wide. "I am not a complete prude. We arranged to meet at the Belvedere. Tomorrow, one o'clock."

Britta nodded her approval. "What is he about?"

"His hair is long, beautiful waves, blond, gold, blond, I don't know. His eyes are blue sapphires, fit for a crown. His lips are nice. Maybe to kiss?"

"And maybe his cock will be nice to—?"

"Britta!"

"What? You don't like sex?"

Audra blushed. She conjured his image and smiled. "I will tell you if we go that far. Now tell me about you, do you have a man?"

"I have two."

"Two? Serious?"

"*Ja.* We drink, have sex, go to clubs...more drinks, more sex..."

"Both at the same time?"

Britta's plump lips puckered. Her topaz eyes glistened with glee as she nodded.

"Two? Really?" Audra reddened at the thought.

"You should try."

"The men, they are good with this?"

"Men like different. I like different. It's fun!" Britta pushed her chest forward until her cleavage popped over the top of her blouse. "I have plenty to share, yes?"

"Yes, and you *are* adventurous, but that lifestyle doesn't appeal to me. I want normal. I want a relationship, not someone just for sex."

Britta's eyes narrowed, she picked up a strudel. "You're still a virgin, aren't you?"

Audra sipped her cappuccino. "One mistake is enough."

Britta stopped mid-bite. "Who?"

"*Who* is not important. I plan to think things through before I get involved."

"This is why you have two men. Not to say at the

same time, but for me, more fun!" Britta raised her cup and clinked with Audra's.

Across town, Rubio Dane slid on a stool beside Giorgi Von Graff, one of Austria's legendary playboys. His Italian-German heritage contributed to his good looks, looks that drew women to him like flies. Today, Giorgi focused on his 'Rotes Zwickl' beer, nodding to the bartender who poured another, and set it in front of Rubio. "You have something for me?" he asked.

"I think so."

Giorgi glanced at Rubio, his lips twisted into a sneer. "You *think*?"

"I'm meeting her at the Belvedere tomorrow at one o'clock." Rubio wiped condensation from his glass with a cocktail napkin. "Have I ever failed you?"

Giorgi's lips relaxed into a smile. "All right then."

"She's beautiful, you'll like her—she's your type."

Giorgi pulled an envelope from inside his cashmere coat and handed it to Rubio. "You'll get the rest when you deliver the goods." He winked at Rubio, tossed fifty Euros on the bar and walked away.

Rubio stuffed the envelope in the interior pocket of his leather jacket, pulled twenty euros from his wallet, switched it for the fifty on the bar, drained his glass and rose to leave, when he heard a smoky voice next to his ear.

"Is this seat taken?"

Rubio glanced over his shoulder. A redheaded woman in her mid-twenties with eyes the color of tumbled jade, blocked his exit.

She smiled and said, "I'm sorry, do you speak English?"

He swiveled in his chair until they were practically nose to nose. "I believe you stole my pick-up line."

"In that case, I should buy you a beer."

Her derriere fit perfect in the seat next to his. She crossed long shapely legs and placed her vintage purse on the bar. "Kitty, From Dayton Ohio. And you are?"

"Alex Mayfield, from California."

"What brings you to Vienna? Business or pleasure?"

"You can do better than that."

Kitty whispered in Rubio's ear.

"Ahhh." He squeezed her hand and smiled. "Much better."

~

EPIPHANY

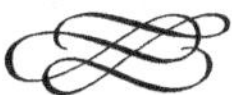

Samson F. Metzger, "Chief Detective," the placard read. The idea of receiving a promotion for bringing down a serial killer was humbling. Knowing the man was once his boss? *Disturbing*.

Sam was introduced to evil at a young age. *Krampus*. He grew up with German folklore about a half-goat, half-devil that appeared around Christmas time to punish naughty German children and bring them lumps of coal, verses St. Nicolas who rewarded good behavior with gifts, and treats. *Good versus Evil*. The line was clearly drawn. And then there were men that blurred the line by managing to play both roles magnificently.

Sam pondered his boyhood and the fear associated with Krampus. He remembered festivals where the horned devil dragged his chains through the streets of Munich, his yellow eyes scouring the crowds for unruly children. Sam's father threatened to turn him over to Krampus for beheading his sister's doll in a tug of war, despite the fact that she was about to dunk the doll in the toilet for a hair wash. For many years, Sam suffered with night terrors. He hated Christmas, and for more years than he wished to count, he hated his father for instilling such fear.

His sister, Audra was never threatened with Krampus, or his dirty deeds. She was the miracle child. The pampered one, favored by St. Nicolas. As much as he loved his sister, a part of him resented the favoritism.

Sibling rivalry lessened once Sam turned sixteen and began to exercise more independence. He and Audra grew closer. Vacations became more amiable, holidays more pleasant.

When Sam finished Gymnasium, Germany's equivalent to graduating high school in America, he chose to attend college in America. Audra never forgave him for preferring the beaches and mild weather at UCSD to the harsh winters in Munich.

Before Sam turned thirty, he had an epiphany. He realized his parents were loving in their own way, and his sister wasn't treated any better than he. Their age difference called for different measures at different stages. He came to appreciate the sacrifices his parents made for him, quit focusing on his sister's blessings, and paid more attention to his own. Unfortunately, his revelation didn't close the gap that distance had put between them, and they grew apart. He still had sketchy memories of giving Audra piggy-back rides and ski lessons.

Leaving Munich at age eighteen was more difficult than he let on to his family. It took five or more years to feel comfortable with the English language, customs, and overcome loneliness. When he turned twenty-two he joined the Sheriff's department. He jumped in, heart and soul, working ridiculous hours to prove himself. During this time, he met a girl, but he couldn't keep up with the demands of a relationship and accomplish the golden boy status to make his papa proud. Depression took its toll, and on his sprint to the finish line, he developed a limp: Alcohol became his crutch.

Sam joined AA before things got out of hand. With the help of his friend Dove Johnson, one of the finest forensic analysts he knew, he found a group that met his needs. Most of the people in his group were professionals. Doctors, lawyers, athletes, he felt his anonymity was protected, safe. Although he carried his sobriety coin with him at all times, the only person he discussed his weakness with was Suzanne. When he confessed his flaw, she didn't flinch.

He didn't plan to fall in love with Suzanne. He knew from the beginning she was married, off limits, yet his heart beat only for her. Time was a virtue, and he was a patient man. He would do anything to assure their future together. Her smile was the rainbow behind the rain. Her kiss healed a thousand wounds. Her touch made the worst day perfect.

He often lingered in the memory of the time they made love. A weak moment, awkward in the beginning. Two warriors laying down arms. Letting go of the pain that built fortresses around their hearts. For Suzanne it had been the loss of Jack, feeling rejected, and then years of abuse from her ex-husband, Ben. For him, it was years of anesthetizing the pain he brought on himself. Blotting out images of torture and evil done to others. Senseless accidents, deprivation, and demoralization of the human spirit. Worrying he wasn't enough. And then, he held her near, and all of his troubles melted away.

He wondered, were they star-crossed lovers? Would the demands of his job, and Suzanne coming to terms with her visions keep them apart? The horror he witnessed on occasion is what she lived with in her head almost every day. How he wished he could be there for her. Hold her in his arms, protect her until the visions subsided, her sanity restored. *Soon,* he told himself daily. Soon she would be rid of her past and ready for a new beginning. He prayed he would be part of her "forever."

Audra dressed carefully for her date. Despite Britta's cajoling, she couldn't bring herself to show more skin than she was comfortable with. She wasn't a prude, but she wasn't cheap. Despite her shocking hair color, and rebellious antics, she was naïve. She didn't know this man well, and didn't want to begin their relationship with an impression that she was a tease. How she longed to be *sorglos* like Britta, but she wasn't raised to be carefree. A difference in their upbringing? Audra only met Britta's parents once, when they picked them up at school. Their laughter was infectious, their bantering, lighthearted, and fun. On the other hand, Audra's family were what Americans called "stiff." They were generous, loving people who guarded their emotions like museum curators guarded the "Ephemera" by Joseph Beuys.

Audra slipped into a plaid mini skirt, net stockings, and ankle boots. Her white sweater hugged her waistline, giving her a nice tailored look. She adjusted a red tam on her head and checked the mirror. *There. Ready.* She grabbed her coat, turned the latch on the green door to her flat and closed it tight, rattling the beveled glass inserts.

She walked three blocks to Prinz Eugen-Straße where she planned to meet the young man from the train at one o'clock. Her palms felt damp inside the pockets of her navy pea coat. For a moment she felt foolish, thinking he may not show. After all, she didn't even ask his name, nor did he ask hers. What did it matter? She came to see Gustav Klimt's work. She had been a fan since she was old enough to walk.

She had spent many summers in Vienna. It was only natural to gravitate to the places she loved as a child.

One of her fondest memories was at the Belvedere Palace with Sam.

It had been a glorious day, sunny, warm, but not hot. Papa insisted on a picnic. Sam let her help carry the basket filled with meats and cheeses, bread and fresh baked goods, and bought her a ginger-orange Bionade from a vendor near the park. She remembered the way the bubbles tickled her nose, and how the sweet citrus flavor danced on her tongue. After lunch, Papa let them play near the fountains.

Sam picked a flower and placed it in her hair. "*Du siehst aus wie eine Märchenprinzessin,*" he said. "You look like a fairy princess."

Sam. She remembered Krampus in the square, her flowing skirts, the tiny tiara, approval in her brother's eyes when he repeated those same words. "*Du siehst aus wie eine Märchenprinzessin.*"

But then something changed. Sam no longer found joy in Krampus. Before she was old enough to understand why, Sam moved to San Diego to begin his schooling, and she felt as though a part of her died. Tender years, spent grieving his loss, as if he were gone for good. By the time he returned to Germany for a visit, she had hardened her heart. And although she was happy to see her brother, she was reluctant to get too close. As years went by, they grew further apart. They corresponded by text, or the occasional card. Deep down inside, she missed him terribly, but was too stubborn to admit it.

Sam could be stubborn too. He never approved of her spontaneity. If she told him she was meeting a man she didn't know, he would've tried to intervene. *"Let me run his name through my data base, make sure he isn't a serial killer."* Just as the thought crossed her mind, she felt a tap on her shoulder.

"Well, hello," he said, grinning from ear to ear.

Butterflies flooded her stomach, her lips stretched into a smile. "Hello, I wasn't sure you would come."

"Nothing could keep me away." His eyes twinkled like sapphires in the sun.

She blushed, and lowered her gaze. "I don't know your name."

"Rubio."

"Audra." She extended her hand. "Pleased to meet you."

"Not as pleased as I am to meet you," he said, grabbing her wrist, and pulling her closer. "My heart is about to leap out of my chest," he said, placing her hand between well-defined muscles.

She felt thumping beneath his silk shirt and pulled her hand away. "It's chilly, shall we go inside?"

He reclaimed her hand. "May I? I'd feel better—the crowd, you know."

"Yes," she obliged, and followed close behind him. She inhaled his scent, clean, not too spicy. She noticed other women glancing their way. She felt good to be at his side.

Rubio bought two admission tickets, and moved her

through the turnstile. Once inside Belvedere Palace, they stopped at the front counter to pick up headphones that would explain the art they were about to see. Audra floated from room to room enjoying each painting, its history, and the warm hand holding hers. They gazed at ornate ceilings, elaborate furniture, and sumptuous living quarters. When they reached Klimt's exhibit, Rubio removed his head phones.

"This one," he said, pointing to "Adam and Eve," a large piece depicting the nude Eve with Adam embracing her from behind. "This is my favorite."

"Why?" Audra crinkled her nose, playfully. "Do you like blondes?"

"No, silly girl, look at Adam's face. Pure bliss. He intends to make love."

Audra felt a tingle. Surely, he was not suggesting having sex on their first date? "Yes, he does look happy, however, I prefer Klimt's earlier work. The Kiss."

"Why?" his rhetorical question made her laugh.

"It seems as though the lover is more—protective," she said. "Are you hungry? There is a lovely café, we could—"

"Are you embarrassed by my observation?" he asked, reclaiming her hand.

"Why no, art is to be appreciated, not scorned."

"Would *you* have posed nude for Gustav Klimt?"

"Maybe."

He studied her face, his eyes penetrating her soul. "I don't believe you. You are pure."

"Nobody is that pure. Adam and Eve made sure of that."

"Then you are not a virgin?"

"I—"

"My apologies. I can see the question made you feel uncomfortable."

"It was a chapter in my life I choose to forget."

Rubio dropped her hand. "Let's find that café, shall we?"

Audra wondered if she spoiled the fun. Dampened his mood. Was he with her because he thought she was easy? She didn't hedge at his invitation. Perhaps she seemed too eager. *Grow up Audra. Men like sex, don't make a big deal of it. The boy who took your virginity was a boy. A lying, cheating, boy. That doesn't mean all males are alike. Rubio was sharing his view about a painting— he wasn't asking you to share his bed.*

They ordered cappuccinos, picked out pastries to nosh on, and took a table close to a large window. The view of the garden was breathtaking and reminded her of Sam. "My family came here when I was a girl. My brother and I played over there," she said, pointing to a garden circling a fountain.

"This is the brother in California?"

"You remembered."

"The cop."

"He's actually a detective. *Sherlock Holmes.*"

"Not Dirty Harry then?"

"He works for the Sheriff's department in Northern California."

"Interesting. Are you two close?"

"We used to be." Her gaze, suddenly drawn to the garden, stirred emotions she fought hard to contain. She turned her focus on her date. "What about you? Do you have siblings?"

"No, I am an only child. My parents died when I was very young. I lived with my Grandmother until she passed away."

Rubio wracked his brain. Did they have this conversation on the train? Did he tell her otherwise? He couldn't remember. He told so many lies that sometimes his memory played tricks on him. "Stop me if I already —" He shifted his gaze for effect, to reel her in, extract information he needed for later. Giorgi expected him to deliver. And he would keep his promise, but first he needed to cover his ass. He wasn't comfortable snatching women with strong ties. It made things messy. Relatives came out of the woodwork to search, gather information. They vowed to find their loved one, they wanted justice. Giorgi would get nervous, make his life a living hell. As much as he detested the man, he needed him to survive.

When she placed her hand over his. The irony almost made him bust out laughing. He controlled the curve of his lips, his smile sincere. "I really like you."

∿

SIBLINGS

Suzanne puttered around the house, boxing up Ben's belongings. They agreed to sell the house in one year, meanwhile, he would spend that year in Camino, living with his retired Aunt Dee. He considered the arrangement his "get out of jail" card. Suzanne considered the arrangement a blessing. Her brother Steven, and sister-in-law Karen would agree. Although Ben was not connected directly to her attempted murder, he was connected to the man who shot her. *Drugs.* Ben was given a light sentence, an ankle monitor, and an iron clad restraining order. If he came within one hundred yards of her, he would go to jail.

Life should've improved without Ben, without his negativity and his outbursts. However, the visions she experienced since the incident with Jim Dixon still left her weary. Her latest vision, the girl with the different color hair, the man in the shadows, the green door, all pieces to a puzzle. She couldn't shake off the notion that something sinister was about to happen. But what? She needed to talk with her psychic friend, Linda Schooler.

"How many times have you had the dream?" Linda's melodious voice put Suzanne at ease.

"Once or twice, but I can't really call it a dream. It's more like I'm there, as an observer."

"Is the intensity the same as the last case you worked on with Sam?"

"Yes, but something is different. I don't know how to explain it, but I feel as though I know this girl, and yet she doesn't look familiar."

"Hmm, interesting. What can you tell me about the man in the shadows?"

"I can't see his face, Linda, that's what makes these visions so frustrating."

"I understand, but there is an answer for everything, you must be patient, keep an open mind. In time, the pieces will come together, and when they do, you will have your answers. Clarity comes with practice. It's like your muscles, the more you exercise, the stronger you get."

"If that's the case, I must be the wimp on the beach getting sand kicked in my face."

"*Hardly.* How's Sam?"

"Okay, I guess. I haven't seen him more than a couple of times since I was released from the hospital, months ago. We talk though"

"He's crazy about you."

"I'm not sure I'm ready to—"

"Of course not. He's not pressuring you, is he?"

"No, not at all, it's just—"

"The visions, the madness, right? I get'cha. Being psychic isn't easy."

"Easy doesn't even equate. It's like living on the edge of insanity."

"It does get better, not easier, *per se*, but you will learn to remove yourself from the emotion attached to the visions."

"Oh, Linda, I wished it all made sense."

"Look for signs."

"Signs? What kind of signs?"

"Time of day, time of year, architecture, license plates, stuff like that."

"Interesting you mention architecture. The green door in the vision is unlike anything I've seen around here. It's large, with an ornate knob in the center, flanked by two leaded glass panels."

"Sounds European."

"Europe? Europe is far away."

"Energy is limitless."

"Geezus, Linda, I hope you're wrong."

"Why?"

"I hate to fly."

. . .

Rubio offered to walk Audra to her flat. He held her hand, guarded her when they crossed the street. *The perfect gentleman,* her mother would say.

"When can I see you again?"

"I'm meeting my friend for dinner tonight—perhaps tomorrow? Or maybe you would care to join us, tonight, say eight o'clock?"

Audra felt awkward when he pulled out his cell and scrolled through his calendar. "Oh, see here, I have an appointment this evening. Tomorrow doesn't look good either. Maybe another time?"

"I would like that."

"May I kiss you?"

Audra presented her cheek. "I had a wonderful time."

His lips barely brushed her skin. "How will we keep in touch?"

"I'll give you my number?"

Rubio handed Audra his phone. She punched in the digits, and hit save. "What about a selfie?" She smiled, holding up her phone.

"No, I don't like photos of myself. May I take one of you?"

"Yes, by the door. I want everyone to know I am in Vienna. The city that captured my heart."

Rubio snapped the photo and returned her phone. "I will call you, then." He backed onto the sidewalk, turned, and walked away.

Audra watched until he was out of sight. She clicked on the photo and blew up the image. His reflection was clear in the glass behind her. She sighed. "You are *one handsome* man." She texted the photo to Britta.

Do you see what I see?

Britta texted back.

Oo-la-la!

PURCHASE

Rubio navigated his way back to Landstraße where he hopped on the U2 train. He rode quietly, his mind strategizing his mission. He would park his car near Audra's flat and wait for her to exit before 8:00. *It will be dark. I'll follow her to the train, invite her into my car.* He envisioned her surprise, and his response, claiming he changed his mind about joining her for dinner. Deprivan *will take seconds. Once she is unconscious, I deliver her to Giorgi. Sinchy.*

He exited the train at Karlsplatz and walked toward Casino Wein, pep in every step. He pushed through heavy ornate doors, transcending from honking horns and street noise to laughter, pinging bells, and piped-in music. He breathed in the scent of expensive cigars, perfume, cigarettes, and *money*. His heart raced with anticipation. By this time tomorrow his debt would be paid. *For now, a little fun.* He bellied up to his favorite Roulette table and placed his bet.

A t 6:00 A.M., Sam awoke, groping for Suzanne's warm body. *Empty.* Another dream, yet it felt *so real.* He could almost smell her delicate scent on his skin. Her soft lips on his cheek. In reality, it had been months since they were together. He wanted to give her as much space as she needed to heal, get things settled with Ben. *Their divorce should be final.*

Sam often wondered if he had been too hard on her. Tracking a serial killer required training. She never had the luxury of attending the Police Academy. In fact, she was thrown into the mix without as much as a crash course in survival tactics. At the end of the day, he wouldn't have changed a thing. Without her help, Jim Dixon would still be on the loose—*more dead girls.* He shuddered at the thought. Without her in his life, he would've never known what it felt like to yearn, ache, *feel.*

Despite his desire to stay in bed and linger in his reverie, he had a meeting in an hour. The Sheriff's Department had received several calls from business owners claiming prostitution was on the rise in Goldorado County —they wanted to know what was being done. "They keep getting younger by the minute," one woman reported. She went on to mention that kids were too promiscuous now-a-days, and it was hard to tell junior high girls, from high school girls with their skimpy clothing and big breasts. "What the hell are they putting in our food?" she added.

Sam remembered how mature Audra appeared at fourteen, and wondered if the woman was on to something. The guys at the academy wanted to know who the "hot" chick was in the photo he kept in his wallet. He didn't envy parents raising kids in this day and age and doubted if he would ever have the chance to experience parenthood firsthand. *Dogs are nice. We'll have two, one for each of us to spoil.* He didn't know if Suzanne would agree, something to discuss with her when the time was right. For now, he was happy knowing she was still in his life.

S uzanne awoke with a start, her heart pumping too hard, every nerve in her body on full alert. "A dream," she said aloud, trying to convince her brain to back off on the adrenaline, and release some dopamine. "It was just a dream."

Still, she climbed out of bed and called Sam. "I saw her again, Sam. The same girl. I'm afraid for her."

"Whoa, slow down. Let's start over. Good morning, Suzanne. How are you?"

"Why are you doing this to me?"

"Because, you're going to have a heart attack if you don't slow down. Breathe."

"You're right. Good morning Sam, how are you?"

"I'm good. How did you sleep last night, Suzanne?"

"I know what you're doing, and it's working." Suzanne placed her hand on her chest. *Much better.*

"Good. Now tell me what you saw."

"I saw the same girl, with the colored streaks in her hair. She's with a man, who I can't identify. She likes him. He's evil. He's leading her into a trap. I can feel it, though I don't know how. I see another man. A dark-haired man. He's beholden to him. The devil's pawn. He's going to do something to the girl."

"Which man?"

A chill skittered up Suzanne's spine to the nape of her neck. She imagined Sam's hand, squeezing her shoulder. His face, too close. She shook off the image. "I didn't hear what you said."

"Which man is going to hurt the girl?"

Suzanne closed her eyes. She summoned the image from her dream. The car, crawling down a dark street—*stalking his prey.* She saw the dark-haired man, sitting behind a desk, counting cash. *That's a lot of zeros.* "The man with the dark hair is wealthy," she said. "The other man—" Suzanne paused, her eyes scanned back and forth as if she were watching an action scene on TV.

"What about the other man?"

Suzanne watched the dark-haired man hand a portion of the cash to the man she had seen with the girl. Suddenly, an epiphany hit her like a brick. "He's going to buy her."

"Oh shit." Sam plopped back down on his bed. She

must be picking up on the trafficking problem, here in the county, he thought. "Do you have any idea where they are?"

"The currency, it wasn't American. Euros, I think."

"Euros?" Sam's head exploded with possibilities. "Damn, that could be anywhere."

"Belvedere. I keep getting Belvedere."

"There's the Belvedere Museum in Austria, we used to go there when we were kids." Sam felt a chill travel up his spine. "How old is the girl?"

"Early to mid-twenties."

"I need to make a phone call. I'll call you back."

Sam ended the call with Suzanne and scrolled through his contact list. He dialed Audra's number. He felt relieved to hear Audra's voice until he heard…*"You say, hello. I say good-bye. Leave a message, I've got to fly. Auf Wiedersehen."*

"Hey princess, it's your brother. Give me a call. <u>Today</u>. Don't worry about the time difference. I miss you." He ended the call and scrolled until he found *Dad*, clicked on the number and listened for the call to connect. He hoped to get them before bed time.

"Samson!"

"Papa, how are you?"

"Good. Your mother is here, let me put her—"

"Wait dad, I need to speak with you first."

"What is it, son? You sound—"

"Where's Audra?"

"She's in Austria, she's working for a lovely family as an au pair. You know your sister—she has gypsy blood running through her veins."

"When is the last time you spoke with her?"

"Why the other—what is this about?"

"I'm not sure, and I don't want to worry you needlessly—can I have the family's name and number where she's living?"

"She's not there yet, son. She's visiting her friend. You know, the crazy one with the large—"

"Britta? Kokettieren. Flirty–"

"Yes, you remember. She's a wild one, that Britta."

"Where are they staying, do you know?"

"No. But Audra's flatmate, Bruno, may know. Give him a call."

"I will. How's mom?"

"She's right here, say hello."

Before Sam could protest, he heard his mother's sweet voice.

"Hello, is this my favorite boy?"

"Yes, mom. How are you?"

"Good," she said, "Why are you asking questions about your sister?"

"Just curious. I was thinking about her, that's all."

"Samson—a mother can tell when her son is lying."

"It's nothing, really mom. Just wanted to reach out—feeling like I've neglected her lately."

"I'm sure she would love to hear from you."

"Okay then. I'm going to track her down."

"Why don't you call her phone?"

"I did. I left a message. I just figured since I was feeling guilty, I'd make the rounds."

"Guilty, shmuilty. Just call more often."

"Love you, mom."

"I love you too, son. And when you speak to your sister, remind her she has parents that worry."

"I will, mom. Say goodbye to papa for me."

"I will. Tschüs."

Sam hung up the phone feeling sick to his stomach. Was there a connection between his sister and Suzanne's visions? He dialed Audra's cell phone once more. This time all he heard was a click.

Audra heard her phone buzz. *Samson.* "Isn't is just like you to invade my space when I'm having fun," she said, hitting the 'End Call' button. She didn't need his big brother antics right now. *Where were you when I needed you?*

She remembered the time she got tangled up with Fritchoff Meister. When she called Sam for advice, her calls went to voicemail. She was attending Realschule, about to move up to Gymnasium. Her hormones were *raging,* according to the Cosmopolitan magazine she kept under her bed, and she decided it was time to 'give it up.' Fritchoff was said to be a good lover, and she believed her sources. Bibiana, a girl from Spain, and

Marta, from Cologne, couldn't get enough of his sex. They said he was very skilled at making a girl feel like a woman. What they neglected to tell her was that Fritchoff was a lug who liked to drink. And when he drank, he got very mean.

He met her at the flat where Bibiana lived with her Grandmother. Bibiana arranged for Audra to be alone with the boy while she and her Grandmother went into town. When Fritchoff arrived, he was drunk. His kisses were wet and sloppy, his penis erect. He forced her onto Bibiana's bed, and climbed on top of her like one of those Monster Trucks she saw at an exhibition in London with her parents. His body pinned her to the mattress, and his groin smashed against her pubic bone. She fought like a hellcat. He struggled with her panties. By the time he was ready to enter her, he had gone limp. He slapped her across the face and called her names, as if it were her fault he couldn't stay stiff. She told him to leave, she threatened to call her brother, have him arrested. She went as far as dialing the phone. Sam didn't answer.

Fritchoff called her bluff. "Suck me, Bitch," he said, grabbing her by the hair. She kicked him hard until he let go. "I'll scream if you don't leave!" Just then, they heard someone pound on the wall. It was the neighbor. The timing was perfect. Fritchoff zipped quickly and ran.

Determined to have another go at losing her virginity, she chose someone less "reputable." Marc worked at the corner market, where he drove their delivery lorry on weekends. Finding the right time and the right place to rendezvous was a challenge, "*Morgon*," he'd say, *always tomorrow.*

She grew weary of his excuses; however, Cosmopolitan assured her the outcome was worth the wait. What the magazine didn't warn her about was the crush that came with the pursuit. The longer she waited for Marc to make the right moves, the more she grew to like him. When they finally made love in the back of his lorry one rainy Saturday, she believed she had fallen in love. Marc was happy to spread her legs, but had no intention of settling in longer than it took to satisfy his itch. Like her brother Sam, he aspired to a vocation that didn't include her. Cosmopolitan didn't prepare her for the heartbreak either, and she considered herself lucky that she didn't get pregnant.

Rubio seemed different. He appeared to be more sophisticated than the other boys she dated. He seemed worldly, knew how to treat a lady, not like Marc who confessed to having sex with many women in the back of his lorry while he kept her at bay. *No wonder he was always busy. Morgon.*

Sam not only felt anxious, the conversation he had with his parents tugged at his heartstrings. Audra hadn't checked in. For many years he managed his emotions with whiskey, tequila, beer, wine. Just about any kind of alcohol you put in front of him. After a while he started having blackouts, and almost lost his job. Recovery took years, but he had finally beat the urge to drink. *Until now.* He pressed his AA token in his palm. He licked his lips. *Just one.* One drink would stop the stampede in his chest. Drown the fear stuck in the back of his throat. He threw the coin across the room, and redialed his sister's number. "Goddammit, Audra! Pick up the fucking phone!"

udra checked herself in the mirror. Looking good, she thought. Britta would be waiting at the restaurant for her. She locked the door and headed down the walk. She breathed in the crisp night air. So what if Sam weren't here to enjoy it with her…she was grown now, she didn't need him, or his approval. *About anything.* As if he were reading her thoughts, her phone rang again. This time she answered. "Who's calling?"

"You haven't lost your sense of humor, I see."

"And you dear brother haven't lost your sense of bad timing. I was about to meet Britta for dinner. Care to join us? Oh wait, you're a million miles away!"

"That doesn't mean I don't miss you."

"Funny, I can't remember what you look like."

"Audra, please—I didn't call to argue."

"Why did you call? Guilty conscience?"

"I called because I love you. And—as much as I try

not to worry about my little sister, well–sometimes I can't help myself."

"You should try calling more often."

"How are you? Papa said you are working as an au pair."

"I start in three weeks. I'm on holiday. Britta and I are catching up. And what about you? Still playing Sherlock Holmes?"

"As a matter of fact, I got a promotion."

"Congratulations! Scotland Yard is lucky to have you."

"Audra, please–you know the only thing that has changed between us is air miles. I plan to visit at Christmas."

"Does Papa know? He hasn't mentioned–"

"Don't tell him. It's a surprise."

"I see. Sure. It will be our little secret. Why should Mama and Papa be disappointed when you decide not to come? Me? *Es geht mir gut.*"

"I won't let you down. I promise. *Du wirst immer meine Märchenprinzessin sein.*"

"I'm too old to be your little princess."

"Never too old."

"Sam, Britta's waiting."

"Okay. Have fun. Tell her hello from me."

"I will. Auf Wiedersehen."

"Auf Wiedersehen. And be safe. Please."

"I'm hanging up now!"

Sam chuckled. "Love you, sis." He didn't wait for

her reply. He knew she loved him. He felt the pain he left behind each time they spoke. Maybe it was time to think about returning to Germany. He wondered if Suzanne would go with him. He'd ask. Soon. For now, Audra was safe. He exhaled, feeling relieved.

Sam plugged in the coffee maker, hit the 'brew' button, and went into the bathroom to begin his morning regime. A hot shower would feel good on his tight muscles. There were few people in the world that invoked physical stress. His sister was one of them. The thought of her in danger made him crazy inside. He'd kill anyone who tried to harm her. And then there was Suzanne. The affect she had on him was intense, but *different*. "Down boy," he sighed, and switched the faucet to 'cold.'

LEWIS

Lewis Howard hovered over his own body, watching as doctors and nurses buzzed around the operating table like a disturbed hornet's nest. One doctor injected a long needle into his sternum, moved aside, another pounded on his chest. Another glanced at the flat line on a monitor. Just then, a surgeon entered the room, barking orders. Everyone stepped aside. On command, one nurse swabbed betadine from Lewis's clavicle to his bellybutton. Another nurse pushed a tray lined with instruments beside the surgeon.

"Scalpel."

Lewis heard him say it, and then heard a smacking sound as the scalpel hit the doctor's hand. Lewis watched as the surgeon slice him open like a Christmas pig. His chest flayed open, the surgeon inserted a metal contraption to keep his thoracic cavity stretched wide. As he reached in, and began massaging his heart, Lewis floated away.

His father and mother stood before him in an ethereal glow, arms outstretched, welcoming his arrival, their faces beaming.

"I guess I've come to a sticky end," Lewis said, looking back over his shoulder at the bloody scene below.

"Y'aven't popped yer clogs just yet," his father said.

"Me missus warned me, she did. Take it easy, she said."

"Let's give it a butcher..." The three stood observing the commotion below.

Lewis shook his head. "Not yer bog-standard death, eh?"

"Come," his father said. "Let's have a chinwag."

Suddenly...

Lewis found himself sitting at a kitchen table, his folks faffing about. He felt as though he had stepped back in time. The room was bathed in warm light. His beagle, Gingersnap, lay at his feet, panting. Just then, his neighbor, Jim walked through the door, lugging a side of beef. "Over-egged the pudding, did ye mate?" he asked, placing the beef on a wooden block. "Ye won't find a better Scotch fillet than on this joint." Lewis couldn't help but notice the ligature marks on Jim's neck were gone. The last time he saw him was the day he went barmy and hung himself.

A sad time for all, Lewis recalled. Mad cow disease brought the whole country to their knees. His own successful meat packing business, paralyzed overnight. His suppliers, neighbors and friends, lost everything.

Lewis was on his way home when he saw smoke billowing above the tree-lined lane leading to Jim's place. Odd, he thought, and decided to see if Jim was on a bender, dropped a fag, and started a bloody fire. Then he heard gunfire. Not just one or two gunshots. He heard what sounded like a bloody war. As he drove further down the lane, he saw military vehicles scattered everywhere. What he saw next etched an imprint, a never-to-be-forgotten image on his brain. Militia formed a line in front of penned animals and commenced shooting until every living cow, goat, pig, chicken, llama, and dog were dead. After each massacre, another group of soldiers dragged the carcasses to the burn pile. The stench of blood, and burning flesh made Lewis want to wretch. Jim stood alone, in shock, tears rolling down his weathered cheeks. He couldn't bear it, and vowed to take the easy way out. A week later he took his life.

The following years proved to be the most depressing times the Brits had experienced since WWII.

Dairy cows had been primarily fed *offal,* a product high in protein, consisting of animal bone and byproducts to promote milk production. When offal was suspected to be the culprit causing bovine spongiform encephalopathy, later known as *mad cow disease,* a term coined due to the animal's abnormal behavior, there was a ban put on feeding it to cattle. But despite the ban, the disease spread at an alarming rate, escalating the death toll to 4.4 million cattle.

Lewis scraped together what savings he had to help his employees, but the coffers were running low, and once winter set in, he was afraid they'd all starve.

Although Lewis was able to procure healthy beef, and other meat products from sources in neighboring countries, news that humans were also contracting bovine spongiform encephalopathy caused meat product sales to plummet. His buyers were afraid to take a chance on importing any meat, possibly risking more deaths. At his wits end, Lewis reached out to the only man he knew that could help him, Dodi Fayed.

Dodi's father had recently purchased Harrods Department Store, which had a reputation for carrying not only exotic merchandise, but also items not available to the common market. Lewis was pleasantly surprised when Dodi agreed to meet.

Although Dodi's first purchase order was minimal, he was willing to take a risk. From that day forward, Lewis began rebuilding his business, grateful for the kindness shown to him by a man who owed him nothing. In years to come, Dodi and Lewis developed a close business relationship.

Jim patted him on the back. "Ye've never been a turnip puller, or a donkey walker, mate, always lookin' out for your pals. This time, the Lord 'imself needs ye.

See that lass?" Jim pointed to a young woman standing in the distance, her long hair gleamed beneath a lamp post. Her short skirt and tall boots made her look cheeky. "She's not in the game, but she's headed for hell. Ye need to find 'er. Help 'er. These aren't punters and derelicts with a few quid, mate. These are men with heaps of dosh from makin' sport of human flesh."

Lewis squinted his eyes, taking in the sight of her. She was beautiful, with an air of innocence that made her that much more desirable. Lewis not only sensed the danger she was in, he *felt* it. He'd never laid eyes on the lass, but he knew she was German, not British. He knew the street lamp, under which she stood, was in Austria, not England. He turned to Jim. "What am I t'do?"

A surge of calamity from below took Lewis out if his reverie. "Time to go back, ol' chap," Jim said, slapping him on the back again. "Ye'll know what to do when the time comes."

A quick glance was the extent of his goodbye to his mother and father. In a blink, he was back in his body, fighting for his life.

"Again!" The surgeon yelled.

Lewis felt something like a cattle prod make contact with his heart.

"Again!"

Suddenly, he felt his heart beat. Faint at first, reminding him of the Aston Martin he bought second hand from a candle maker in Manchester. Once the car warmed a bit, she ran tickety boo. And so did he.

T he next day, Lewis was commended for a jolly good outcome. Nurses and doctors popped in and out of his room to congratulate him for surviving, for coming back to life, for being a "miracle" patient. By evening, the parade dwindled. All that remained was peace, quiet, and Trudy, the love of his life.

"I saw Jim. Mum, and Dad," he confessed.

"Ye must be knackered," his wife said, reluctant to leave his side.

"And m'dog—Gingersnap was 'er name. Had 'er from a wee pup, I did."

"Ye were in surgery for six hours, luv, four of which yer heart refused t'beat."

"Tosh."

Trudy's eyes welled; her nose turned red. "'Twas a miracle the doctor didn't give up, Lew. By the grace of God 'twas four bloody hours!"

"Don't be getting all collywobbles." He reached for her hand.

She sniffed, pulled a handkerchief from her pocket, and dabbed her eyes. "Yer here now. That's what counts."

"Can't get rid of m'now, can ye?"

She brought his hand to her lips and let her tears fall.

"Jim told me 'bout a girl. She's in trouble."

"Jim never made a lick 'a sense," she said, wiping her tears.

"I saw her with me own eyes," he pleaded with Trudy, his eyes wide. "I felt it! I felt the evil lurking nearby! I—"

"Hush now. No need t'get in a tither."

"Jim said I must help 'er."

"Jim was off 'is nut, he was. Now rest. Ye need t'get better. *I* need ye to get better."

Lewis squeezed her hand. He closed his eyes, and fell in to an abyss.

~

THE DEBT

Rubio waited outside of Audra's flat. When he saw her emerge, he slouched down in his seat. *Pretty.* Prettier than the other girls he procured for Giorgi. She was taller too. He hoped that didn't present a problem. The containers used for transport only came in three sizes. It would be a shame to cram her into one that wouldn't allow her any movement. Although she would be heavily sedated, it was a fifteen-hour drive to the dock in Lecce, Italy, where the transport containers were transferred into shipping containers, loaded on trains, and taken to Brandisi. Giorgi said, once the ship was out to sea, the 'precious cargo' would be released to stretch and use the toilet. So why should he be concerned. His only worry should be what the *schlägers*, or thugs, would do to him if he didn't pay up.

When Audra stepped under the lamplight, he felt a moment of regret. She was the kind of girl he could've brought home to meet his mother. The fleeting feeling disappeared without a trace. Who was he was kidding? He didn't have a mother. *You are who you are.*

His car crept up alongside of Audra, window rolled down. "Would I sound too eager if I said I missed you already?"

Audra kept walking. "As I recall, I extended an invitation for you to join us."

"Then I am selfish to want you all to myself?"

"One would certainly question your motives."

"Oh, you wound me with your words, my fair lady."

Audra smiled. "I merely meant to remind you that I don't ditch my girlfriends—however, I am willing to share my time."

"Can I at least give you a lift to the restaurant?"

Audra stopped to consider his offer. "Perhaps you can give my friend a lift as well? She's there, up ahead."

Rubio's flirtatious demeanor dropped like a hot rock when he saw a woman in the distance walking towards them. What to do? He wanted to grab Audra, throw her into the car and be done with it. He had a debt to collect, a debt to pay before midnight. He pulled over to the curb. "I'd love to meet your friend, but I'm getting the feeling that you don't trust me." He paused, a smile blossoming on his face. "Or is it that you're afraid to be alone with me?"

"I'm not afraid of you, it's just—"

"I'm listening—" He hoped his smile, in full bloom now, would seal the deal.

She stepped closer to the car. "You're right. I am a bit nervous."

"Do I look like the 'big, bad wolf', or perhaps *Krampus*?"

She laughed. "No. I'm sorry. It's just—"

He raised one eyebrow.

"Okay. Yes. A ride would be nice."

"And your friend?" He nodded toward the woman still in the distance, but heading right toward them.

Audra got into the car. "That's not her," she said, "I must have been mistaken."

Rubio shook his head, his smile never wavered. He knew the woman was not her friend. She was at least sixty, and walked with a limp. "Naughty girl."

BONES

Suzanne scrolled through the Want Ads. She needed to find something to keep herself occupied, out of her head. The visions of the young woman were becoming a distraction. She couldn't get them out of her mind. She was about to jot down a phone number from the list of job ads when suddenly she felt woozy. A man's face swam in her vision like a kaleidoscope, fractured, blurry, then everything went black.

She dialed Linda Schooler.

"I'm afraid for this girl," she said, hardly giving Linda a chance to say, 'hello'.

"Whoa! Slow down."

Suzanne took a deep breath and exhaled. "Sorry. It's just that I feel something terrible has happened, but I don't know what. I saw a man, well at least he appeared to be a man…it was hard to tell, his image was shattered, like glass, or one of those tubular thing-a-ma-jigs that you look into."

"A kaleidoscope?"

"Yes. Like that."

"This is where meditation comes in, Suzanne. Quiet your mind, see if you can put the pieces together to form a complete picture."

"I hate this, Linda. This isn't a gift, it's a curse!"

"Remember the good you've done in the past. You found those girls, stopped a serial killer from killing again. When you change your perspective, the universe will point you in the right direction. Trust me."

"Where have I heard those words before?" And then it dawned on her. "That's it—she trusted him."

"See? That's what I'm talkin' about, Willis. Let it go, and it will flow."

"Gosh, Linda—I don't know where to start."

"The information will come. Let it happen, don't force it."

"I still feel like this is happening far away."

"You mentioned that before. Like the setting was in another country. Plant the seeds, let them grow."

"Easy for you to say."

"Hah! I wish. It took me years to filter out the garbage, you know, self-talk, negative chatter. You've got to learn to tune it in. Visualize getting a crystal-clear picture. Believe me, the more you fiddle with the tuner, the better reception you'll get."

"I'll try."

"If you need help, try gardening. Nothing like connecting with Mother Nature."

Suzanne hung up the phone feeling better. Linda was spot on, she needed something to focus on other than herself. A walk would do her good. She grabbed a light jacket from the hall closet, filled a water bottle, and stepped into the sunshine.

A block or so from her house, she turned to see a woman walking behind her. The woman was older, maybe sixty. She walked with a limp. Suzanne covered her ears. The cry of kittens was deafening.

Lewis, newly released from the hospital, hobbled to the window. "Ye shouldn't be up, Luv," his wife called from the kitchen.

"Ye got eyes in back of yer 'ead, now do ye?"

Trudy walked into the room, her hands on her hips. "Y'know I do—and ye 'ave rocks in yers! What do ye mean by getting up to fancy a glimpse out the window? The doctor said to keep yer rump in the chair for the next few days. Yer stitched to the brim."

"Ye know, I'm not a teetotaler. I feel like I have bees in me bum."

"Well, lucky bees, I say—how 'bout a game of rummy?"

"Ye'll beat me again, like ye always do."

"I promise to go easy on ye. Now please, come sit down."

Lewis hobbled his way back to his chair. "I can't seem to shake this feelin'."

"What feelin' is that, Luv?" she asked, shuffling a deck of cards.

"Doom." He plopped into his chair. "Ah, git ye chin off ye chest, Luv—not doom for me. It's what Jim said. The girl. Something happened. I feel it in me bones."

LECCE

Audra couldn't move. Her hands and feet were bound. Her mouth, taped. A dank smell permeated her nostrils. She felt movement beneath her. It was dark. But nothing was more terrifying than the sound of whimpering that surrounded her. At first, she thought she heard kittens, crying, mewling…then she realized, the sound was human. *Children.*

A wave of nausea hit her. A scream stuck in her throat. *Don't be a fool.* Her brother's voice entered her head. *If you vomit, you'll choke.* She certainly didn't want to do that. Wasn't that how John Bonham and Jimi Hendrix died? She remembered Sam telling her their story when she was ten or eleven. She drew in a deep breath and willed herself to overcome the nausea. *I don't want to die.*

A short while later, the movement stilled. She heard coarse voices issuing commands in *Italian.* She smelled fish. Suddenly, she was being hoisted into the air. A man said what sounded like, "that side, put it on that side, you idiot!" Her Italian was weak, so she wasn't sure. All she knew is when the container she was in came crashing down, pain shot through her hip and shoulder. She cried out.

"*Stupido*!" The man sounded like he was seething. "*Rompi la merce*!"

Merchandise? She wasn't sure that's what he said until another man chuckled and said, "*Rompilo, l'hai comprato.*" *Break it, you bought it.*

Audra heard containers slide on something gritty. *Fish, grit,* they must be near water, a port perhaps, off the coast of Italy. The cries of the children grew louder when a heavy door slammed, and chains clanked, metal to metal. And then...*silence.*

An hour or so later, she heard the chains being removed, the door was lifted, and more containers were loaded on board. Although Audra couldn't see what was going on, she could sense that the containers were filling up the space around her, the air becoming dense. A chemical smell, something used for cleaning mingled with the fish. The door slammed. The chains slid in place. The vehicle started to move.

She could tell the road was winding by the way her body sloshed back and forth. The engine labored each time the driver shifted gears. *Hills.* She listened for sounds that would identify the region they were in, whether they were headed inland or to the coast. The scent of fish grew stronger. She wracked her brain to remember her lessons in geography. Pictures formed in her mind, cities along the coastline.

She gathered from the production of her natural bodily functions that they had traveled less than twenty-four hours. Although she felt dehydrated, she had peed twice. Traveling from Austria to Italy's northern coast would've taken maybe five hours. Which meant if her estimations were correct, they were going south. Why Italy? Why the coast? *Why Rubio, why?*

R ubio stepped into the Casino Wein seven minutes before midnight. Before he reached his favorite roulette table, he was hoisted off his feet and ushered through a door leading to a room he was well acquainted with. A man only known as Ivan sat behind a heavy wooden desk counting euros.

"Either you have my money, or you are completely mad coming here. He checked his watch. "Five minutes to spare."

Rubio straightened his rumpled coat and removed an envelope from his breast pocket. "It's all there, count it."

Ivan's snarl relaxed into a sarcastic grin. "I trust you." His eyes like steel traps latched onto Rubio's. "We have an understanding you and I. If you try to cheat me, you die. Simple." He gestured to one of his goons, "Get him out of here."

Rubio felt the blow to his kidney, but he didn't go down. The man flanking his right side made sure of that, as he pushed him out the door. Rubio caught his breath and moved along. Wein wasn't the only casino in Austria. Casino Graz was 197 kilometers away. Far enough away from Ivan and his spies. He crossed the road, got in his car and pulled away. The drive would give him time to atone for his sins. *Until next time.*

Rubio was in deep with Giorgi. Rubio saw too much, knew too much.

He served as bait—the guy who did the dirty work.

When he delivered Audra to Giorgi, Giorgi seemed pleased, paid him on the spot. Rubio was still in earshot when Giorgi ordered his men to get her caged and on the truck for the midnight run. Normally, Giorgi liked to sample the merchandise, this time he didn't. Rubio wasn't sure if it was because of the time crunch, or whether he had a buyer who wouldn't accept damaged goods. He knew Giorgi could be sadistic.

'Regret,' was a word that didn't belong in Rubio's vocabulary, yet he felt guilty about Audra. *She was different.* The others were mostly runaways, orphans, losers. The clientele didn't care, as long as they were clean and didn't put up a fuss. Drugs took care of the 'fuss' part, most of the grabs didn't know where they were, or didn't care. Once they were hooked on drugs, they would do anything for their next fix. *Like trained seals, begging for fish.* Rubio knew the drill. He was once just like them. It was Giorgi who recognized his potential. It was Giorgi who changed his life. And it would be Giorgi who could make his life a living hell if he didn't do as he was told.

Rubio was six when he was taken. A woman posing as a social worker snatched him from his home in Bakersfield, California. She claimed he was being neglected, that his parents weren't capable of taking care of him.

His mom worked in a bakery; his dad was a roughneck on an oil rig in Santa Barbara. Rubio wasn't the best dressed kid in school, nor was he the worst. There were times when he didn't bring a lunch and had to rely on charity, but those times were few and far between. So, when Miss Nester came to the door and insisted Rubio go with her, he was confused. "My parents are good—they love me!" he screamed. At least he thought so, until they didn't come for him. How could they love him? If they did, they would have stopped Miss Nester from taking him to a foreign country where he was beaten, sodomized, and forced to do unspeakable things.

When Rubio was twelve, fifteen-year-old Giorgi was being introduced to adult pleasures. His father hosted a party on one of his many yachts, and procured flesh in various ages, shapes, and genders. Giorgi overheard Rubio negotiating with one of the older girls for a bite of her cake. He told his father Rubio was a smart one, pleasing to the eye, and one day the boy would work for him. Three years later,

Giorgi's father purchased Rubio for five hundred Euros. He fed him, clothed him, and made him watch Giorgi transcend into adulthood. Rubio came to know Giorgi's cruelty, his idiosyncrasies, kinks, and deepest desires. By the time Rubio was eighteen, he was rounding up Giorgi's merchandise, and personal concubines. Later, Giorgi took him into the business. Like his father, Giorgi was immersed in human trafficking.

The first thing Giorgi did was get Rubio clean. He had no tolerance for druggies, or fuck-ups. However, Rubio found another addiction, *gambling*. He loved the adrenaline rush when he won, the low when he lost. Life became a roller-coaster ride. He'd won big, lost big, and ultimately became tethered to Giorgi.

Rubio convinced himself that the kids he snatched were better off. Giorgi made sure they were well fed, and groomed for pleasure. Those who did not abide by Giorgi's rules were beaten and immediately sold to other traffickers. As much as Rubio hated Giorgi, hated the business, Giorgi paid well, which afforded Rubio the freedom to destroy his own life.

Giorgi had clients all over the world—Princes, diplomats, powerful players. He supplied entertainment for high profile people from every walk of life. His "kingdom" stretched far and wide, and those who sought his services not only kept a tight lip, many of them made it possible for Giorgi to operate at an overwhelming capacity. It boggled Rubio's mind how much perversion there was in the world. Giorgi's number one rule—it wasn't his place to judge.

Rubio checked his watch. Audra should be in Lecce soon, the first stop on her long journey. He had to laugh at the irony–by morning, she'd be heading for the US. He wondered if her brother would start sniffing around once he realized she was missing, or if he even cared. The thought hardened his heart. No one looked for him. *No one cared.*

Lewis writhed in his lounger. Eyes squeezed tight, he moaned, mumbled, tossed and turned. "I can't move!" he cried. "I can't move!"

Trudy shook him awake. "Lewis! Wake up, Luv–yer havin' a mare."

Lewis' eyes rolled around in their sockets, as if searching for answers. Trudy shook him again. He awoke with a start. "Lecce!"

"A cat in a flour sack, ye are–"

Lewis took a moment to get his bearings. He swiped his face, wiping away whatever image plagued his sleep. "It's the strangest thing–"

Y'gettin' y'self all lathered up over somethin' Luv, what is it?"

"The girl–they've taken 'er to Lecce!"

"Lecce? Where's that?"

"Italy. We have t'call somebody."

"Call who? The Bill? What y'gonna tell 'em, Lew? Ye

'ad a 'mare 'bout a girl y'never met? 'They,' whoever 'they' is, 'as taken her t' Lecce?"

A tear rolled down Lewis' cheek. "She's in a god-awful place." He wiped the tear with his palm. "I keep seein' Euros, and American money. I think they mean t'sell the lass."

"Lew, let me call the doctor. Yer beginning t'scare me outa me wits."

"I don't need a doctor. I need the Vicar."

Trudy disappeared from the parlor, and reappeared with a pot of tea, her worried brow, relaxed. "I rang my sister…she 'as a friend."

"Y'didn't tell 'er I was bats, did ye?"

"No, of course not. Tess has a knowin'—she understands such things." Trudy filled each cup with tea, a lump of sugar, and a dab of milk. "She said, she'd give 'im a ring."

She met her husband's scowl with a warm smile. "It wouldn't hurt."

"It's so real, Tru." He shook his head. "Never experienced anythin' like it."

Trudy smoothed his hair, hooked a finger under his chin, and lifted his face to meet her gaze. "I believe something 'appened to ye. Not sure what. But I pray that Tess' friend can give ye the answers y'need."

PASSION

Suzanne lingered in a hot bath. The bubbles had melted, but the water still felt wonderful on her aching muscles. She had taken a part time job at *Face In A Book*, a local book store, stocking shelves, counter work and whatever was required. Although she had only worked a few days, she enjoyed the vibe and the clientele. *I need to get back in shape*, she told herself. It had been awhile since she did any heavy lifting, or exerted herself. Psychic work didn't require muscle. At least not the kind of muscle she was used to.

She received a check from the Sheriff's department once a month, as a retainer fee. She felt undeserving each time she endorsed the back and made a deposit. She'd talk to Sam about it later, at 6 p.m. when they met for dinner.

She hadn't seen Sam in months. They spoke on the phone once or twice a week, but that was all. She knew as soon as she let him into her life, she would want him in her bed. Once she let him into her bed, there would be *commitment, ownership.* Rushing into a relationship could only lead to disaster. *He's not Ben,* she reminded herself. *Take it slow.* Even her therapist agreed. Yet, Sam held a place in her heart that she couldn't deny. *You love him.* "No, I don't," she said aloud. She let her head settle against the terry pillow and her mind wandered. It didn't take long for a vision to spoil the moment...

She could see narrow streets, lined with a myriad of interesting architecture. Modern dwellings mixed with historical refurbished, and crumbling structures. Cobblestone streets gave way to concrete roads, rail yards, shipyards, and buses. A golden sky, streaked with salmon pink, cerulean, and azure blue gave her a peaceful feeling—until a box truck barreled up the street, its gears grinding with the climb. The vision of the girl popped in and out of her mind's eye, along with the fractured image of the man she had seen in an earlier vision. The sound of kittens mewling was deafening. She covered her ears and slid beneath the water.

S am splashed hot water on his face, squirted a dollop of shaving cream in his hand, and lathered two days' worth of stubble. Once he was clean shaven, he stepped into the shower. His heart was so happy that he burst into song. *"Does Suzanne love me? How will I know? How can I tell if she loves me so?* Just the thought of kissing her made his body react. He hit his falsetto, *"That's what it is!"* He sang a few more bars as he soaped up and rinsed.

He had waited patiently for Suzanne to agree to a dinner date. The ache in his heart did a quick recovery every time he heard her voice, but he wanted more. He wanted to relive the intimate moment they shared when they were vulnerable, needy, *irresponsible*. He'd start with a kiss if allowed, *take it from there*. He wanted it to be right between them. "Right" meant acquiescing; giving her space. Opening the door as wide as it would swing in hopes that one day she'd walk through, hang her hat, and stay awhile.

Work kept him busy, he didn't have time to wallow over *what could be*. He would take "what is," and be satisfied, regardless of the outcome. "You're in a good place," he convinced the image in the mirror. But as he combed his salt and pepper hair, he noticed more silver had crept along his temples in the last few months, and his mom's voice recited an old adage in his mind, "Every man needs a good woman to keep him young."

He planned to take Suzanne to one of his favorite places, Los Pinos, in Cameron Park, a little town in the foothills of NorCal. The Mexican cuisine was authentic, the atmosphere homey, yet elegant. It was far enough from the city to allow them time to talk during their commute. *You'll have her all to yourself.* What more could he ask for?

He wasn't expecting the phone to ring.

He towel-dried his hair, and wrapped it around his waist. "Metzger," he announced. All he heard was gibberish, a crackle. Then the line went dead. He looked at his caller ID. *Audra.* He looked at the clock. *1:19 a.m. in Vienna. Maybe she butt-dialed me.* Was she at a party? She said she was having dinner with Britta. *What's Britta's last name?* He couldn't recall. He'd wait 'til morning, try calling back again…but it was no use… unease reached the pit of his stomach. *Gonna give yourself an ulcer, buddy. She's not your little princess anymore. She's an adult. She's smart. She can take care of herself.* Why wasn't he convinced? He redialed her number. His call went to voicemail.

Suzanne dressed in a sapphire blue pullover sweater, black slacks, and black suede boots. The two-inch heel gave her just the right height. She pulled her chestnut colored hair into a sleek ponytail that settled at the base of her neck, and finished with a little mascara, pink lipstick, and a pair of silver hoop earrings.

Sam rang Suzanne's bell promptly at six. Suzanne took one last look in a mirror that hung by the door. *Why am I so nervous?* Her rosy glow was a dead give-away. Her heart beat to a rhythm only lovers can feel, like a thousand butterflies fleeing at once. By the time she opened the door, all her senses were on full alert.

When she heard his deep resounding voice utter, "Hello," her color deepened.

"Hello yourself, stranger." Heat pooled in her cheeks.

Sam remained frozen; his eyes glued to hers. "Can I just kiss you and get it over with? Otherwise I won't be able to focus on anything else, and I certainly want to enjoy the evening, you know, without staring at your lips, or imagining how incredible your body would feel against mine."

"Would you like to come in?"

He stepped inside, closed the door, and took her face in his hands. His kiss was slow, tender, loving. When he released her, he stuffed his hands in his pockets. "Sorry. I couldn't help myself you look so beautiful. Are you hungry?"

"Famished." She pulled him to her, her lips tingling at the touch of his. His scent worked its magic. Every fiber in her being wanted to take him upstairs, devour him, instead, she set him free. "It's really good to see you, Sam."

Audra assumed they had arrived to their destination. It seemed as though the truck had backed into a confined space, the outside noise, suddenly muffled by the barrier surrounding the vehicle. She no longer heard traffic, road noise, or seagulls. What came next, chilled her to the bone. The first cry came from what sounded like a toddler. Whimpering escalated into uncontrollable wails, and hiccups. The whimper lasted a few moments longer, and then Audra heard a scream, a loud smack, and a thump.

One by one, the containers were emptied. When it came her turn, her hands were bound, and a black sack was thrown over her head. "*Mossa!*" A voice demanded. Audra scooted forward, her feet navigating the space below her. Someone grabbed her arm, pulling her forward until her feet met the ground. She twisted her ankle on impact, falling forward on her knees, her palms. The floor was smooth, greasy. She smelled exhaust fumes, and more distinct odors. Fennel. Vinegar. *Finocchio marino.* She knew the fragrance well. Her mother made it often, using a variety of fennel grown along the rocky coast of Apulia, and white vinegar. She stored the concoction in glass jars, and served it with antipasto salad, or used the finocchio in a pasta dish called, *pasta con le sarde e finocchietto*, made with sardines, saffron, raisins, and *pinoles*, pine nuts. In a pinch, finocchio marina could be purchased in the *Lebensmittelgeschäfte* back in Germany, and Sam said he found it in California grocers as well, but it wasn't as good as their mother's.

Audra concluded this location was a holding center. *For what purpose?* Her pulse quickened. She wanted to call out to Rubio. *Was he even here?* She recalled getting into his car...he told her she looked nice and leaned toward her as if to give her a kiss. She closed her eyes, anticipating his lips, but instead of a kiss, he jammed a needle into her leg. She didn't have time to question his motive, the drug paralyzed her senses, and she blacked out.

Now, a meaty hand pushed her forward, she bumped into a wall. She stretched her hands out in the darkness, only to have them knocked away from the wall, but not before she discovered the structure was rough. Puglia was known for their *trulli's*, stone structures built without mortar. Navigating Puglia took experienced travelers. It was easy to get lost in the maze of unmarked streets. She remembered going uphill, hearing seagulls, trains. No. She was closer to the coast. Lecce was known to import finocchio marina. Lecce also had ports nearby.

Where were they taking her? The others? *Children.* She felt sick. Sam had warned her of the traffickers in Cologne, Berlin, Hamburg, how they hung around the bus depots, train stations, luring young girls into prostitution. But she wasn't *dumb.* She knew to stay away from *riff raff* as Sam called them. Rubio seemed like a regular guy. He was educated, well-dressed, handsome, charming. She imagined him a little naughty, but never evil.

Audra became aware of the temperature change, and smell in the air. The fennel smell mingled with the smell of urine. Hers?

"Tutto spento! Usa il bagno. Mettiti questi," a raspy voice

said. Her handler thrust a bundle of fabric at her chest. *"Capiche?"*

Audra nodded her head. Her clothes were wet, they needed to be changed. A wrinkled hand guided her to a toilet, lifted her skirt, pulled down her tights and panties. "Sit."

Audra obeyed, her bladder let loose, following orders. She had barely finished her business before she felt her boots being tugged off her feet. Then came her tights and panties.

"Apri le tue gambe," the raspy voice directed. Audra played dumb. She didn't want to open her legs, but warm water gushed upward, and Audra was caught by surprise.

"Mettiti questi," the raspy voice commanded. Washed clean, her boots and garments were replaced with dry panties and a loose shift. No bra, no shoes. *No running...* "Where are they taking me?" A blow to the head knocked the question from her lips. She saw stars, and hit the ground.

When she awoke, she was back in her crate, surrounded by what sounded like *mewling kittens* all around her. She wasn't the only one. The nightmare was real. She drew her knees to her chest and covered her ears. A scream lodged in her throat.

. . .

"I have to confess," Sam said, glancing from the road to Suzanne, and back again. "I didn't choose Los Pinos just for the food, which is excellent, by the way, I chose it because I wanted you all to myself, with no distractions."

"I'm happy you did. I love this drive." She turned toward him, placed her hand over his. "I missed you."

Sam couldn't contain the grin that appeared on his face. He withdrew his hand and placed it over hers. Suddenly, Suzanne pulled her hand away, drew her knees to her chest, and cupped both hands over her ears. Sam pulled off the freeway, and stopped alongside of the road.

"Suzanne? What is it? What's happening?" He slipped his arm around her and drew her close. "Let me help you. Tell me what you're seeing."

"It's dark. I can hear them, they're everywhere!"

"What are they? Describe them to me."

"I can't see them," she cried.

"Tell me what they sound like, can you do that?"

Suzanne flattened her palms against her ears. "Kittens. I hear kittens. But they're not kittens! They're—"

"What, Suzanne?" He gently implored. "You can tell me."

Suzanne removed her hands from her ears, her eyes haunted, her face pale. It was as if the word coming from her mouth was not her own. "*Children.*"

Sam placed a hand on her shoulder, his tone softened, sounding hypnotic. "Breathe." Gently, he massaged her shoulder, focusing on the trigger point between the rotator cuff, and the crook of her neck.

"I'll be fine," she said, glancing at his hand, then meeting his stare. "Why does this happen whenever we're together? Why can't we just have a quiet dinner without one of these visions hijacking our evening?"

The lines creasing his forehead relaxed. "I'm beginning to feel special." The grin that followed eased her mind. *He understands.*

"I have no explanation for this one," she said, taking his hand in hers. "I've seen this girl before. It's almost as if she's been with me since my near-death experience. I have no idea what our connection is…she wasn't one of Dixon's victims. At least I'm not feeling that she is."

"We can put all of that behind us, Suzanne. Dixon is dead."

"The man I see—I sense he's another Dixon. Charming, good looking…a predator. I feel she's in danger, but I don't understand, why am I hearing kittens, or children cry? It's maddening."

"Could it be spousal abuse? So many kids get caught in the mix of anger, and insanity. One of the most difficult parts of my job as Sheriff are the 10-16 calls. You never know what you're walking into."

"I don't know. There's something about the crying. It's muffled, or indistinct. It reminds of the time I approached these kids outside of a grocery store. They had this box, and when they lifted the lid, I saw it was filled with these adorable fluffy kittens." She smiled. "Maybe the universe is trying to tell me I need a cat in my life."

"What do you say we discuss it over dinner?"

"You sure you don't want to take me home?"

"And miss gazing at you by candlelight? No way!"

"How do you always manage to make me feel better?"

"It's something I enjoy doing?" He patted her knee. "I live for these moments."

They pulled back onto the freeway, feeling as though the storm had passed. But in the back of Sam's mind, niggled the phone call he received earlier, the faint prattle and crackle before the hang-up.

"How would you feel about taking a trip with me?"

She returned his question with a salacious smile. "Don't you think we should get through dinner first?"

After what seemed like an eternity in hell, Audra heard movement outside of her crate. The chain, keeping the lid secure, slid to the floor with a clang. A small hand reached inside with a bottle of water, and a sandwich. "Toilet," the small voice said, dropping an empty plastic bag into her lap. Audra could see the barrel of the AK47 strapped to the kids back.

It had taken a few seconds for Audra's eyes to adjust to the light, but she assessed the child was male, between 10 and 12, possibly Asian. She could barely make out his features. His skin was pale, his arms seemed too thick to be female, his fingernails, bitten to the nub. Angry scars circled his wrists. The command in his voice when he said, "toilet" resonated authority that comes from fear. Audra had worked with enough children to recognize the symptoms.

During her schooling, she worked at a Grundshule near her home in Frankfurt. The children's ages ranged from 6 to 10. Once they finished with Grundshule, the kids were divided into three categories, the slower kids went to Hauptshule, Realschule prepared kids for vocational work, and Gymnasium prepared students for University. Working with children in Grundshule gave one a pretty good idea of which kids would end up where. One boy in particular stood out to Audra. *Martin.* He was frail, suffered with asthma. Bullies love to tease, ridicule, play mean tricks on him, but Martin always seemed to outsmart the best of them. He spoke quietly, 'Martin the Mouse,' they nick-named him. One day he had taken enough of their abuse. She saw his hands shake, his knees clench together, his voice took on a deep tone, it sounded tough, and strong. But Audra knew this façade was out of anger, shame, frustration, and wouldn't last long…*like this boy.*

"*Danka,*" she said to the boy, before light transcended into darkness.

"Welcome," the boy mumbled back, closing the lid.

American, she thought. *How did he get here?* Wherever 'here' was. And— *what do they intend to do with me?*

. . .

Dinner was relaxing for Sam and Suzanne, the booth cozy, their conversation intimate. Star crossed lovers converging at last. "I've never felt this way," Sam said, reaching for Suzanne's hand across the table. "I swear you've put a spell on me."

"I think witches cast spells, not psychics," she said.

"Are you sure?"

Suzanne chuckled. "Yes, I'm sure. But I do have to agree with you, this evening has been rather intoxicating."

"Intoxicating? Dear God, how much alcohol did they put in your drink?"

She could feel her cheeks warm. "Hardly enough to make me feel this good. It's you, Sam. I feel good around you."

"Good enough to go to Germany with me?"

"You were serious!"

"I was thinking about visiting my folks, and my sister."

"And here I was thinking Seattle, the Grand Canyon, San Diego— Germany is far, I don't speak the language!"

"I do. And I know my parents would love you. My sister, eh, not so sure."

"I'm flattered to be asked. Can I think about it?"

"Of course. No pressure. I thought May would be a nice time to go. It's still a bit chilly, but spring is a beautiful time of year. There are many festivals, and gardens to visit."

"Sounds lovely."

"I like to go before the tourist season."

"When you're in Germany, do you feel like you're home?"

"I haven't been back in years. The last time wasn't so pleasant. My sister and I had a falling out."

"Tell me about your sister."

"Audra is—how can I say this nicely? She has a mind of her own, and she believes life should be the way she wants it."

"Sounds like a spirited young lady."

"Somehow, I think the two of you would hit it off. You both seem to be—"

"Stubborn?"

Sam's full lips parted, revealing straight white teeth. "Finish your drink. We may be able to catch the sunset heading home."

Suzanne took a sip and pushed the drink aside. "I love a good sunset, let's go."

Sam paid the bill and escorted Suzanne out the door. Before she got into the car, she took his hand and placed it around her waist. "Before we go any farther, there's something I would like."

"Say the word, it's yours."

"A kiss. I would really like another kiss."

Sam pulled her close. His eyes seized hers, setting

her on fire. His lips were gentle, sweet. "I thought you'd never ask," he whispered.

"Let's go home," she said.

Audra nibbled on her sandwich. She sipped her water, and waited. It seemed too quiet. Minutes had turned to hours. Day had turned to night. Audra could tell by the ceased activity. No more hustle bustle. The trains became less frequent, airplanes, less frequent. She strained to hear voices. Strained to hear clues concerning her destiny. She wracked her brain, reliving her date with Rubio. The way he acted, his questions, his demeanor. *He set me up.*

Suddenly a phone rang. The person receiving the call paced back and forth, his voice loud, then soft. He spoke in a language Audra was not familiar with. It wasn't Italian. *Farsi?* Maybe. The one word she understood was "ship".

Her body shook. Tears stung her eyes, yet she didn't cry out. Wherever they were taking her, she would remain strong. She relied on Britta's sensibility to track her down when she didn't show up. To tell someone. But, *who?*

When they arrived back at the house, Suzanne couldn't get inside fast enough. Sam quickly locked the door behind him, cupped Suzanne's face in his hands and covered her mouth with his. His tongue slipped between her teeth, exploring his boundaries. Suzanne welcomed him, pressing her body against his. Together they probed and prodded, finding the right rhythm, the right amount of pressure, and thrust.

"I forgot how good you taste," he said, nibbling his way along her jaw, down her neck, and returning to her lips.

"In that case, I think we should go upstairs for a refresher course."

"Just a heads up, I'm a slow learner. This may take all night."

Suzanne took his hand, leading him up the stairs, and into her room. A nightlight glowed from the corner of the room, casting their shadows on the wall. Sam noticed the room looked very different from the time he rescued her from Ben. The bed now faced the window, where she could greet the morning sun. Pillows, in muted shades covered half of the bed. The detective in him longed to turn on the light, note the changes, but his lover side didn't dare spoil the mood. He felt like a college kid about to make love to his high school sweetheart.

Suzanne began to undress, but one hoop earring caught in her sweater. "Great," she grumbled.

"Here, let me help," he said, releasing the thread from the metal. He pulled the sweater over her head, and tossed it on the bed. His eyes feasted on the swell of flesh spilling over black lace. He bent down to kiss each mound before reaching around her back, unhooking her bra, and setting her free. "Let me look at you," he said, filling his eyes with her beauty. He removed his shirt, and drew her close, skin to skin. His kiss, gentle at first, increased in urgency. Shedding their clothes between kisses, they stood naked, holding each other so tight, their hearts beat as one.

Suzanne lifted the bedspread, sending pillows and clothes tumbling to the floor. She gasped at the giant shadow the mound created on the wall. "If that thing moves, kill it," she said in jest.

Sam laughed, easing Suzanne onto the bed, touching and tasting her, on the way down. He moved her into a comfortable position, maintaining his stride. She moaned with each stroke, each nibble, until his lips found hers, and their passion ignited.

"Please," she begged, "I want you inside me."

Sam gazed into her eyes as he prepared her for his entry. Once inside, he moved slowly, feeling her rise up to meet each thrust.

Suzanne had dreamt of this moment, but never expected to feel such ecstasy with a man she had spent so little time with. Sure, they had grown close pursuing Dixon, even had unbridled, needy sex. But this was different. As he moved inside of her, she felt as though he was healing her from the inside out. She felt loved, safe, cherished, desired, *whole*. When he whispered the words, "Come with me," she knew he referred to more than a physical release, he was inviting her to be with him forever. She cried out, answering his call, as their souls soared to great heights and exploded into the ether.

"I wasn't expecting—" Sam caught his breath and propped himself up on one elbow. He traced Suzanne's lips with his finger. She returned his gaze.

"Dessert in bed?"

"It's more than that—it's—" His eyes traveled the length of her body and back. "I never imagined—" Suzanne pressed her fingers on his lips.

"Yes."

"Yes?" Confusion creased his brow. Suzanne laughed.

"Yes, I'll go to Germany with you."

VISION

Lewis had no patience when it came to waiting on a woman. Trudy learned years ago that when he was ready to leave, it was time to go. No dinking around.

Waiting on her cousin, and her cousin's friend, was torture. "Y'said she'd be here at noon. It's 'alf past."

"Keep yer britches hitched. She'll be 'ere." Trudy picked up a basket filled with yarn and several gages of knitting needles. She selected a set already attached to a strand of grey wool. The clickety clack sound of the needles, and the repetitious movement, eased her mind. Two rows in, she heard the buzzer. She tossed the project back into the basket and rose. Wagging her finger she said, "Don't ye be sayin' nothin' 'bout the time. Tess is doin' us a favor."

Lewis peeked through the peephole. "'E looks pretty dodgy, 'e does."

"The two of ye can 'ave a good chin-wag in the parlor."

"And where will ye be?"

"In the garden with Tess."

"I feel like a barmy ol' fool."

"Puddle mush. Open the door before they grow roots."

Lewis opened the door and forced a smile. "Tess! Good to see y' gal. Come in."

"This 'ere's Martin Joseph, a good friend of mine."

"Welcome." Lewis ushered the couple into the parlor. "I'm Lewis, m' wife Trudy."

Trudy grabbed Martin's hand and shook it. "Thank ye for coming, my Lew 'ere's been 'avin' these dreams—"

"Not exactly dreams…more like—"

"Visions?"

"Yes. Visions."

Trudy wrapped her arm around Tess. "Let's walk in t'garden, 'ave a chat?"

Lewis gestured for Martin to sit. "Sherry?"

"None for me, thanks."

Lewis took a seat directly across from Martin. "What d'I need t'do?"

Martin's lips curved into a warm smile. "Tell me what happened."

"Well, I saw m'self on the operating table, splayed open like a prize pig. I saw me mum, and me dad…like it was yesterday. And my friend—hung 'imself he did, when the plague hit in '96. Damn shame. 'E was a good ol' chap. Lost everythin'."

"Did they speak to you?"

"Yes. They spoke of a lass. Said she's in trouble. Said they took 'er to Lecce."

"Italy?"

"Yes. I saw money. Euros. Lots of 'em. It felt as though she'd been sold."

"Did your neighbor tell you who 'they' are?"

"No." Lewis bowed his head. "Feels like I'm watchin' someone drown, and I can't swim."

"Sounds like you had a near death experience. When that happens, a person steps into the other side, where all things are revealed."

Lewis's eyes narrowed. "Don't believe in that 'ogwash."

"It's pretty far-fetched. I was eight years old when a livery truck went rogue and smashed our Fiat like a cockroach. I was comatose for three and a half weeks. When I awoke, I knew Jack Brabham won the British Grand Prix, I knew his time was 1:34.4 on lap 56, I knew that John Surtees placed second, and Innes Ireland placed third—six months before the race took place. I've seen horrific crimes weeks before they happen, but going to the police has only made me a prime suspect.

Lewis' head dropped into his hands. He covered his eyes. "I feel so helpless. Why show me somethin' I can't do anythin' about? Why torment me like this?"

"It's a bloody mystery." Martin clasped his hands behind his head. "Do you want answers?"

"Yes, but I may be pushin' dirt or bonkers before the answer reveals itself!"

"Don't beat your head. The answers will come. Do you meditate?"

"Thought that rubbish went out with John Lennon?"

Martin unclasped his hands and slapped one knee. "Rubbish is it?"

Lewis chuckled. His mood lightened a bit. "I've heard the term—not so sure I'd know how to go 'bout it."

"Go within. Be silent. Listen to your thoughts. There's plenty of books, listen-ups. You can find something that works for you, man. Relax, let the information flow." Martin leaned forward, his eyes narrowed, his pitch dropped a notch. "I walked in your shoes. After a few miles, I found my stride." Martin winked. "It helps to write your thoughts down, no matter how willy-nilly they seem."

"Does this ever go away?"

"It's not the flu. You've changed. You died; you came back. Ask yourself why? You feel helpless, I understand, but the more information you collect, the more pieces of the puzzle you'll have to work with."

"And y'think I'll get the whole picture in time?"

"Maybe. Maybe not. It may take a month—it may take years. All I know is for me, my job here wasn't finished. Perhaps I was meant to have this conversation with you, and for that reason alone I was spared. We're like one big machine. Every part is integral. I may be the cog in your wheel. Tomorrow you may be the cog in someone else's. It's the way the universe works, man."

Lewis reached for Martin's hand and shook. Although he felt a wee bit better, darkness lingered in his soul. When he rose, he felt unsteady. *Moving.* His stomach turned sour. He wanted to lie down. *Disappear.*

Audra struggled to keep the meager meal she had eaten from erupting. She never had a problem with motion sickness—until now. The crate pitched and swayed. Waves pounded the vessel. The wind howled, drowning out the cries around her. She closed her eyes and prayed. Prayed the storm would subside, prayed she wouldn't choke on her vomit, prayed she wouldn't die in her sleep.

JACK?

The phone rang, startling Suzanne out of her reverie. Her night with Sam was extraordinary. She could almost feel his touch on her skin. She clicked on her phone without a second thought, ignoring the caller ID.

"Suzanne? Suzanne Cash?"

"Yes. Who's calling?" she asked.

"It's Sheena. Sheena Bradford, do you remember me?"

"Yes! How are you? How is the baby?"

"Emmett is fine, he's cutting teeth, into everything…"

"Before you know it, he'll be asking for the keys to your car!"

Sheena laughed. She sounded good. Happy. "You're probably wondering why I'm calling," she said, her voice suddenly serious.

"Tell me." Suzanne sat up, and braced herself for what was to come.

"Emmett is starting to display—how can I put this? He has a gift. One I don't fully understand. I thought perhaps, you could meet him. Give me some insight on what to expect."

"Sheena, geez, I don't really know how it all works myself, perhaps—"

"Please, Suzanne? I trust you." She paused. "Besides, I've never had the chance to thank you in person."

"I don't know, Sheena, New York is—"

"I'm in Sacramento. I moved back. There was no sense staying after Dixon murdered my cousin. I wanted to go back to school, finish my degree at Sac State."

"In that case, I would love to get together. Unfortunately, I'm busy this week, how about next?"

"Excellent! And Suzanne?"

"Yes?"

"He says your name."

S uzanne ended the call, her mind reeling. She thought Jack was finished with her once he reincarnated, moved into a new body, a new future. Did he intend to hijack her mind again? *He's a baby. How could a baby be a problem?* Only one way to find out.

Suzanne practically jumped out of her skin when the doorbell rang. She glanced out the window. *Sam.* She ran to the door.

"You'll never guess who—" She stopped mid-sentence. Sam's face was stone-cold serious. "Sam? What is it? What happened?"

"I was hoping you could tell me," he said. "Can I come in?"

"I don't understand, what's wrong?"

"My father called this morning. Audra's friend Britta called my parents to see if they had heard from my sister. They had dinner plans three nights ago. My sister didn't show up, and Britta hasn't been able to reach her."

Suzanne's blood ran cold. Chills ran up her spine. The image of the leggy girl with crimson hair flashed across her brain.

Sam could tell by Suzanne's expression she was getting a hit. His heart stampeded in his chest; tears filled his eyes. "You saw her. You told me about the girl, you mentioned the Belvedere. Is that where you saw her?"

"I saw a young woman. I had no idea who she was." Tiny hairs prickled on the back of Suzanne's neck. "I don't know the location, it was dark, someone was following her. That's all I saw."

Sam took a step toward her. "Think Suzanne, think. There must be more!"

Suzanne flinched. Sam's intensity caught her off guard. "I had asked you if there were any missing girls, you said 'no'."

Sam took a deep breath and exhaled. "I'm sorry.

How could you know?"

"Know what?"

"It's my fault, I should've followed up."

"I don't understand."

"I got a weird call from my sister's number. I thought maybe it was a mistake. I didn't follow up."

"Don't do that to yourself, Sam. Not calling back doesn't necessarily equate to a problem."

Sam nodded. He looked miserable. "You warned me. I didn't listen. I thought it was just *coincidental*."

"You're right—what I saw <u>may</u> be nothing."

"No, Suzanne, you've never been wrong. You're my only hope."

MISSING

Lewis stared out the window. A storm swept through London, flooding the streets, and slowing traffic to a crawl. Headlights bobbed below, smearing light in both directions. Every now and then, the wind would whistle through the trees, shaking them senseless. In the distance, bells eerily tolled from Westminster Abbey. He didn't hear Trudy enter the room.

"What'cha staring at luv?"

Lewis startled. "Damn, Tru, don't sneak up on me like that."

"For the love of muffins, yer an oily skillet. I brought y'tea, thank y'very much."

"Sorry, luv. I feel like I could jump out of me skin, these days. Like I got a grasshopper in m'knickers."

"I know, luv. Come. Sit. Tell me 'bout it. I'm a good listener."

"Wish I could explain it t'where it makes a lick 'a sense."

"Try me, luv. I promise not t'judge."

Lewis settled into a chair. He poured a dab of cream into his cup; Trudy poured his tea. He sipped gingerly, blowing between sips. "I'm afraid to close me eyes—it's like I'm trapped in a horror movie. The kind where y'feel the evil gettin' stronger, the music gets louder, and y'just know there's somethin' waitin' 'round the corner that's gonna make y'crap yer knickers, and scream like a teenage girl."

"What do y'think is 'round the corner, Lew?"

"I don't know. That's the horror of it all. I feel it, but I just don't know."

"Did Martin Joseph give any advice?"

"Humph. 'E said t'meditate. Reminds me of when the Beatles lost their minds to that Maharishi back in the day. Maybe I should get m'self stoned."

"May be fun!"

"Oh Tru, isn't it like y'to see the sunny side of things?"

"I feel blessed yer still here, Lew. There's always that."

Lew smiled for the first time since Trudy stepped into the room. "I'll figure it out luv. Somehow, I'll figure it out."

• • •

Sheena Bradford pretended to dust around Emmet's chubby legs with a feather-duster. "Does that tickle?" Emmett giggled with delight. "I talked to our friend today. She said she would love to meet you. What do you think about that?"

Emmett climbed off the coffee table and toddled to the bookshelf across the room. He navigated the books on the shelf, babbling to himself. Sheena grabbed her phone and turned on her camera.

"What'cha looking for buddy?" She moved closer to capture his expression and garble for future reference. "Can you smile for mommy?"

Sheena watched him pull each book half-way out, check the title, and push it back in. "Are you looking for Barney? Those are mommy's books, Bud, your books are down below." Emmett didn't veer from his mission. When he found what he was looking for, he pulled the book onto the floor, plopped down, pointed to one of the photos on the cover, and grunted. His expression was so intense, Sheena zoomed in.

"That's Big Ben, Em. Do you like the clock?"

Emmett opened the book, featuring landmarks all over the world. He carefully turned the pages until another photo caught his eye. He pointed and grunted again.

"That's the London Bridge, sweetie, like the song," she sang, "*London Bridge is falling down, falling down, falling down, London Bridge is falling down, my fair lady.*"

Emmett turned to another page, and another, his tiny features intent on something specific. Through the viewer, she saw his eyes light up. He pointed to the Westminster Abbey and got all excited.

A chill skittered up Sheena's spine. "Why those photos, Em? What are you trying to tell me?" He closed the book and perused the shelf. He settled on a dog-eared paperback. "Let mommy see, honey. Whatcha got there?" Emmett handed her the book.

She couldn't believe her eyes. Goosebumps gathered on her flesh. Out of all the books Emmett could have chosen, this one gave her the creeps. A girl running for her life, the title scrawled across the cover struck a nerve: "Missing."

∾

BROTHERHOOD

S am sighed. "I'm sorry things didn't work out. I hope you understand." Suzanne straightened his shirt collar. Worry, and lack of sleep stole the sparkle from her eyes, and the smile from his lips. "I'll be back as soon as I can."

Suzanne walked him to the escalator, rode one floor up and stopped. Airport security wouldn't allow her any further.

"I pray you find her, Sam. And I pray that she is unharmed."

"I'll call you when I get to Austria. Let me know if you get anything, I don't care how trivial it seems, or what time of day or night. Britta is meeting me at the airport. She is going to help me trace Audra's steps." He pinched the bridge of his nose. "She said my sister met someone on the train. They met up at the Belvedere Palace—some art exhibit."

"Klimpt."

"Yes, that's the one. How did–"

"I saw the Belvedere the first time I met you. The Klimpt exhibit banner hung by the entrance. Oh Sam, if I had only known." Suzanne hung her head.

"How could anyone know?" He pulled her close. "Drive safe. I gotta go." He kissed her tenderly and waved goodbye. She was still waving when the tram doors closed. She felt as if a part of her left with him.

ART

The plane landed at Sacramento International Airport at 3:00 p.m. Passengers from all over the world snaked their way around the roped off area for their turn to have their passports stamped, and enter the U.S.

Giorgi Von Graff stood behind a woman from Salinas, chatting as if they were long-time friends, her brown eyes sparkled as he spoke.

"Where would you recommend that I dine first?"

The woman's reply dripped with snobbery. "The Fire House on 2nd Street is lovely, if you want American cuisine."

"I will take your suggestion," he said, his dazzling smile winning her over.

"There's Morton's on Capitol Mall, if you like steak and seafood."

"Yes, I do love both."

Just then, she turned to acknowledge the Customs and Border Protection Officer calling, "Next?"

"Enjoy Sacramento," she said, smiling, and scooting her luggage in front of her.

Giorgi offered to help. "May I?"

The woman blushed, and flipped her blond hair to one side. "I'm fine, but thank you."

A CBP Officer motioned to Giorgi, and he stepped up to the booth. "Reason for entering the U.S.?" he asked, his tone dry as toast.

"Business. I am an art dealer." Giorgi produced his passport. The Officer thumbed through it, lifting his gaze.

"You've made several trips this year, Mr. Von Graff. The art business must be quite lucrative."

"It can be, yes. Staying afloat requires constant attention."

"I see. And how long do you intend to stay in the U.S.?"

Giorgi handed the Officer his itinerary. "My return ticket is for one week from today. I expect to leave accordingly."

The Officer stared at Giorgi for a moment longer, then stamped his passport. Slowly, he handed the document back to Giorgi, his face transforming from stoic to friendly. "Welcome to the U.S., have a nice day. His smile vanished. "Next?"

Giorgi picked up his suitcase, and moved through the turnstile.

Outside the airport, Giorgi saw the woman he chatted up in line getting into a car driven by a familiar face. She nodded. He nodded back. Business as usual.

He hailed a cab, and gave the driver an address. "Westlake Village."

Giorgi checked into his hotel, unpacked a few items, and dressed in a charcoal suit, and white shirt. He pulled one of the many red ties from the drawer, looped it through his collar and tied a perfect knot. He examined his image in the mirror. He looked like your typical business man, as he would expect the men he was meeting to look as well, with one difference, the red tie, red ascot, red shoes they wore would speak of the brotherhood they shared.

He slipped into a cab, and instructed the driver to take him to Morton's House of Steaks.

When he entered the restaurant, he greeted the hostess with his charming smile. "I am meeting—oh there they are!" He slipped past her and joined two men at the bar.

The man wearing a red ascot slid to his left, offering Giorgi the seat in the middle. Giorgi looked down, spying red shoes worn by the man on his right. "Gentlemen," he said. "What are we drinking?"

The two men exchanged glances. Red ascot spoke up. "What do you recommend?"

Giorgi plucked the wine list from its brass holder,

opened it up and began pursuing the vinyl covered pages. "I hear the red wines are the finest in this establishment. Says here, plump, juicy grapes, picked at the peak of perfection."

"Local or imported?" Red Ascot asked with utmost curiosity.

"I prefer reds from Italy." Giorgi proclaimed. "I am told shipments arrive regularly through the port of Sacramento."

"And the vintage?" Red Shoes turned to Giorgi, his lip quivering slightly.

Giorgi studied Red shoes piggy eyes. "Aged 6-14 years. Does that meet your satisfaction?"

Red shoes could barely contain his excitement. He gestured to the waiter. "We'll have three glasses of your best red wine." He rose, and gestured with a head nod. "And bring them to our table." A grin spread across his face. "Suddenly, I'm very—*hungry*."

Red ascot agreed. "Famished."

WATER

Suzanne glanced at the clock. Sam had only been in the air 4 hours, and already she missed him terribly. She returned her dinner to the kitchen untouched and turned on the TV. She scrolled through the listings, hoping a program would catch her attention and take her away from her angst. She couldn't imagine the pain Sam felt knowing some monster had kidnapped his sister.

She clicked on BBC. Maybe old reruns of "Are You Being Served" would lighten her mood. Strange dialog caused her to increase the volume. It was as if another conversation was layered over the existing dialog. Did that even happen? Was it possible to dub the sound of one program over another? She listened carefully.

"I keep seeing her, Tru. Each time I close my eyes, she's there."

Suzanne turned the volume up another notch.

"I'm afraid what they'll do to her."

"Lewis, y'can't be in your right mind after what happened."

"Trudy, I saw her. Jim said she was in trouble, and she is!"

"Y'died, Lew! They had to resuscitate ye, y'lost oxygen to your brain."

"It's real, Tru, y'got t'believe me."

Suzanne dropped the remote.

Once she composed herself, she googled "near-death experiences." The list of prompts was endless. She had to narrow it down. She typed in "Lewis" near death experience. Again, pages of websites popped up on her screen. *Perhaps Lewis is British?* She typed in more key words and scrolled through the prompts, one by one. After viewing 34 websites to no avail, she found one that could be beneficial. A small article was printed in a London Journal a couple months earlier. Lewis Howard from Kensington pronounced dead for four hours after open heart surgery regains consciousness. Wife Trudy claims his survival is a miracle.

When Suzanne googled Lewis Howard, Kensington London, little came up. Beneath the same article was a photo of man in his early forties posing with Princess Diana and Dodi Fayed outside of Harrods of London. The previous article didn't mention Lewis was famous, sharing the same name had to be coincidental. For the next hour, she perused the internet, astounded at the number of people who shared her plight. One man from

Russia reported waking up 3 days after he was pronounced dead, others reported hours, minutes.

Some recounted their visit in heaven, others described the depths of hell, a number of people had no recollection at all. What surprised her were how many people there were who had stories similar to hers. What the articles didn't divulge was how many came away with visions like hers. And what about Lewis? Was he out there experiencing visions of brutality? Crimes against helpless women and children? Or was he getting lottery numbers? Hitting it big on the crap tables? Her brain hurt from thinking too hard, her eyes burned, her lids felt heavy. She laid her head down on the desk and began to dream…

She dreamt she was riding along, surrounded by lush, green countryside. Sunlight dappled Sycamore trees and a sweet scent filled her senses. Suddenly she caught a whiff of something unpleasant. A burning smell. Flesh. She rolled up her car window, but it was too late. The odor permeated her nose, grew stronger by the minute. *Meat. Burnt meat.* There was no escaping it, she looked for the source. In the distance, a plume of smoke. Then came the sound, bleating sheep, barking dogs, cows, moaning in pain. Horses added to the cacophony. Gun shots rang out in succession. *Turn around.* Turn around before you reach—*the slaughter.*

Suzanne woke with a start. Her fingers hit the

keyboard, bringing her computer back to life. She typed the words "slaughter in London." She got more than she bargained for.

Her screen filled with newsworthy items; MAD COW wipes out England's cattle industry. British outbreak affects about 180,000 cattle and devastates farming communities. Creutzfeldt-Jakob Disease—a fatal disease that slowly destroys the brain and spinal cord in cattle…the list went on. But what did Mad Cow have to do with Lewis, his near-death experience? And what was Lewis Howard's connection to Sam's missing sister?

"I'm tired," she said, flipping off her computer. A hot bath with scented oils seemed like a needed reprieve.

She turned on the faucet, lit a candle and turned out the light. Shedding her brushed cotton tee and faded jeans, she stripped down to bare skin, and accessed her image in the mirror over the sink. *Not bad.* Her full breasts were still perky, her stomach flat, and lean. She was one of the lucky ones who didn't contend with cellulite, and her buttocks were firm. She hadn't scrutinized herself in a long time. Her shape was never topic for conversation with Ben. But now? Now she appreciated her body, and the way it fit together with Sam's, like a puzzle piece.

She splashed cold water on her face, and blotted it dry, but her flushed cheeks remained. She wound her hair into a top-knot, secured it with a tortoise-shell pick, and stepped into the tub. The temperature was perfect. Not too hot, not too cold.

She lathered a sponge and glided it over her smooth skin, leaving a sudsy trail. She imagined Sam's lips following the trail, his hands exploring her body, cupping her breasts, massaging the crevice between her legs. She closed her eyes to relive their lovemaking. His hot kisses, finding places she had forgotten existed. His weight pinning her down as he ravished her inside and out. The way their bodies moved together in sync, puzzle pieces, made from the clay. The intensity of their climax, waves, crashing again and again upon the shore, as they clung together, their hearts beating as one. His scent, clean and spicy, still lingered on her bedsheets. She longed for his return.

She submerged deeper in the tub, rinsing the memory from her skin. She prayed for his sister's safety, but the vision that flitted through her sixth sense said differently.

The water in the tub began to pitch, sloshing over the sides. Suzanne sat up, trying to erase the image from her brain. "Nooo," she cried, hanging onto the side of the tub, but the water swelled and receded. Suzanne closed her eyes, facing the message head-on. Crying, mewling, echoed in her ears, the stench of urine, feces, and vomit assaulted her nose. Another sound, creaking, metal against metal...and then it stopped. The water stopped moving, the odors, gone, the sounds, gone, with the exception of one voice, that sounded as if it were coming from the bottom of a well. "Help me."

Audra squeezed her eyes shut, opened them, and repeated the exercise a few more times. *I'm still alive.*

The seas seemed to have calmed as they glided along. It was hot. Humid. *Somewhere tropical.* But where? They had been at sea for seven days according to the tally marks etched on her leg with her fingernail. If her geography served her right, if the ship was heading north, it would be cold. If it were headed south, they most likely would dock in the next week. If they were heading West, much longer. And if she died along the way? Who cared?

WAVES

Sam checked into the Lindner Hotel, next to Belvedere Palace. It was a newer property, not the hotel he remembered from childhood. He took a quick shower, changed into jeans, a coral polo shirt, and navy suede jacket he only wore when abroad. Despite the pleasant daytime temps, evenings could be cool.

He had fueled up on airplane food, Salisbury steak, mashed potatoes, and broccolini, two cups of coffee, a cheese Danish, boiled egg, and two slices of bacon. Jet lag was not an option. He texted Britta when he landed. She would meet him in the lobby in ten minutes. Time was of the essence.

"Sam?" Britta's vivacious personality was reduced to 'scared kitten.' Makeup smudged beneath her eyes indicated she had been crying.

"Britta. Thank you for meeting me," he said. Britta buried her head in his shoulder, and sobbed.

"I should've called sooner. I didn't know what to do. I thought maybe—"

Sam lifted her chin, brushed away her tears with his thumbs. "You didn't know." He slipped an arm around her and lead her to a one of the lobby's chairs. The modern design reminded Sam of Nina Levitt's work. A combination of punk and porn. Britta looked perfectly at home, her leather clad legs crossed, her bosom overflowing an electric blue bodice, her blonde hair wild and free.

"What can you tell me about the guy she met?"

"I can do better." She scrolled through her phone. "Look. It's him." Sam took the phone from her hand.

"This is the guy she went to the Belvedere with?"

"She sent me the photo after he dropped her off at her place. She thought she was a clever girl for catching his image in the glass."

Sam checked the time code on the photo, 5:53 p.m. "What time were you supposed to meet Audra for dinner?"

"Eight o'clock. I waited until Nine. I texted her several times, then I thought maybe she was busy having sex or something, so I called. Three more times. I gave up and went home. No big deal. I was happy for her. I figured she was finally—" Britta stopped when she saw Sam's expression. "She said you wouldn't approve."

"Approve?"

"*The sex.* Handsome man, lonely girl. Audra liked him."

"Send me the photo. I'm going to the police, file a report. Is there anything else you can tell me?"

"She met him on the train. I think she got off at Karlsplatz, that's where we met, the café around the corner."

"Thank you, Britta. You've been very helpful." Sam pulled 50 Euros from his wallet and stuffed it into her hand. "Grab a taxi home. I'll call you if I hear anything." Sam pulled Britta to her feet and into a warm brotherly hug. "We'll find her," he vowed.

Outside, Sam hailed a cab for Britta, and one for himself. He slipped inside and gave a command. "Take me to the police station."

"This is rather unusual, Detective," the policeman replied, his accent as thick as the mustache under his nose. "You're welcome to fill out a missing person's form, but it sounds to me that you are not sure if your sister has gone missing, or if she is holed up with her lover."

"No one has heard from her in three days. She doesn't pick up her phone." Sam swiped his hand over his stubbly face. "Do you have children?"

"Yes. And I do understand your predicament, but I see no reason to suspect foul play."

Sam pulled his phone from his pocket, and offered it to the policeman. "Have you ever seen this man?"

The policeman squinted, put on a pair of reading glasses and looked closely. "Yes. He looks familiar. Let me check." The policeman disappeared through a secured door, shutting it behind him. Sam heard voices. When the policeman returned, his demeanor had completely changed.

"I cannot help you," he said, thrusting Sam's phone back at him as if it were going to blow up in his hand. "Fill out the form, your choice."

Sam didn't argue. He filled out the meager form, and handed it back to the policeman. "Thank you," he said, looking deep into the policeman's eyes. He thought he saw a flicker of remorse. He looked closer at the policeman's name: *Irlich von Steuben.*

The temperature seemed to have dropped 10 degrees in the last hour. Sam pulled his jacket closed and zipped it half-way. The wind blew, reminding him of his childhood. Of Krampus, the Christmas devil. *Where can she be?* He saw the sign for the U-Bahn, and headed down the stairs. Even if he had to ride the trains all night, he would find this pretty boy his sister was involved with.

A taller policeman opened the door to the secured room. "What did you tell him?" he asked von Steuben.

"To fill out a form or leave."

"Good. We don't need some American Rambo sticking his nose where it doesn't belong."

"I have a feeling he's not going to quit until he finds his sister."

"We don't need Giorgi Von Graff getting wind of this. Rubio is his boy. He goes down, our tits are in a ringer."

"The detective showed me his credentials. He has dual citizenship. He can make waves."

"Well, let's make sure he doesn't."

GREEN DOOR

Suzanne woke to the phone ringing next to her pillow. *Sam.* "Hello?"

"Did I wake you?"

"What time is it there?"

"Afternoon, 3:30 p.m. Rode the trains all night looking for this guy my sister met—I just got up myself. How are you?"

"I've been getting snippets, but it's too weird to even explain."

"Try me."

"I heard a conversation going on over a TV program I was watching on the British Broadcast Channel. It was a man talking to his wife about someone hurting a girl. What are the chances of that? Get this—she mentioned his near-death experience. I hopped on Google to see if I could find anything."

"And?"

"I'm not sure. This man, if he is the same man that died, was also in a photo with Dodi Fayed, and Princess Di."

"I don't see a connection."

"There lies the problem. I drifted off for a bit and had a dream about Mad Cow Disease. I'm stumped."

"You're beautiful when your stumped."

"I think I'm blushing. How did your meeting go with Britta?"

"She said my sister was lonely, and horny."

"How was that information helpful?"

"It's been years since I saw my sister. I really don't know her that well anymore. Maybe she is shacking up with some guy."

"Do you really believe that?"

"No. The police were no help. Except—"

"I'm listening."

"The policeman I spoke to seemed to recognize the photo Audra took, but acted like he didn't."

"Send me the photo, let me take a look."

Sam clicked on the photo, and forwarded it to Suzanne. "I'll wait until it comes through."

"How is your hotel?"

"It would be better if you were here with me."

Suzanne heard the ping and opened the attachment. "This is the door I saw in my visions! This is the man!"

"What else can you tell me about him?"

Suzanne closed her eyes. Nothing. All she saw was the light filtering through her bedroom window. "I don't think it works that way, Sam." She could hear his audible sigh. "I'm sorry."

"No, no—I can't expect you to—damn, I was hoping."

"If I get anything, I'll call you."

"Yeah. Okay. Fine."

Suzanne felt his disappointment. She struggled for positive words to end the call, but nothing good came to mind, instead, a feeling of foreboding washed over her. "Be careful," was all she could say.

CLIENTS

Giorgi climbed into his Mercedes SUV rental and headed for the freeway. He glanced in the mirror at his polished appearance. His clients loved him. He was their sex Santa, ho, ho, ho. *The naughtier, the better.* He catered to the twisted, insatiable, perverted, and cruel. Who was he to judge? He provided something for every palate.

He'd been doing business in Sacramento for twenty years. He serviced millionaires, politicians, celebrities, businessmen and women alike. Young, old, and in between. In his line of work, money talked. You want a fourteen-year-old virgin? Older? Younger? Girl? Boy? Dark skinned, light skinned, blue eyed, brown eyed, long hair, short hair, no problem. *I'm the candy-man.*

Soon, a fresh load of flesh would be arriving in Sacramento. The crates would be off-loaded from the ship before they reached port and were distributed accordingly. But first, he would meet with his minions, arrange for black market videos to be made in L.A. He had several buyers clamoring for their piece of the action. Those sold into the active sex slave industry would be taken to various locations, checked by doctors, and taken to their new homes. Giorgi was known for his high quality and compensated handsomely for his discretion. This shipment proved to be exceptionally profitable, with an order placed for a "babysitter" at triple the price. Rubio promised Giorgi the girl he captured fit the bill. A virgin, brunette, beautiful, nubile, and intelligent.

The buyer lived on a ranch in a rural area. He bred race-horses, owned properties all over the world, including little remote islands, he used for his escapades. When the buyer called earlier that day with a dinner invitation, Giorgi couldn't refuse. "Just a few 'close' friends," he said. Giorgi exited east on Highway 50, anticipating a very interesting evening.

Audra took small bites of the sandwich her handler threw into her crate yesterday. *Or was it the day before?* Peanut butter and jelly. Evidently, the crew hadn't considered the risk of peanut allergies. Earlier, Audra had heard a commotion. Someone screamed something about blowing up like a balloon. "

Sta esplodendo come un palloncino!"

Angry voices cursed in Italian. Then came footsteps.

Keys jangled; chains dropped to the floor. A metal door squealed opened, then closed. A shushing sound, like something being dragged across the floor. Another door opened to a balmy breeze. Then came a splash. *Dead kid overboard.*

TRANSACTION

Suzanne filled a kettle with water for tea and placed it on the stove. An image popped into her head of lighting the fire with a wooden match instead of the knob. The hands were not hers. Older. Steady. A phone rang, the same hands picked up the call.

"Who's this y'say'? And how do y'know me husband, Lew?"

Suzanne closed her eyes. She felt dizzy. But not round and round dizzy, but up and down dizzy. The feeling swelled, receded, then swelled again. *Ocean.*

Sam rode the U Bahn to the last stop, switched cars, and waited for the train to repeat the route. Three young girls got on, giggling, and speaking rapidly in French. Two sat down in one seat facing forward, the third sat across, in the aisle seat, facing the girls, and

Sam. The car filled fast, and soon very few seats were available. The door closed, and the train began to move. Sam heard a shush and a thump behind him. A young man traversed down the aisle, struggling to keep his balance. He stopped next to the girls and gestured to the empty seat.

"*Ist dieser Platz besetzt?*"

The two girls facing front giggled. The one facing Sam slid over. The young man sat down, turned and smiled at the girl next to him.

"*Danka*," he said, flashing a dazzling smile.

Sam couldn't help but notice his eyes, the shape of his face. His hair was shorter, but there was no mistaking his eyes. Sam held up his phone, pretending to text. He snapped a photo, and compared it to Audra's. *It's him.* He watched the young man flirt, despite the language barrier. Sam refrained from jumping up and ripping out his throat. When he heard him introduce himself as Rubio, he made a note. The guy moved fast, working his magic on the young girls. By the time they reached the next stop, the spell was cast.

Sam rose and grabbed the pole next to Rubio and the girls. He nodded at Rubio, gesturing toward the girls.

"*Du bist ein Glückspilz.*" *You're one lucky guy.* Sam fixed his eyes on Rubio. "I have money. I can pay."

The girls gave Sam a dirty look.

"*Pervertieren,*" one girl said to the other. Rubio laughed.

The girls turned to one another and giggled, oblivious to what he just inferred. Rubio on the other hand seemed curious.

"Pervert? Me? I have a daughter your age. <u>This</u> man is a <u>pimp</u>."

One girl looked as if Sam struck her in the face. Her eyes grew big. She grabbed her friend's hand and moved toward the front of the car.

Rubio's expression soured. "You're a cop."

"No, just a man," he replied sliding next to Rubio. "I like them a little older. Sweet. Brunettes are my favorite." Sam looked around to make sure no one was paying attention to their exchange. "I meant what I said. I have money."

"Not here," he said. "Get off at Schönbrunn. I'll meet you at Herzog's on Sechshauser Strasse in twenty minutes."

Sam winked. A sly smile spread across his face. "Maybe today is <u>my</u> lucky day."

Sam stepped onto the platform. He navigated his way to the staircase, and out into the open air. He turned this way and that to get his bearings before heading west. When he saw Herzog's, he crossed the street, and went inside. "*Zwei*," he said to the hostess. She grabbed two menus and led him to a corner table. "*Danka*," he said, and took a seat facing the door.

The large window provided him with an excellent

view of the foot traffic outside. Sam would be able to spot Rubio quickly. Or so he thought. When Rubio came around the opposite corner, ten minutes later, Sam was surprised.

Rubio didn't greet the hostess, instead, he snapped his fingers at the bartender, who dropped his bar towel, and hustled over. *They know him,* Sam thought.

"What are you drinking, American," he asked, his cavalier demeanor bordering on cocky.

"Clausthaler," Sam replied.

"Becks." Rubio waited until the bartender was out of earshot before sharing his glib observation. "The pervert is an alcoholic as well? Interesting."

Sam's hazel eyes turned to pitch. He chuckled. "Ah, another assumption. Alcohol impedes the performance, I'm looking forward to an exciting evening."

"And what makes you think I can provide that for you?"

A cunning smile slid across Sam's face. "This isn't my first rodeo."

Rubio returned a like smile. "What do you want."

"I'm partial to brunettes. Preferably one who speaks my language." Sam leaned closer, his voice, barely a whisper, "I want to be able to understand the dirty talk, *verstehst du?*"

Rubio nodded. "Anything else?"

Sam steepled his hands on the table. "Slender, au pair, college girl, you know the type, innocent on the outside, tigress on the inside." Sam closed his eyes, his mouth relaxed into an *ahhh*, as if he was conjuring an image. When he opened his eyes, Rubio was staring. "I'm very particular, " he said, "but as I said earlier, I can pay."

Rubio leaned back in the chair. A darkness washed over him. Was it regret? Sam didn't want to speculate. His agenda was to save his sister, not heed this moron's guilty conscience. At least, not yet.

"Why not hire a prostitute?" Rubio's eyes narrowed. "There are plenty to be had."

"For the same reason I don't buy my wine at the local market."

"I see, you are an elitist."

"I thought I was a perverted alcoholic?"

Rubio, nodded. "Same difference."

"And you speak very good English for a—pimp."

"Touché!" Rubio chuckled. "I consider myself more of a—" He thought for a moment, his lips puckered, "—a collector of art."

"Then we are on the same page."

"Meet me at St. Stephen's Cathedral at ten tonight. Don't be late."

"How do I know you are not setting me up?"

Rubio's eyes hardened. "You don't. Bring cash." He took a swig of beer, rose, and hurried out of Herzog's.

Sam texted Suzanne: Found the guy. Pray I find Audra.

· · ·

Suzanne sat at her desk, deciphering her scribbled notes. She needed to find the man in the photo. Lewis Howard. She started her computer and began to search. UK phone book. She typed in his name, Kensington, London, and hit return. Six names scrolled across the screen. She dialed the first.

On the fourth try, she heard the familiar voice. "I'm trying to reach a Lewis Howard—he was in the meat business..."

The words echoed the voice in her head, "Ow do y'know m'husband, Lew?"

"Mrs. Howard, I don't actually know your husband, I know of him, I know he had a near death experience, I know a girl is missing...I keep seeing him, hearing his voice..."

Trudy nearly collapsed on the floor. She caught herself by grabbing onto a kitchen chair. Her voice was weak when she called, "Lew–Lew come, it's for you."

Lewis answered with a suspicious, "'ello?"

"My name is Suzanne Cash, I'm calling from America. I too, had a near death experience. I see things, hear things, they don't make sense half the time, but as I told your wife, there is a girl, she's in trouble–I need your help."

"I know what yer sayin,' woman, but 'ow can I

help?"

Words tumbled out of Suzanne's mouth, faster than anticipated. "I don't know—she was in Austria when she disappeared—are you getting any visions? She's a dark-haired girl, in her twenties…"

Lewis took the phone to his chair and sat down. It seemed the weight of the world had lifted off his shoulders. "Then, I'm not daft after all."

Suzanne exhaled, "I know how you feel. I thought I was losing my mind! And then there was my dead boyfriend…" Suddenly there was silence on the other end of the phone. "Lewis? Are you there?"

Suzanne could hear the angst in his voice. "I saw me friend—'E told me 'bout the girl."

"He's guiding you from the other side. That's how it worked for me."

"I feel the need t'travel. I kept hearin' Lecce, had a bad feelin' 'bout the place. And water. It's all so strange. The missus thinks I popped me cork."

"No. You're fine. It was explained to me that dying changes your frequency, we pick up energy, thoughts are energy, so are visions. It's our job to figure out what it is we are supposed to do." She heard the quiver in his voice.

"Are they goin' t'find the girl?"

"With our help, yes they will."

"Then I'm beholden for y'ringin' me. What's next?"

"We share notes. Lecce must mean something…any ideas?"

"Lecce is a walled city, a bit dodgy if y'ask me. They say there's 2000 years of bloody history waitin' t'be discovered in the underground tunnels. She's a bloody perfect place for criminal activity."

"What about water? Is there water nearby?"

"Several ports. Brandisi is one of the largest."

"It's a start. The big question is, where are they taking them?"

"'Tis a 'them' then, is it?"

"I'm afraid so."

Suzanne texted Sam: Found my London source. He believes Audra was taken to Lecce. She may have been put on a boat.

Suzanne was about to fry herself an egg when the phone rang. She expected it to be Sam, and didn't check the caller I.D. The voice on the other end of the phone caught her by surprise. "Suzanne? It's Sheena."

"Sheena, how are you? How is little Emmett?"

"He's fine, except his behavior has been a little odd. He keeps showing me pictures, specific pictures in books. I thought it was just fascination, until he showed me a book with a missing girl. It gave me the creeps. I thought maybe you'd be able to give me some insight."

"What else did he show you?"

"The London Bridge, Big Ben…"

"Can I come and see him?"

"Of course, I would love that, when?"

"I can come now."

"Now? You're scaring me."

G iorgi woke to the sound of a rooster's crow. He surmised, by his surroundings, it had been quite the party. Breakfast awaited under an assortment of silver domes. He lifted one lid discovering a frittata made with lobster claw meat and topped with caviar. The second, Crème Brûlée French toast with golden raspberries. The last, poached eggs, displayed on a rasher of thick smoked bacon, covered in Béarnaise sauce and topped with roasted asparagus. He closed the lid and poured a cup of coffee, lifted it to his lips, reconsidered, and set the cup down.

He remembered eating a decadent dinner of veal medallions with roasted fennel and butternut squash last evening, followed by whiskey and cigars. Must've been the liquor served in the delicate cordial glass that knocked him on his ass. He vaguely remembered warm bodies crawling all over him like puppies, nipping, sucking. All of which had been recorded on video, of that he was sure. *Leverage.* They wanted to be sure <u>all</u> the balls weren't in his court. Although, he was sure that when it came to blackmail, he held more clout. Everything these people did was in excess. Their lifestyles, a constant game of one-upmanship. Desensitized, and soulless. Preying on the weak made them feel alive. Giorgi understood. After all, misery loved company.

Giorgi showered, dressed, and headed back to the hotel. No need to overstay his welcome. The deal was made. The merchandise would be delivered in ten days. Once the ship reached the port in Oakland, and the cargo was assessed, and stabilized, delivery would take place. Meanwhile, he'd work on his tan.

Emmett greeted Suzanne at the door, his bib, wet with drool. "He's teething, Sheena said, scooping him up and closing the door. "It's nice to see you, she said, leaning in for a hug. Emmett reached for Suzanne.

She stared into his fathomless eyes. One green, one brown. He didn't blink. He circled his arms around her neck and rested his cheek against hers.

Sheena stood slack-jawed. "He doesn't react that way with anyone." Suzanne gave him a gentle squeeze and set him down. "I don't think I'll ever fully understand the nature of our relationship, but what I do know is he is trying to tell us something."

"For sure! I can't tell you how many books he goes through a day trying to communicate. He hasn't been sleeping very well, either. I thought it was because of his teeth breaking through his gums. But now, I'm beginning to wonder."

"Right before you called, I was speaking with a man who had a near-death experience. We were comparing notes. Sam Metzger's sister is missing."

Sheena's jaw dropped. "No way! She was kidnapped

in London?"

"No, Austria, actually. But Lewis lives in London."

Emmett giggled and clapped his hands. Both Sheena and Suzanne smiled. He crawled over to the book shelf. He pulled himself up, and began rummaging through the books, tossing the ones he didn't want on the floor.

"Here we go again," Sheena said, stacking the discarded books in piles on the floor. "What are you looking for this time, buddy?"

Emmett grabbed a children's version of "Noah's Ark" off the shelf. The author kept the bible theme, but instead of animals on the ark, there were children from all over the world. He opened the book to an illustration of the ark bouncing on the waves, some of the children looked delighted, their hands in the air, others looked miserable, their faces colored green with discomfort. Emmett pointed at the arc, and handed the book to Suzanne, grunting what sounded like, "Here."

Suzanne opened the book, and studied the page. "Is this where she is, Emmett?"

The boy clapped his hands. He toddled to Sheena, crawled up in her lap, and buried his head in her bosom. Every now and then he would peek at Suzanne and giggle.

Sheena wrapped her arms around him, and squeezed. "What does it mean?"

"It means Jack can still communicate with me. I believe that although he's been reincarnated into a new body, his soul remains the same. He knows things."

"Will he grow out of it?"

"I don't know. I'm new at this myself." Suzanne ruffled Emmett's hair and smiled. "He helped me find those girls–and *you*."

"Me?"

"Yes. He led me to you."

"How is that possible? He wasn't born yet?"

"I believe the reason he was so adamant to save you was because he planned to reincarnate into your womb. I saw it. He showed me."

"That's crazy."

"I know. What's even more crazy is getting help from a toddler." Suzanne clasped her hands together. "What else do you want to show me Emmett"

He climbed down from Sheena's lap and hurried across the room. He ran one tiny finger along the books on the shelf. He stopped, listened, as if a voice from another world guided him. He shook his head, his eyes flooded with tears. He ran to Sheena, and buried his head in her lap.

"Hey baby boy, what's wrong? It's okay, mama's here." Sheena glared at Suzanne. "Maybe this wasn't such a good idea."

"I'm sorry. Perhaps he's not ready to share."

"Or—he's frightened."

"Either way, time will tell."

DUTY-BOUND

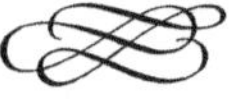

"Have y'popped y'cork, Lew?" Trudy blocked Lew's attempt to fill his suitcase. "Y'just had heart surgery. Y'aven't completely healed. What if y'get infected, or go pear-shaped?"

"I won't be goin' pear-shaped, Tru. I need t'help the lass."

"Why you?" She pleaded. "Why not let The Bill handle it, or that woman? She knows as much as y'do about the poor girl."

"Did ye ever feel so strong about a thing that if y'don't follow through, y' won't be able t'live with y'self?"

"No, Lew. I've lived m'life on the safe side. Takin' care of m'self and the man I love. I can't imagine m'life without ye, and if that's not enough to stop y'barmy ways, y'not the man I married 52 years ago."

Lewis stopped in his tracks. "I'm <u>not</u> the man y'married 52 years ago. Somethin' 'appened t'me. And if y'can't understand, then we've gone sideways."

Sam walked six blocks to St. Stephens Cathedral. He stared up at the regal structure in awe. The "Mozart's" were busy hawking tickets for various operas. Sam stood near the entrance, and waited for Rubio. After 2 hours, he had the feeling he wasn't going to show. Fear gripped the pit of his stomach. Rubio was his only chance of finding his sister. And now? He figured Rubio would lay low until Sam no longer posed a threat. Or perhaps he would change his route, conduct business as usual. Sam headed back to the hotel, his tail between his legs.

Suddenly, he heard footsteps, following very close. He turned to see Rubio in his wake. "What the fuck, man?"

"Did you really think I was going to show up with the goods without checking you out first? What if you were a cop?"

"Right, why didn't I think of that?" Sam curbed his anger. "Now what?"

"Meet me here in an hour." Rubio slipped him a piece of paper with instructions and an address written in black fine-point marker. "Don't be late."

. . .

S am found a bank kiosk and withdrew 600 euros in cash, three 100€ bills, the remainder in small denominations, just for show. He folded the bills strategically, and stuffed them inside his breast pocket. If Rubio produced Audra as his evening entertainment, it would be over, if not, he needed to play along, at least until he could grab Rubio by the throat and convince him to tell him where she was. The rendezvous place was three blocks away—he had 15 minutes to kill. His last meal churned in his stomach, his senses, on overdrive. Blood coursed through his veins, thrummed in his temples. Hair prickled on the back of his neck as he neared the dingy building where his fantasy was to play out. He checked his watch. Five minutes. He walked across the street and waited.

Rubio walked briskly, practically dragging a young woman in his wake. When they slipped into the doorway, Rubio backed her against the door and held her face in his hands. Sam couldn't hear what Rubio was saying, but by the resonance of his voice, Sam imagined it was a warning.

Sam ran toward Rubio, grabbed him by the hair, spun him around, and wrapped his arm around his neck. "Where's my sister," he seethed in Rubio's ear. "Where's Audra?"

"You're a fuckin' lunatic, man. I brought what you asked for."

"I want the girl you met at the Belvedere Palace. Where is she?"

"I don't know what you're talking about!"

"I saw you. You were visiting the Klimt exhibit," Sam seethed, his forearm pressing against Rubio's windpipe.

"I don't know where she is. We had one date, that's all–I haven't seen her since."

"You're a liar." Sam tightened his grip. "Where is she?"

Rubio struggled to no avail. "He'll kill me if I tell you," he said, gasping for air.

"I'll kill you if you don't." Sam squeezed tighter.

"She's long gone, man. You'll never find her."

Sam ground his heel into Rubio's instep while tightening his grip on his neck. "Tell me where she is!"

Rubio squealed. "She was shipped out, some rich guy bought her, that's all I know!"

"Where?" Sam dug harder, this time sliding his heel toward Rubio's toes. Rubio whimpered. Sam was about to do it again when the young woman slipped behind him, and jabbed something into his back. Sam loosened his grip. He reached behind him and came away with blood on his hand. "Damn," was all he said before he sank to his knees.

"*Nimm sein geld!*" The woman shouted. Sam clutched the wad near his breast.

"Fuck the money, let's go," Rubio said, and the two took off running.

Sam dragged his bleeding body to the curb, and hailed a taxi. "Take me to the nearest hospital—I've been stabbed."

LACERATIONS

Sam woke up to a middle-age woman in baby-blue scrubs checking his vitals. "What—?" he asked, his voice weak.

"You came in last night with a lacerated kidney. You were rushed into surgery—you're going to be fine. The doctor should be in soon. Until then, rest. You've lost a lot of blood. Anyone we should notify?"

Sam thought a moment. "No. I'm fine," he said. No use getting Suzanne all riled until he knew the extent of his injury.

"Okay, then. The police are going to want to speak to you when you're up to it. We don't take kindly to tourists being stabbed on our streets."

Sam closed his eyes, reliving the scene. He had a few questions of his own. "I was attacked from behind. I didn't see who did it."

The nurse patted his hand. "I'll be back later to check on you."

Sam was grateful he'd booked his room for an indefinite time. No need to contact the hotel. The only one who would be concerned with his whereabouts was Suzanne. He didn't suspect Rubio would hunt him down and finish him off. Right now, he was probably pissing his pants knowing Sam was on to him. Rubio answered to a higher power. *Someone who has all the answers.* Answers that would save his sister.

Rubio dipped his hand in one embossed leather pocket and opened his phone. He tapped in a number and waited. "It's Rubio. There's a cop here from the states inquiring about one of Giorgi's purchases." He paused, spied his surroundings, and lowered his voice. "One of my girl's poked him last night. If he's alive he's probably at Vienna General." Rubio listened, nodding his head. "Yeah, well, he's your problem now. If Giorgi finds out we're both fucked."

Rubio pressed "ENDE" and stuck his phone in his pocket. He walked past the Opera House teaming with tourists. Casino Bar was calling his name. It closed at 3 a.m. He had three hours to work through his frustration. One big win and he'd hop a plane to Tahiti, cut his hair, change his name. *Change my luck.* He said too much. Either "Dirty Harry" was going to put his ass in a sling, or Giorgi would. He knew Audra was a big mistake.

Girls with families were always trouble, but Giorgi didn't give him much choice, and Audra checked off every box on the list. Except one. *I hope she reaches California before they find out she's not a virgin.*

A udra pried her sticky eyes open with her fingers. Her throat felt parched. How long had she been knocked out? Loud noises bled through her comatose state. A clanking sound, followed by scraping, screeching, and a thump. The kittens were quiet. Too quiet. She wanted to call out to them. Make sure they were still there. *Still alive.*

She lost track of their route. The scratch marks blurred in front of her. From the stench assaulting her nostrils, she had lost more than a day. Once they started moving again, they would hose down the crates, open the doors, give them water, and food. How she had come to appreciate the little things.

SATAN

Suzanne checked her phone. No new messages. *Where is he?* She hadn't heard from Sam in three days. Her text messages to him, left unchecked. *Something's wrong.* She closed her eyes, wishing now, more than ever, a vision would assure her that Sam was safe. *Nothing.*

"Linda, it's Suzanne."

"I know. Kinda goes with the territory."

"I'm worried about Sam. Any reason I should be?"

"I wish I could give you the answer you want to hear, but I can't. At least not without more information."

"He's in Germany. His sister is missing."

"That explains the euros you were seeing earlier."

"Yes, but he went to Vienna. I haven't heard from him since he found the guy he suspects snatched his sister."

"Have you tried the hospitals?"

"No. I didn't want to go there."

"No one wants to think the worst, but trust me, if you don't cover your bases, you're going to drive yourself nuts."

"Sage advice, once again. Thank you."

"Try connecting heart to heart. See if that works for you."

"Thank you, my precious friend. I will let you know how it goes."

"And when you find him, tell him the blood between the sons of Satan can be thicker than the brotherhood of man."

S am swallowed two pills and a few sips of water. The pain had subsided enough to get off the intravenous meds they were giving him. "When can I leave?" He asked the pretty young nurse. She returned a nervous titter.

"No English," she said.

"*Wann kann ich abreisen?*"

"*Demnächst.*"

Sam nodded. "Soon. Great. *Danka.*"

She tittered again and hurried out of the room.

Sam reached for his phone. After the excruciating feat to grab it, he discovered his battery was dead. He tossed it back on the nightstand and laid his head back. Within minutes the pain killers kicked in and his eyes slammed shut. Suzanne appeared behind his lids. Her face, drawn with worry, tears filled her eyes. "I'm fine, my love. I'm going to be fine," he heard the voice inside his head say. He wanted to rush to her, hold her tight, reassure her that forever was their fate…but her face morphed into Audra's…and worry turned to terror… and tears turned to blood.

When Sam awoke, Irlich von Stuben, the policeman he saw at the station, stood over his bed, his piercing eyes lacking compassion.

"*Wer hat Sie Detective erstochen?*"

"I didn't see her face. It was dark. *Zu dunkel.*"

"You came to the station. About a missing girl."

"Yes. I remember you. I was inquiring about my sister. Do you have any news?"

"*Nein.* I suggest you go home."

"Why would I do that?"

"Meddling in police business can get you hurt." He nodded toward Sam's wound. "Wouldn't you agree?"

"Where I come from, when someone is missing, we don't threaten the family…that is unless we know something we aren't sharing."

"Be careful, Detective. Krampus still roams the streets looking for those who disobey the rules."

"You have a predator in your midst, and you're okay with that?"

"I don't remember you mentioning—"

"And if I did?"

"Go home, detective. This isn't America. The streets are filled with runaways, and wayward girls who go missing every day. Frankly, I blame the parents. They are responsible for teaching them not to talk to strangers."

Sam struggled to sit up. He wanted to punch the policeman's smug face. Choke him until his sharp little eyeballs popped out of their sockets. *"Fick dich!"*

"Your passport will be confiscated in three days," he said, patting Sam's foot. He lifted his gaze, his eyes, glued to Sam's, and continued, "The blood between the sons of Satan can be thicker than the brotherhood of man." He turned to go, adding, "Feel better, detective."

Following the policeman's departure, the sweet nurse came back in to fluff his pillows and take his blood pressure. He pointed to his phone with pleading eyes, *"Hast du ein Ladegerät das ich mir ausleihen kann?"*

She nodded, and opened the drawer on the night-stand. Inside, was a chord with various phone jacks. She found the one that fit Sam's phone and plugged it in.

"Danka."

She smiled. *"Krampus stiehlt jeden Tag Kinder."*

"Where does Krampus take the children once he steals them? *Bringt sie wohin?*"

"America."

Sam rethought the warning he received from the policeman. Maybe it wasn't a threat after all. *Perhaps he was giving me a heads up.*

∽

THE RACKET

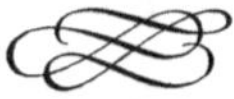

"**D**o you speak English? *Um sprichst du Englisch?"* Suzanne rolled her eyes. Her attempt at speaking German failed on all levels.

"Very little. Can I help you?

"Do you have a patient by the name of Samson Metzger? He's an American. A German born American."

There was a moment of silence. "*Nein.* I'm sorry."

The phone went dead before she had the chance to ask any more questions. This was her fourth try. Either the operator didn't speak English, or Sam was not listed as a patient. She dialed his cell number, just to hear his voice, but before the call transferred to his voice mail, she heard a faint "hello."

"Sam? Can you hear me?"

"Hey, sorry I haven't called, my phone—"

"You're hurt."

"I keep forgetting you have that super-power."

"Dear God! What happened?"

"I got stabbed."

"When? Where? Are you all right?"

"I'm fine. Any news?"

"Yes, the man I told you about, Lewis, Lewis Howard, he wants to help look for Audra. It's a start. And it feels right. I don't know why, but—"

"The nurse mentioned America, she said children are stolen every day, and taken to America."

"Lewis thinks your sister was taken to Lecce, he said there's a port in Brindisi."

"I'll see what I can do about checking myself out of here. I'll be home as soon as I can."

"Did they arrest the woman who stabbed you?"

"How did—"

"I don't know, it just popped into my head."

"No. I haven't given the police any information. I believe they know who took my sister."

"Why would—"

"It's a racket, bigger than I imagined, a multi-billion-dollar business. Finding someone who's not on the take may be a challenge. For now, I have to have faith that Audra is still alive."

"Linda said to give you a message. She said, 'The blood between the sons of Satan can be thicker than the brotherhood of man.'"

Sam's spine tingled. "I'm coming home."

PAPER

Audra's menstrual cramps kept her rolled up like one of the bugs she remembered flicking off of the benches at Belvedere park with Sam. He'd usually initiate the flicking competition, but her long slender fingers acted quickly with precision, matching his tenacity. She got him in the eye once—he got even by smashing a bug in her hair. How she wished she had taken his advice. She knew the questions Rubio asked her were inappropriate, yet she let her girlish ego override her sensible self. It had been a long time since someone as attractive as Rubio paid attention to her.

Most of her friends were what Americans called "nerds." Her flat-mate Bruno knew very attractive men, but they were more interested in her fashion sense, and each other, than her. *Bruno.* She'd give the moon and the stars to be cuddled up on the sofa with Bruno, his cat Latté, and a classic Rita Hayworth movie. How she took the small things for granted, considered her life boring. Britta lived a life she envied, always a new man, a new job, a new adventure. Getting the job as an au pair and coloring her hair was the extent of her adventurous side. Her parents thought that moving to Budapest was rebellious…*what would they think of me now?*

The latch above her head opened and closed long enough to throw in an orange, a peanut butter sandwich, and a bottle of water.

"Hey!" she called. "I'm getting my period. Can I get something? For the blood? *Sangue?*"

Twenty minutes passed before the lid opened and a roll of paper towels bounced off her head. When she looked up, she caught his eyes. Brown, vacant, small. *It's him.*

"Thank you," she said. "*Danka.*"

The lid didn't slam, instead it eased down like a warm breeze on a summer night. She didn't cry. She didn't yell. She tucked a wad of paper towels between her legs, *just in case,* closed her eyes, and prayed.

When morning came, Audra's head pounded from waves slamming the ship, knocking her against one side of her cage, then the other. She was cold, achy, sick to her stomach. The drugs they mixed in the peanut butter had given her nightmares. Her body shook. Tiny lights appeared in her peripheral vision. *This is bad.*

Suddenly, the lid opened. She felt a plastic bag hit her shoulder. *Maintenance.* "First we clean, then we eat," she heard her mother say. "No, first we pee, then we clean, Mama," she said aloud. She squatted over the bag, and hoped for the best. The rocking made it difficult to aim, but she was determined to void in the bag, and not on the floor.

When she finished, she gathered wet paper towels, plastic wrap, and a water bottle, stuffed them into the bag, and knotted the top. She wondered how the little ones managed, and began to sob. Bits of conversations she had overheard from the crew suggested child trafficking. Her heart hurt for their stolen innocence, stolen humanity, for the pain they would endure *all for the sick pleasure of some deviant*. For the first time since Sam announced his vocation, she understood his calling. It was men like him that made a difference. *If only I had said, 'No' to Rubio.*

PRAYER

Sam hailed a taxi, instructed the driver to take him to the hotel, where the driver would wait until Sam grabbed his belongings, and settled his bill. They would then head to the airport. However, when Sam entered his room, he discovered it had been ransacked.

"Son-of-a-bitch!" He winced as he shoved the strewn mess into his suitcase. His side ached with every move. He reached in his pocket for the small white envelope he received from the discharge nurse, tossed two tablets in his mouth and chased them down with a miniature bottle of water he grabbed from the mini-bar.

When the driver saw Sam exit the building, he jumped out, deposited Sam's suitcase into the trunk, and started the engine. "*Und es geht los.*"

Sam shook his head. "Yes. Away we go."

Beneath his cool exterior, Sam was seething. The only people who knew which hotel he'd been staying in was the hospital staff, and the police. He had no doubt who trashed his room. But, why? Only one answer, the police were part of the operation, and wanted to send a message. Without allies, he was sunk. His badge, obviously, meant nothing, and he knew first hand, crooked cops felt they were above the law. Linda's words rang true, as did the policeman's warning. He was dealing with an evil so prevalent in every walk of life. It was no secret that children were being trafficked by and to world leaders, respected politicians, Hollywood's elite, and those with deep pockets. The thought made him sick.

He paid the driver, and maneuvered his suitcase through the revolving door. He followed the signs to the Air Berlin ticket desk where he produced his passport, badge, gun permit, and credit card. He opened his bag, extracted a hard Pelican case, showed the contents to the agent, and repacked the case in his bag, already missing the weapon he was forbidden to carry on board.

While waiting for his flight, Sam surveyed his surroundings with the scrutiny of a bounty hunter. A small figure, dressed in a black niqab stood by a partition, flanked by two tall figures dressed in three-piece suits. When she turned, Sam could barely see her young, sad eyes. Ten? Twelve? Sam wondered about her escorts. Were they taking her to somewhere to be sold? Was she being offered as a bride to a wealthy sheik? The thought churned his stomach, and he looked away.

Near a coffee kiosk to his left, was another young

girl, her skirt so short, you could practically see what she had for breakfast. Her escort was older, tattoos, piercings, disguising his true age. He hovered over the girl as if she were his prey. If she moved further than a foot from his side, he yanked her back, and secured her wrist in a tight grip. The girl didn't object, she merely obeyed, her head hung low. Sam wanted to box the guys ears, scream in his face. How dare he treat the girl that way. Would his sister's fate be that which he was witnessing? Would some goon tether her to his side with brute force? Transport her from one buyer to the next? He closed his eyes, remembering Audra's sweet face. *Please, God…let me find her before*—he couldn't finish his prayer. The thought of someone hurting his sister paralyzed him. *I will find you,* he vowed.

AUDRA

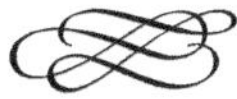

"Do not lie to me Rubio," Giorgi said, his voice as tranquil as blue waters in Sardinia, Italy.

"The guy was a dick! He tried to kill me!"

"Perhaps I'll finish the job myself."

"I didn't tell him anything, Giorgi, not a goddamn thing. And I didn't stab him, Blondi did. She was trying to protect me—the guy had his hands around my throat."

"Rubio, Rubio. You fucked up. You brought me a girl with ties…a brother who is a cop no less. He's not going to stop looking until he finds her."

"He has no idea where she is—and no one is going to help him find her. In a few days, she'll be in Oakland. Then she'll be <u>yours</u> to deal with."

Giorgi released an audible sigh, as if he were bored. "True. And Rubio? If she gives me any trouble, I won't hesitate to have you killed. Capisce?"

"Understood."

Giorgi ended the call, and moved to the window to enjoy the sunset. His southwest view overlooked the city. Now bathed in a golden hue and glittering lights, ribbons of red and gold shimmered against the river bank. The evening was too lovely to waste anticipating trouble. Very rarely did he involve himself with the details of a delivery. That's what his minions were for. However, this one was an exception. His buyer, a long-time friend of his father's, was paying a handsome price for a virgin with a specific look. He didn't intend to disappoint his client or his father. If everyone did their job, he would get his product to the buyer, collect his fee, and go home.

L ight blinded Audra's eyes for a split second before tattooed arms slipped a black hood over her head, and lifted her from her container. She committed the artwork to memory for future use. The head of a goat transfixed on a reversed pentagram had symbols on each point, but she couldn't make them out. She had seen the symbol in her history books, *the mark of Satan*. Krampus.

The man led her through a short hallway, and into a doorway, in which he told her to duck. "Don't want to bruise the merchandise," he said. "The boss would have my ass." He pushed her head down, and through the opening. He closed the door behind him, and removed the hood. His face was hidden by a mask, and when he spoke, his English was perfect. "Remove your clothes, shower, and put these on."

She turned to see a pair of black pants, and a long sleeve black T-shirt arranged on a cot, next to a pair of KEDS, a sports bra, and a pair of cotton underwear. "Yeah, not Victoria Secret, but they'll have to do," he said. "I'm going to stay right here, so don't be stupid. *Non essere stupido. Capiche?*"

Audra wanted to tell him she understood English, but the less he knew about her, the better. She did as she was told.

The water not only felt glorious on her aching muscles, she was determined to get the stench off her body, and wash her hair. She lathered, rinsed, lathered again, and rinsed until she no longer felt the filth of her own body waste clinging to her skin. The water trickling down her face, mingled with her tears. If God had heard her prayers, he kept silent. Days turned into weeks. And now?

"*Sbrigati!* Hurry up!" She heard him shout. "Your chariot awaits," he said, and burst into laughter.

She shivered as she toweled herself dry. She stepped out of the bathroom, covering herself as best she could. The tattooed man had the decency to turn around.

"This isn't my favorite gig," he said. "I spent five years in Susanville, no one wants to give a guy anything legit once he's been in that place." He sighed. "But that's not your problem. You got enough problems without worrying about me." He tapped his feet on the floor. "Yeah, I gotta sister. She's a junkie piece o'shit, but I wouldn't humiliate her either." He paused. "You done? *Finito?*"

He didn't wait for an answer. He turned as she was pulling the pants over her hips. "Lucky guy, whoever he is. You're really pretty. And older than the others. Too bad things worked out for you this way. It's strictly business. Don't take it personal or nothing."

Audra remained silent; her eyes cast to the floor.

"Let's go," he said, placing the hood back over her head. "He's waiting." The tattooed arms reached for her wrists, retied them together, and guided her to the door.

When they stepped back out into the hall, it was quiet. Too quiet. Her heart hammered against her chest. She felt as though she would internally combust. The ringing in her ears grew louder, and louder until she could no longer bear it. "Where are the children?" she screamed.

PRIMAL

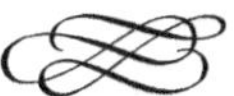

Sam's flight proceeded smoothly. A two-hour layover in Frankfort allowed him time to regroup. *Construct a game plan.* He looked forward to seeing Suzanne, hearing what she had to say about the Englishman. What a crazy situation…accepting Suzanne's visions had taken time to get used to, buying into a stranger's visions made him feel like he was back at square one. This was his sister they were talking about. Neither of them knew Audra, how could he trust the information coming from a stranger? And why were they thinking about Audra in the first place? Suzanne mentioned a girl fitting his sister's description when they first met. Premonition? And how did she find this guy so quickly? She said she heard him talking in her TV. And Sheena's baby! How did Emmett figure into the mix? *God, I need a drink.*

And as if thoughts were things, a stewardess magically appeared with a small tray filled with beverages. "Wine? Beer?" His blank stare made her repeat the question.

"Uh, I—no thanks." He reached in his pocket, grasping his sobriety coin in his hand. He needed to keep his head. As much as he wanted to go on a bender, crawl into a hole, and forget the world, now was not the time. *Evil will not prevail*, he told himself. The knot in his stomach competed with the throbbing in his side.

And yet? Evil ran rampant. He dealt with evil every day. It never ceased to amaze him the destruction and pain humans inflicted upon one another with blatant disregard. But this—selling humans—for sex, for organs, human sacrifice—*whatever*—<u>this</u> he would never understand. *Children*. He shuddered recalling Suzanne's vision, *mewling kittens*. How did Audra become a target for such evil? Was it her innocence? Her beauty? Did her petite frame and youthful looks fit a certain profile?

He'd never understand human smuggling. Worldwide, prostitution had become more acceptable. His beloved Germany itself had its fair share of laufhauses, brothels, and sex clubs. In fact, "Pascha," a brothel in Cologne, had been the largest brothel in Europe. Las Vegas and Pahrump, Nevada supported *legal* brothels… but that wasn't enough. There were infantophiles, those attracted to children under five years old, hebephiles, who liked children eleven to fifteen, ephebophiles, who like them older, fifteen to nineteen. They even formed their own group, "MAP," minor attracted persons. One thing he had learned in AA, pick your battles. Right now, the most important thing was to find his sister, and if it meant believing in purple dinosaurs or little green men, he would follow every lead possible.

Trust. A word he was beginning to reassess. He trusted Suzanne, he just didn't always understand her gift, *or curse, as she would put it*. He prayed that whatever the universe was imparting to her about his sister was enough to save her life.

His sorrow was so deep, he felt as though he were drowning. The only escape from his dark void was to relive the moments he had shared with Suzanne before Audra went missing. As he stared out the oval window at the nothingness below, his mind conjured the scent of her hair; the touch of her soft, smooth skin; the way her tongue tangled with his, probing with longing, as her breasts heaved against his chest. Her long legs, wrapped around his hips as he thrust inside her, gently, rhythmically, satisfying a primal hunger, and absolving themselves from any hinderances that came before.

His reverie lulled him to sleep. He awoke to an announcement from the pilot that they would be landing within the hour. *Sacramento.*

Suzanne planned to meet him at the terminal.

FILTHY

"Commune with nature." Isn't that what Linda said? Suzanne wandered through the rose garden at Capital park. Squirrels dashed up and down the trees, chittering playfully. The air was crisp, and the scent of roses faint. Suzanne walked from bush to bush determining which one she liked best. Her way of not forcing the images, she desperately needed to see, to form in her mind's eye. *Relax, let your mind receive on its own accord.*

Suzanne sat down on a bench facing the capital. As the hour reached eight, more people hurried along the perimeter, heading for work. The sun, still in the east, crept over high-rise buildings, spilled along the walkway, and warmed the back of her head. She tried her best to clear her mind and focus on Mother Nature. She spotted an odd-looking bird perched on a branch to her left, and a bee buzzing around a white rose bud, tipped in pink. The grass, still wet with dew, was a myriad of tiny rainbows, and clover. It had been ages since she indulged herself in the beauty that surrounded her. She almost felt sad for the time she had lost as she appreciated what a beautiful city she lived in. She made a mental note to visit the park more often, and turned her body so she could feel the sun on her face. She winced. Too bright. She turned away, but the bright light remained imprinted on her "screen." As she inhaled, exhaled, and relaxed her shoulders, she saw tattooed arms, pushing a long-legged, petite figure into a white van. She couldn't see their faces, but somehow, she knew. *Audra.* The image told her nothing, other than the girl was alive.

"Show me more," she said aloud.

"I'm sorry, are you speaking to me?"

Suzanne's eyes flashed open. The man standing before her had a quizzical look on his face.

His smile gave Suzanne an uneasy feeling. He was movie-star handsome, with jet black hair, and violet eyes, trimmed in long lashes. He had a faint accent, but Suzanne couldn't distinguish its origin.

"No! I mean, I was thinking out loud, I guess."

"Ah," he said, a slight twinkle in his eyes. "I thought I was the only one who did that." He looked away. "Beautiful day."

"Yes," she agreed. She wanted to know more about this man, but didn't feel inclined to ask. His clothes were expensive, his tanned skin accentuated his striking features, and the ruby, blue sapphire, and clear crystal point-encrusted watch circling his wrist was the most exquisite time piece she had ever laid eyes on. It had to be a Rolex.

He followed her eyes to his wrist, and tugged at his sleeve. "My father's a jeweler. I'm an only child," he said, the twinkle returning. "Mind if I sit?"

Suzanne was stunned by his proposal. She moved to the far end of the bench, allowing plenty of space between them. "Not at all, I was just about to—"

"Please don't tell me you're leaving," he said, his voice, a cool breeze on a summer's day. She felt herself hypnotized by his gaze.

"I must. I'm picking up a friend at the airport."

"I see—girlfriend?"

"No, boyfriend, actually."

"Ah—then it would be obtuse of me to invite you for a drink this evening."

His smile challenged her better sense, but her commitment to Sam kept her strong. "Thank you, but that won't be possible."

"Are you sure? A drink with a new friend, surely there is no harm in that?"

"Harm no, more like inappropriate. It's not who I am."

"And who are you?"

Suzanne rose from the bench and smiled. "Enjoy your day." She heard him sigh as she walked past him and headed toward toward 'L' Street, where she was parked. She could feel his eyes watching her. He took her breath away, but not in a good way. He made her feel— *dirty*.

Suzanne waited in the Sacramento Airport at the bottom of the escalator, near baggage claim. Her palms were moist, her heart fluttered in her chest. Love? Or anxiety? The jury was still out. She had long forgotten what it felt like to be in love, and her relationship with Sam often led to dangerous waters. Her experience with the man in the park left her perplexed. How could anyone that good looking, invoke such an ugly vibe?

And his watch...she typed the description into Google, and was flabbergasted with the results. It wasn't a Rolex, after all. The watch was made by a jeweler in New York, appropriately named, "The Mystery," and retailed for $1,457,063.19. What was a man of his caliber doing in Capital Park so early in the morning? Was he a diplomat? He did have an accent. Perhaps he was visiting a California Senator, or the Governor, himself. Why invite her for a drink? Certainly, a man of his stature dated woman of the same ilk. Unless he mistook her for *easy prey*.

Sam's voice took her by surprise. "Suzanne!" He beelined toward her, arms open wide. As he held her tight, he whispered, "I missed you."

Suzanne hugged him tighter. "And I missed you." She broke the embrace. "How was your flight?"

"Long." He looped his arm through hers, and steered her toward "Baggage Claim."

She could tell by the way he walked that something was amiss. "What are they giving you for pain?" she asked.

"I don't remember the name of it, nothing we have here in the states. It works great, and doesn't seem to have many side effects." He checked his watch. "I fell asleep on the plane. I should have taken one hours ago."

When Sam's luggage popped out of the hopper, and onto the belt, Suzanne insisted upon lifting the suitcase off of the carousel. "I'm not helpless," Sam complained.

Suzanne rolled the suitcase toward Sam. "Is this it?"

"No, I have to go to the baggage office to claim my firearm."

Sam slapped his I.D. on the counter, along with his claim slip. Suzanne noticed when the TSA officer handed him his gun case, Sam seemed hesitant to take it, as if it were a newborn or a bomb.

Suzanne kept her feelings in check because she was familiar with Sam's moods. She had seen him struggle with impending depression mixed with determination and grit. Once they were alone, she hoped he'd open up to her. Allow himself to unleash his demons, talk about his pain. "I'm parked in the garage." She didn't wait for him to protest, she grabbed his gun case, set it on top of his suitcase, and rolled them behind her.

When they reached the car, he pinned her against the door, his mouth urgently seeking hers. When she opened her eyes, she saw the angst in his. She cupped his face in her hands. "We'll find her."

"How can you be so sure?"

The image of the well-dressed man in the park came to mind. "I have a feeling she's here. Here in Sacramento."

KITTENS

The tattooed man struck Audra so hard, she felt her teeth rattle. She couldn't control the sobs that were long overdue. "Geezus," he said in a huff. "You can't go screaming like that!"

"Where are they?" Her voice dwindled to a whisper.

"You speak English."

"A little," she said regretting her outburst.

"The children are safe. They are being taken to their new homes."

Audra knew their "new" homes would never replace their real homes, nor were they safe. Their lives would be forever changed. She wanted to ask *why?* How could a human being do such despicable things to another, especially a child?

"We need to get going." He lifted her hood, stuffed her mouth with a wad of fabric, and tied another strip of cloth around her head to keep the gag in place.

Although she couldn't see his face, his eyes shown through the small holes of the mask. They were ice blue, and no doubt matched his heart.

"Watch your step," someone growled. *A new voice.* Audra stepped down, assisted by strong hands. The hands gripped her flesh so hard, she cried out. A blow to the back of her head silenced her immediately. She wanted to scream, lash out, kick, scratch, bite, use whatever strength she had to gain her freedom, but instinct told her this wasn't the time, or the place. They were still on water. She smelled mold, fish, suntan lotion, and beer. The place she was confined to reeked of cigarettes, and body odor. She sensed she was in the cabin, surrounded by engine noises, as well as footsteps, shuffling, and laughter above her. Another language, she recognized as Spanish, spoken by three different voices. She heard what sounded like a casting reel, a high pitch squeal, and a click. Was she in the custody of fisherman? On a fishing boat. But where? Spain? Portugal? Lisbon? What did it matter? Between her bondage, not being allowed to see, and menstrual cramps, her thought was, *I want to die.*

When she awoke, it was dark. The boat rocked gently, bumping into a padded surface. It reminded her of the time she and Bruno took a river cruise down the Danube in a friend's yacht. They docked in different slips along the way, and each time they tied up, the crew threw out rubber bumpers to keep the boat from crashing into the pier. One afternoon it rained, and she opted out of the monastery tour in Bratislava. The wind picked up, rocking the boat until she felt sea-sick. The sound of the boat bumping against the rubber buoys sounded like the sound she was hearing now.

The door opened to the cabin, and she smelled food. The hood was removed from her head, then the gag. A hollow voice spoke from behind a mask. *"Mangaire."* Audra shielded her eyes against the bright light shining in her face. She accepted the plate with her bound hands, and set it down. She held out her wrists to be untethered. She was surprised when the man obliged her wishes.

After using the toilet, she washed her face and hands, and returned to her place. The man sat waiting in the corner, texting on his phone. She could see he was young, even in the dim light. His hair, the shape of his ears, his fair skin was smooth, and firm. Audra guessed early twenties. His voice too, sounded young. She wondered if the men on the boat were illegals, working for some rich man, staying under the radar? Guys like him, like Rubio, what was their objective? Did they have goals in life? Were they addicted to something that prevented them from being upstanding citizens? Were they too lazy to enter into a vocation? Or were they just plain evil?

As if he heard her thoughts, he looked up. "*Manga!*"

Audra could barely open her mouth. Her throat was parched, emotion brewed at the surface, constricting her muscles. She felt as though she had swallowed a brick. "Water?" she asked, softly. Again, the young man granted her request. She wanted to grill him for information, but was afraid if she did, he'd punish her. Take away her food and water. She needed to regain her strength. She lifted the plastic spoon to her lips.

Her belly cramped. *Too much, too soon.* The food too spicy, too heavy. Her mind supported her ravenous state; however, her stomach didn't agree, and it all came out of her like a volcanic eruption.

"Goddammit, pig!" He shouted. He grabbed Audra by the hair, and pushed her into the muck. "Clean it up!"

Audra's stomach erupted again, this time barely missing his shoes. He danced away from her, cussing and swearing. All Audra could do was cry.

Another man banged on the door. "*Culerto*—what's up in there?" He turned the knob and barged in. "Sick."

"It's the food, man. She don't like your cookin'."

Audra buried her face in her hands and sobbed, shaking her head, "No".

"Aw, *chica—chica*. You okay?" The man bent down and helped Audra to her feet. Go lay down. We will take care of the mess."

Audra didn't refute the kind gesture. "*Grazzi*," she said.

The kind man shoved the other one into the corner. "Clean it up, and be nice to our guest. If our boss catches wind of any mistreatment of his goods, he will cut off our balls and feed them to us on a spoon —*comprendez?*"

Once the mess was cleaned up, the two men left her alone. Unmasked, untied. She stretched out on the long, padded bench, closed her eyes and fell asleep.

When she awoke, it was morning. She shivered from the cold. The sound of waves lapping alongside the boat, and the hum of the motor, indicated movement. She looked out one of the portholes. Trees. Houses. A pot of tea and crackers caught her eye across the room. A change of clothes hung over a chair. She may still be a prisoner, but at least her captors acted less like barbarians, and more like humans.

She inspected the cabin. The commode was small, old, in need of a good cleaning, but usable. A nozzle hung from a hook, with enough hose to rinse below her waist, but no more. A dirty bar of soap, and a small scrub brush occupied a rusted dish. She pushed up on the handle, water sprayed her face.

She listened to the action going on above board, debating whether to risk a shower before redressing into clean clothes. She felt the teapot. Hot. She hurried into the small cubicle, and stripped out of her clothes.

She clenched down, keeping the scream from

escaping her mouth. The water was icy cold, and stung her skin. She scrubbed with such speed her body was red from head to toe. She dried herself with her dirty clothes pulled inside out, and dressed. She was done in three minutes.

She held the pot in her hands, then lifted the lid to inhale the steam. She poured herself a cup, and drank, enjoying the warm sensation traversing down her throat, into her stomach. She bit into a cracker, and spit it out. The taste was offensive. She vowed never to eat again.

"Come!" The kind man said, standing in the doorway. "Time to go."

AMERICANO, FLAT WHITE

"His name is Lewis Howard," Suzanne said, lifting Sam's suitcase out of the car. "He has one helluva story."

"How does his story tie in with my sister?"

"You know how Jack would tell me things?"

"Yes, I remember," Sam said, his brow bunching into a frown.

"Lewis has a deceased friend that shares information with him."

"What does his friend have to do with my sister?"

"I don't know, maybe he's like Clarence, the angel in *It's a Wonderful Life.* He needs to earn his wings." She set the suitcase down on the walkway, and sighed. "I don't know, Sam," she shaded her eyes from the sun, "I'm new at this. All I can do is relate what is happening as it comes to me."

"I apologize. It's not your fault—I—"

"Sam, don't. It's the fault of the person who took her." She picked up the suitcase. "Let's go inside. You need to rest. You're as pale as a ghost."

It was the first time Suzanne had been in Sam's apartment. Her eyes roamed about the room, getting a feel for the man she knew little about, yet cared for so deeply. His apartment was sparsely furnished, warmly decorated with a few antiques. She could feel his sentiment toward his homeland by the elegant paintings, hanging on the walls. She recognized the serenity of Caspar David Friedrich's, "The Monk by the Sea," and the "The Wanderer Above the Sea of Fog." Both pieces spoke of Sam's isolation, and his reconciliation with who he had become. She knew it wasn't easy for him to face death, demoralization, and destruction every day. *And now this.*

She moved from the living room into the kitchen, impressed by his tidiness, and organizational skills. *Everything in its place.*

"Sit, make yourself at home," he said, rolling his suitcase out of sight. "Coffee?" he asked.

"Please, you sit and let me make you a cup. All you need to do is point."

"I'm not an invalid."

"No, you're a stubborn man who needs to rest. Otherwise—"

"Otherwise what?"

She could tell by his tone he wasn't one to be threatened. "Do you remember the first time I made you a cup of coffee?"

"Yes. Your husband came home, and caught us in the kitchen talking. I must admit, he had every right to suspect I had more than coffee on my mind."

She laughed. "I think a re-do is in order. Please? Let me do this one simple task?"

"You know me too well."

"I want to. I want to do more, Sam. I want to make your world right again, find your sister, catch the bad guy, and fix you coffee."

He grabbed her hand, and pulled her near. His eyes reflected the sadness in his heart. "Can you? Can you really do all that for me, Suzanne?"

"I want to," she said, placing her lips on his.

He threw up his hands and winced with pain. "Okay then," he said through his gritted teeth. "You win."

Suzanne plugged in the coffee pot, placed a filter in the holder and scooped grounds into the basket. She filled the pot with water, and poured it into the top of the machine. She pressed the "brew" button, and set the canister on the shelf. She caught a teapot out of the corner of her eye, and turned, as if the teapot had magic powers. She moved closer, touching the spout. Her hand was not her own. She removed the teapot from the shelf, and wrapped her hands around the round body. Her hands felt warm. She lifted the lid and inhaled. Although the pot was empty, she sensed the steam escaping the pot was soothing. Next to her, the water filtered through the basket into the coffee pot. In her mind's eye, she could see water streaming from a metal hose. Suddenly, she felt unsteady, and grabbed onto the counter. The rocking motion stopped.

"She's on a boat. She's safe." Suzanne turned to Sam, "She's safe for now."

"How do you know?"

"She showered. They served her tea. I saw it."

Lewis took a deep breath and exhaled. "Your ticker sounds good," the cardiologist said, as he listened through his stethoscope. He squinted at the scar on Lewis' chest. "Knittin' looks good too. You've healed quite nicely."

Lewis began buttoning his shirt. "I'm okay t'travel then?"

"No heavy liftin'," he said, "and don't be gettin' too excited over those pretty flight attendants." He winked. "I don't expect any further trouble."

"Can I ask y'somethin' Doc?" Lewis' gaze dropped to the floor.

The cardiologist stopped writing, and gave Lewis his attention. "What's troublin' you then?

"Do y'think there's an afterlife?"

"Seen some inexplainable things in my career, including what happened to you. Why do you ask?"

"I think I went t'heaven and back. Now I'm haunted by what 'appened."

The doctor's bushy brows gathered in the middle of his forehead. "What did you see?"

"Well, I didn't see the man 'imself, mind ye, but I did see me dead neighbor, and me mum and dad."

"It's not unusual to have that kind of experience, I've heard it before. But not often. Most of my patients don't die during surgery." The doctor patted Lew's hand. "You're not off your nut, Lew, I'm sure something happened…I just can't explain what, or why."

"Thanks, doc, it's reassurin', y'know."

"You're going to live a long life if you take care. Glad to hear you're not stewin' at home." The doctor placed one hand on Lew's shoulder, easing him toward the door. "I neglected to ask, where is it you're off to?"

"America."

"*America*?"

"I'm off t'find a missing girl."

When Lewis arrived home and shared the good news with Trudy, she went into the bedroom, slammed the door and bawled for thirty minutes.

"Are y'bawlin' for m'leavin' or because y'ave to put up with m'ol' sorry arse for another twenty years?"

"Both. I can't believe 'e's lettin' y'go. What if—"

Lewis grabbed Trudy by the shoulder's and shook her. "If the good Lord saw fit t'take me 'ome, 'e had 'is chance." He lifted her chin. "Please, ease yer mind, Luv. I'll be fine." Lew picked up two sweaters from the pile of clothes on the bed. "Now 'elp this ol' chap out and tell me, the blue? Or the brown?"

Trudy pointed to the blue sweater, her eyes glistening. "Yer an 'onorable man, Lewis Howard. 'ard-headed as they come, but 'onorable all the same. But know this, if y'die in America, I will never forgive ye. And don't be thinkin' 'bout showin' up as no ghosty. Do y'ear me, man?"

Lew's lips tilted into a sheepish grin. "I'll come back as a cat, scratchin' at yer door…that way I know ye'll let me in." Trudy rushed into his arms and held him tight.

PICTURES

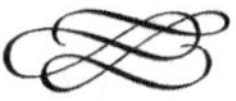

"How many?" Sam scribbled a number on his pad. "Uh, huh, I understand. How many more are you expecting?" Perplexed, he turned to Suzanne, who was listening to the conversation. "Who does know?" His upper lip clamped down on his bottom lip, holding back the words he wanted to say. "Thank you for your time," he said, and tossed his phone on the table.

"No luck?" Suzanne rose, her hands clasped on top of her head.

Sam blew out his frustration. "Nope. The Port of Sacramento isn't set up for containers. They handle mostly auto imports, farming equipment, stuff like that."

"Lewis mentioned Italy…"

"It's like trying to find a needle in a haystack. The

nurse I spoke with in the hospital didn't indicate any specific location in the states, and the cop was just as vague."

Suzanne bent down, and took Sam's hand. "We'll find her."

Sam rose, side stepping Suzanne. "The guy I just spoke to asked if I checked with the FMC, or the UNODC."

Suzanne raised her brow. "The what and what?"

"The Federal Maritime Commission, and the United Nations Office on Drugs and Crime. Evidently there's a Container Control Programme that was initiated some years back to monitor the containers coming from other countries for the very purpose of catching smugglers bringing drugs, weapons, and humans into the country. Obviously, the system is flawed."

"I have a feeling that however she arrived, she is no longer a part of the scene."

"How can you tell?"

"I just got a visual of a leaf falling from a tree."

"I pray that you're right." He pulled her close. "I have faith in you, Suzanne, I hope you know that."

"And I you. You're one helluva detective." She kissed him lightly. "We make a good team." She lifted his chin. "Tell me what I can do. Who can I call?"

"Let me check in with the office. I need to connect to some of the task forces in Sacramento and Stockton. They may have a jump on any new activity."

"Lewis Howard arrives tomorrow from London. He's just as determined to find your sister as we are."

"I'll leave Lewis to you. Meanwhile, I'll be checking with the other agencies." He smiled, and took her hand. "When I got stabbed, all I could think about was how upset you were going to be with me for not calling. I'm glad I was wrong."

"And I was sorry I didn't see it coming." She let go of his hand. "I didn't tell you about Jack."

"Jack? I thought—"

"I went to see Sheena. Emmett was showing me pictures in books…he showed me Big Ben, and a book titled, "Missing." I know it's crazy, but it's Jack." Suzanne paced while Sam listened. "He showed me Noah's Ark—he's getting images, I know it—showing me pictures is his way of communicating."

Sam shook his head. "Crazy is right. He's a baby! He shouldn't be—God!"

"I don't know if Emmett knows what it all means, and I pray that he never finds out, but at least I know that if I can't—"

"YOU found Dixon, Suzanne, not Jack."

"And <u>you</u> found me." She cupped his face in her hands and kissed his lips, nipping his bottom lip with her teeth. He pulled her onto his lap, and drew her closer, bending her backward into the crock of his arm. His eyes held her gaze as he took control, kissing the corner of her mouth, her jaw, nibbling her ear. Her chest pressed against his, their hearts thumping like rolling thunder. "I've never seen your bedroom," she whispered.

"I'd be happy to give you a tour."

SPECIAL ORDER

Giorgi waited for his turn to be seated at one of the Rio Café's deck side tables. Once seated, he ordered a vodka martini with a twist, and set his sights on his view of the Sacramento River. He smiled to himself knowing his "merchandise" arrived late the previous night. He turned at the sound of a familiar woman's voice, and nodded. The woman sashayed onto the deck. Giorgi rose and pulled out a chair. "I ordered you a martini."

"Aren't you a love," she said tilting her sunglasses, revealing chocolate brown eyes. Her blond hair, tucked beneath a wide brim hat. "What did you think of Morton's Steak House?"

"P-lease." He opened his napkin and laid it across his knee. "How is everything going?"

"One of the items was damaged in transport, but

that's to be expected, given the fragile nature..." She shifted her gaze to the water. "The Vermont order has been filled, three pieces were sent to DC, seven to New York, and forty-seven to L.A." His eyes, like magnets, drew her back into his gaze.

He steepled his index fingers, and raised his brow. "And my special order?"

"Not to worry, that one is being prepped for delivery."

The waitperson brought her martini. "Are you ready to order?" she asked.

"Oh goodness, we've been so busy chatting..." The woman opened the menu and browsed the selections.

Giorgi intervened. "Bring us two of your stuffed salmon dishes. And I'll have a glass of your finest chardonnay."

"You have a choice of rice pilaf or–"

"Just salads for both. Olive oil and vinegar on the side, please."

The woman handed the menu to the girl and smiled, "Well, that settles that."

Giorgi ignored the woman's indignant look. "You have two days. Two. I expect nothing less than perfection."

"Have I ever let you down?"

Giorgi drummed his fingers on the table. "How's that lovely home in Salinas?" He checked one manicured hand, nonchalantly. "And that beautiful granddaughter of yours? How old is she now, twelve? Thirteen? Such a *tender* age.

The woman gasped. "I don't find your joke amusing."

Giorgi's dazzling smile disappeared. His eyes turned to flint. "Who's joking?"

FIZZLE

Audra had lost all conception of time. Her head swam, her vision was blurry, her limbs, heavy and limp. "Am I dead?" she asked, in a voice that didn't seem to fit her mouth.

"No darlin' just a little *relaxed*." Lilly, the woman from Salinas lifted one of Audra's eyelids, then the other. She turned to the man guarding the door. "How much did you fuckin' give her?"

"I followed the instructions you gave me to a tee. She should be coming down by now."

"Don't give her anymore until I tell you to. Help me get her undressed and into the shower. I need her ready to go in an hour. I pray to God this shit wears off. Get her some coffee. No—Get her a flumazenil. And remind me to get a hold of Dave at the compound pharmacy. We're running low."

Lilly paced the room, observing Audra's behavior. "Shit, shit, shit!"

Each time she moved, Lilly's image smeared across Audra's vision. Audra struggled to focus. Her face felt frozen.

She couldn't lift her arm, or stop the man invading her space. "C'mon babydoll," he said, "time to make you all perty."

Long slender fingers pried Audra's lips apart. He placed a small lozenge on her tongue. "Close," he said. She obeyed. The tablet fizzed inside her mouth, and she wanted to giggle. She felt like a rag doll, as he tossed her onto the bed and began removing her top, her sports bra, and pants. She could feel his eyes feast on her body. He took liberty, touching her breasts as he worked. When she was naked, he lifted her from the chair, and carried her into the shower.

She melted under the hot spray, like a popsicle in summer. She looked at the bottom of the shower to see what flavor she was, disappointed she didn't see cherry-lime, her favorite.

TIMEPIECE

Lew kissed Trudy one last time before pushing through the turnstile. He checked over his shoulder to see her frozen in her knickers, her eyes leakin' like a busted radiator. She waved as if he were going off to war. He waved back, hoping his smile reassured her he would return.

When he reached his terminal, he took a seat facing the window. Watching planes land and depart eased his anxiety. He hadn't flown since he sold his meat-packing company twelve years ago. Back then, he was strong, confident. *An Ace.* Now those around him thought him one sandwich short of a picnic. He was the chap that died and came back to life. *Frankenstein.*

He wasn't chuffed at the thirteen-plus-hour flight across the pond.

Sitting on the runway, he second-guessed his decision to get involved with a girl he'd never met. *What if we don't find the lass, what then?* Was he all mouth and trousers? Somewhere in his refurbished heart lie the answer. The only thing that kept coming to mind was a watch. *Gaudy. Expensive.* He hadn't had a vision of the girl in days.

HUNGRY

Suzanne reached for Sam's shoulder, but her eyes gravitated to the bandage an inch above his waist between his hip and buttocks. She startled when she closed her eyes and witnessed the knife enter his flesh. A groan stuck in her throat. Her body trembled.

Sam rolled over, wincing slightly. "Hey, what's wrong?"

"My God, Sam," she cried.

Sam brushed the hair from her face. "Talk to me," he said softly.

"Hold me," she said, burying her head against his bare chest.

Sam pulled her close, shifting his weight. His fingers massaged her neck and shoulders. He never thought he'd be one to console another person. *Until Suzanne.* He opened his heart, brushed the dust off his feelings, allowed himself to feel compassion. He wanted to surrender to love, hold her until years crumbled away, like the chalk cliffs in Jasmund National Park on Rügen Island, a place he visited as a boy with his family. *Audra.* Rocks, fossils of sea urchins, sponges, and oysters tumbled into the sea, the rugged landscape as fragile as the human condition. *Time.*

"I saw it happen." Suzanne pulled away. "I saw the knife—"

Sam reached for his wallet on the nightstand. He opened it and pulled out the most recent photo he had of Audra. He flipped it toward Suzanne. "She is what's important, not me. If I had been allowed to stay in Austria, I'd still be searching. The fact that you, and your friend Lewis, feel my sister is here is a revelation, I would have stayed in vain. I will heal. I'm eighty percent better already. But this girl—" He tapped on Audra's face, "this is the only pain that needs tending to." He exhaled his frustration. "How about some coffee?"

"Isn't that how we ended up in bed in the first place?"

He kissed Suzanne's nose. "I am not complaining."

Suzanne brewed coffee, drank a quick cup and left. Sam had phone calls to make. He started with Andrew James, a guy he met at the police academy years ago. Since then, Andrew joined the FBI in the bay area.

"Rumor has it, she was put on a ship out of Brindisi, Italy."

"Did you call Interpol, or the Homeys?"

"No, I know technically it's not your department, but I'd thought I'd start with you guys." Sam sipped his coffee. "Any reports of a human smuggling ring bringing a shipment in?"

"Geez, we get tips all the time. Let me check if there's been any activity in Oakland. If we're talking L.A. or Long Beach, I can give you the number for a friend of mine, Roger Blitz. He's a good guy. Hang on."

Sam finished his coffee listening to canned music on the other end of the line. He admired Andrew for his dedication to the bureau. It wasn't a job for sissies.

"Well, you're right, there was a report of a shipment that came in this week, however by the time we reached the docks, the containers were empty. We alerted the coast guard, but chances are the traffickers have already unloaded the goods…which means we now have to put boots to the ground, check with all our informants to find out who went where. It all takes time, my friend."

"What do you mean, who went where?"

"Some are brought to the US to work, you know, slave labor, farming, restaurants, factories…then there's sex trafficking…we check the brothels for underage kids, roust up the pimps, heat 'em up until they talk. It's like shining a light on cockroaches, they tend to scatter. But we have a really good team that gets results. How old is the girl you're looking for?"

"Twenty-five."

"Hell, her age makes it harder. She's legal. Won't be easy getting a conviction. I assume there's a missing person's report?"

"She disappeared in Austria. The authorities consider her an adult making bad choices."

"And your thoughts?"

"I know better."

"In that case, send me a profile. I'll do some digging."

Suzanne drove home, showered, and dressed in a pair of high-waisted jeans, and an almond color cashmere sweater. She twisted her hair into a long rope, and piled it on top of her head, securing the loose bun with a clip. She swiped mascara on her lashes, and painted her lips rose petal pink. She grabbed a sheet of white card stock, and a black marker from the drawer. She printed LEWIS HOWARD in neat block letters, and blew on the ink to dry. In twenty minutes, she would be meeting the man from London, whose life, like hers, had been changed forever.

While Audra's photo floated through the ether, Audra floated in and out of reality. Intermittent bursts of laughter, followed by intense paranoia, and fear. Her brain fought to make sense of her situation. *Sheisse. Where am I? Where's Britta?* She saw Britta a few minutes ago.

"Britta?" she called.

Lilly entered the room. "Britta? Is that you?" Audra repeated.

"Are you hungry?" Lilly responded, walked across the room and parted the drapes.

Audra squinted. "Britta?" she whispered.

"No, darling. I am not Britta. I'm your new best friend." Lilly snickered. "I am taking you to meet another friend. He's going to take good care of you… providing you take good care of him, that is."

The woman's words whirred in Audra's head like an egg beater.

"Britta?" She looked like Britta. Blond, busty. Audra squinted. Maybe not. The woman's nose was narrow, sharp. Witchy. Her dark brows matched her roots. Britta was blond, through and through. Audra knew, she had showered alongside Britta in *hochschule.*

The woman was talking, *English,* not German, or Viennese. Audra strained to understand. "Not Hungary, Munich."

"I didn't ask where you were from, twit," she grumbled. She brought her fingers to her mouth. "Eat? Food?" She rubbed her tummy. "Hun-gry."

Audra's gaze darted around the room. It locked onto a ceiling sprinkler, and froze. The next thing she knew, she was *moving.* Her hands and feet were bound, black cloth covered her face, and a gag kept her from screaming.

S uzanne held up her home-made sign. She spotted a man wearing a bowler hat in the distance, navigating his way to baggage claim by reading the signs along the way.

"Lewis?" Suzanne smiled, hoping she had identified the right man.

"Yes, yes of course," he chuckled, extending his hand. "Suzanne, I presume."

"Yes! So nice to meet you," she said, accepting his enthusiastic hand shake. "I'm parked in the lot," she said pointing over her shoulder. "Can you manage? Or shall I bring the car around?"

"I promised me wife that I'd accept a hand with m'baggage."

"I'd be happy to help. How was your flight?"

"I closed me eyes 'alf way across the pond. I managed a film, can't bloody remember the name of it."

"I'm happy that you chose to stay in my guest room rather than a hotel. It will give us time to talk, and perhaps figure things out."

"I 'ave to say, yer quite generous puttin' up an ol' codger such as meself. The missus, she's not so keen on the idea."

"I'm happy to do it, and if Trudy isn't comfortable

with the arrangements, you can always stay at Sam's. I'm sure he wouldn't mind."

"Sam?"

"Yes. Sam is an undercover detective for Goldorado County. It's his sister that is missing."

"She's not missin', she's been taken."

Terror shimmied down Suzanne's spine. "Any idea who took her?"

GLUE

Sam entered his office at noon. A handful of employees stayed behind to cover the others who went to lunch. One dispatcher, one desk clerk, one desk sergeant. They all nodded as he crossed the room.

His desk was the same as he left it. Papers piled neatly to one side of his leather mat. His coffee cup, rinsed and dried, sat approximately six inches to the left of his phone, right above his favorite pen. The calendar on the wall still on the page of the day he left. He walked over to the wall, crossed six days off the month, making note of the small notations written by his secretary, Julie. He missed an appearance at the Crab Feed sponsored by Goldorado County Search and Rescue. Bummer, it was one of his favorite events. He had planned to take Suzanne this year. The tickets were in his top drawer.

He sat down, already feeling the burn in his side. He

picked up the phone and dialed the first number on the list he pulled from his breast pocket. The voice on the other end launched into a greeting, "California Department of Justice Sacramento, how can I direct your call?"

"This is Detective Sam Metzger, Goldorado County Sheriff's Department, can you connect me with someone in the human trafficking task force division?" Sam waited patiently for a voice to magically appear on the other end of the phone. He wasn't expecting a recording. "Leave your message at the tone." He slammed the phone down on the receiver. *What to do?* He picked up the phone and re-dialed Andrew. "Hey buddy, it's Sam again...I need your help."

Sam and Andrew arranged to meet at 4 p.m., when Andrew's shift ended. Until then, Sam trolled the internet looking for suspicious ads. Sometimes trafficking was a click away. With the social media boom, criminals were able to work the system, eluding law enforcement. One just needed to know the lingo. "Puppies for Sale," "Babysitter Wanted," "Models Wanted." The possibilities were endless. The ads that piqued his attention were "Crate Trained Puppies" 4-6 weeks.

He worked an investigation back in the day where a woman in Jackson kept her children caged, and rented them out like power tools. When the Feds busted her, she had six kids ranging from five to fourteen that she trafficked for sex, slave labor, and childcare. Other than being caged, the kids seemed oblivious to the abuse. They were polite, well-mannered, and educated. The older children taught the younger ones how to read, write, spell, and do math. The mother seemed like your typical soccer mom. No one suspected, until the twelve-year-old became pregnant, and almost died behind a grocery store after trying to abort the baby herself. His drinking at the time anesthetized the horror.

S uzanne fixed a green salad with figs, feta cheese, and cucumbers. A chicken baking in the oven, dressed with red potatoes, fennel and carrots smelled divine. Lewis watched her work, but she knew his mind was elsewhere.

"Would you like to phone your wife to let her know you arrived? If I were her, I would rest easy knowing you were safe."

"Y'know the missus all too well. She's probably bit through both thumbnails by now."

"She seems delightful. Would you care to use my cell?"

"Much obliged." He said, rising from the kitchen chair. "I 'ave this 'ere gadget that works just fine." He produced a flip phone from his pocket and left the room.

When he returned from his call, his face looked relaxed, and his smile warmed Suzanne's heart. She imagined what it must be like being married, and in love. She never had that with Ben, but she felt sure if she and Sam were to marry it would be different. Then again, there were no guaranties in life. "Live in the now," Linda had said. Right *now*, she was content, but worried. "I haven't heard the kittens cry in the last couple of days."

Lew's eyes grew large. "They've parted ways," he said. "Don't know 'ow I know, but it feels right as rain t'say it."

"Do you still believe she's on the boat?"

"No," he said, shaking his head. "Can't get a clear picture. Like m'glasses need a good wipe."

Suzanne nodded. She understood. Neither of them wore glasses, and yet the images she saw in flashes weren't clear. "I'm expecting a friend to join us for dinner. Her name is Linda Schooler. She's a psychic. I don't know what I would have done without her help. She understands what we are experiencing. I believe she can help us put the pieces together.

"Glue. Huh." His attention wandered once more. "Glue," he whispered.

RICH

Audra sat alone in a room. An ostentatious room, filled with trophies. Animal heads lined one side of the room, a bookcase with metal figures, with marble columns, and wooden bases. The many fixtures hanging from the ceiling were made of deer antlers, those from young bucks. *Children.* Audra's body began to shake. The person associated with this room had no regard for life. Krampus. She was sitting in a devil's den.

Audra couldn't remember being dressed. The filmy prairie dress she was now wearing made her feel uneasy. Her long tresses, now fixed into two braids, were adorned with pink ribbons, and hung over each breast. She felt like a little girl again. *Prinzessin.* Tears rolled down her cheeks.

The smell of cigar smoke wafted up from behind her. She didn't turn to look. His voice reached her ears. Deep, gravelly. "Well, aren't you perty."

Perty. That's what he said. The kind one. But it wasn't <u>his</u> voice. *Coincidence? Did they know each other?* Her body stiffened.

"Don't you be afraid now, young lady. Ol' Jake is gonna take good care of you. Yes siree…*real good care.*"

Audra cringed when he fondled one braid, brushing a knuckle across her breast. She could hear a wheeze coming from his chest. His breath a foul combination of cigars and gingivitis. His greying hair, thin, greasy, and long, parted down the middle, accentuating dark blue eyes. His cheeks were ruddy, his nose bulbous, like the drunks that hung out at the local pub on the corner back in Budapest. Her appearance seemed to please him. She squeezed her eyes shut. Her body trembled. "Please don't, I—" she whispered. The slap came so swift and hard, it knocked the rest of her words out of her reach.

Linda Schooler arrived just before the oven timer went off. "I'm Linda Schooler," she said, reaching for Lewis' outstretched hand. "Welcome to the US." She gave him a package.

Lewis raised the package to his nose. "Lavender soap?"

"Yes." Linda said, excitedly, her Shirley Temple dimples showing. "I hope you like it. Sometimes it's nice to have a bit of home when you're in a strange place."

"'Ow did y'know? It's m'favorite."

"She's psychic," Suzanne said. "And my mentor."

The threesome conversed over dinner, mostly recounting Lewis' near-death experience. Lewis interrupted with, "Do y'smell that?"

Linda and Suzanne exchanged glances. "Smell what?" Suzanne asked.

"Cigar smoke," he said.

Suzanne closed her eyes. "I hear gunfire, but it's from long ago."

Linda fingered the cloth napkin absently. "Yes, it feels like we're going back in time."

Lewis slipped into a trance-like state. "The lass, it's as if she's a prize of some sort."

"What else do you see?" Linda asked.

"Trees, water. Wildflowers. Purple ones." He cupped one ear. "I 'ear dogs barking...I know that bark, I do... the Queen Mum has dogs like—" He stopped, his eyes flashed open. "Huntin' dogs."

"Lupines grow wild, but it's a little early for them around here. There's water all up and down the coast," Suzanne said, clearing the table. "We have rivers, lakes streams..."

"There are areas that are less progressive, where people live on acreage so they can hunt and fish." Linda rose, assisting Suzanne with the dishes. "That may account for the hunting dogs."

"The mutts I'm talkin' 'bout are pure breeds. Set y'back a pound or two."

"Trafficking <u>is</u> a rich man's sport..." Suzanne loaded the dishwasher.

"Let's make a list," Linda suggested. "Cigar smoke, hunting dogs, wild flowers, trees, water—sounds like we're looking for someone who owns property, someone with money."

Suzanne called over her shoulder, "We can have Sam check to see if anyone prominent has been busted for solicitation."

Linda nodded. "It's a start. Lewis? Anything you want to add?"

Lewis thought for a moment...*that watch. That big expensive watch.* "M'mind is on trinkets. All the posh stores at the airport, I suspect. Quite fancy, they are." He cleared his throat. "Need to keep me mind focused on our girl. I feel like we need to take the *reins*." Lewis steepled his fingers. "Don't know why that word popped from me mouth. *Reins.* Huh."

Suzanne brightened. "I get it, Lewis—it's like getting the hiccups. Random words pop out of me too. It takes a bit of concentration to decipher their meaning. If I'm lucky, they come with an image."

Linda scratched her head. "I associate reins with horses, power."

Suzanne slipped back into her chair. "So far, we have wealth, property, fields, dogs, horses..."

Linda tilted her head, as if listening to someone beside her, except no one was there. "What is one thing that money <u>can't</u> buy?"

Suzanne spoke up. "Character."

RUMORS

"Listen," Andrew said. "You didn't hear this from me."

Sam nodded. "Of course."

Andrew took a swig of beer, and set it down carefully. "This shit is deep. Real deep. We have all these task forces set up, but sometimes, it feels like we're tripping over one another. It's rare that we all show up on the same stage. Meanwhile, these traffickers are ruling the roost. I can't tell you how many botched stings I've been on. We're either too early, or too late."

"So, what you're saying is your numbers don't match."

"In a nutshell. We get a tip on a freighter coming in with a couple hundred immigrants. We don't know how many of them have paid a smuggler to bring them into the country, how many are being smuggled in to sell, all we know is once the sting is set up, we end up busting a few dozen."

"What about the tunnels? Kids? Little kids?"

"Don't believe everything you hear on social media."

"Are you saying it doesn't happen? There are no children being brought to the US as sex slaves?"

Andrew leaned back in his chair. His eyes pierced through Sam's. "Yes. It happens." He leaned forward, his jaw working back and forth. "We work our asses off to make sure it doesn't."

Sam sat up tall. "And when it does?"

"The shit hits the fan. That means someone, somewhere, dropped the ball." He leaned back again, and lowered his voice. "Or—someone's on the take."

"Say the ship comes in…how easy is it to unload the merchandise before they hit US waters?"

"Ever see one of those ships? It takes special equipment to unload the containers. It takes a huge crane. There's no way a smuggler is going to bring one of those monsters to the party."

"But if they have access to the cargo, they wouldn't need to move the container, only the contents, right?"

"I suppose."

"What's to stop them from taking some crates off the freighter and loading them onto say– a yacht, or a fishing boat?"

"They'd have to get past the Coast Guard."

"What if the Coast Guard is paid to look the other way?"

"Like I said. It happens."

"I need to know if it did."

Andrew ordered another beer. When the waiter was out of earshot, he continued, "I checked around. No one has heard anything about a girl that age. We did get a tip on some kids that were displaced when an orphanage closed down in Kyiv. They haven't been located yet, but we're working on it."

"What's the protocol? I know we bust up rings in the boonies, but I've never worked an investigation dealing with international traffickers…what am I looking for?"

"These people, men and women look like ordinary business people. You would never suspect them. Hell, there was a high-profile lawyer that just got arrested for trafficking and kiddie porn in Virginia. Most of the perps buy their way out of charges that stick, or you have guys like Epstein that would rather die than sing. It's all about money. If someone took the risk of bringing this girl to the US, she must be a prize. An <u>expensive</u> one." Andrew's eye narrowed, "Oh, and you left out one little detail."

"And what's that?"

"That the girl *is your sister*."

SLASHERS

Audra's breath came in ragged waves. Below her, dogs jumped and barked, trying to nip at her heels. Fear paralyzed her. She hugged the trunk of a tree so tight the bark tore at her skin. A spider danced above her head, warning her to keep her distance. She heard horse hooves galloping toward her.

"Ye-haw, you sure are one scared little bunny." He said with a hardy laugh. "Bunnies don't climb trees though, where'd you learn to do that?" He steadied his horse underneath her. "Time to come in for supper young lady, and I won't be takin' "no" for an answer. There're bobcats out here, and hell, they know how to climb trees too." His belly jiggled with mirth. "Hop on," he said, his smile morphing into a serious slash. "Now."

Audra shimmied down the tree, grabbed a branch, and swung herself onto the back of the horse. The horse lunged forward, forcing Audra to latch onto the man's waist. As they rode swiftly to the house, she spied her surroundings, the terrain treacherous, and desolate. *What were you thinking—there is no escape!*

Suzanne walked Linda to the door, then showed Lewis to the guest room. "There's a bathroom across the hall…fresh towels next to the shower. Make yourself at home. Help yourself to food and drink in the refrigerator, and if you need me just call out. I'm a light sleeper."

"Yer very kind," he said. "Is there a telly I can look at for a bit. I don't think I'll be able to catch a wink just yet."

"Of course. Let me get the remote." Suzanne opened the drawer in the small table beside her sofa. "I'll fetch a throw for you, it still gets cold in here at night. I keep the thermostat down low, but if you need more heat, feel free to kick it up a notch."

Lewis stared at her as if she were talking Greek. Of course, she thought. *Gadgets are different from what he is used too.* She clicked on the TV, and gave him a quick lesson on how to navigate the buttons. Lewis punched the up arrow, landing on a movie channel. A western. They glanced at each other as if a miracle happened before their very eyes. Both took a seat, mesmerized by the scene unfolding before them.

A man on a horse lassoed a young squaw. She fought with all of her might to get free, but it was no use, the man's strength won out, and she was his captive. He rode back to his cabin, holding her tightly to his chest. When they arrived, she fought against him again, this time he used violent means to disarm her fury. He carried her like a rag doll into the cabin, and threw her on the bed. He climbed on top of her, and began ripping at her clothes.

"'At's not 'ow 'e's gonna take her," Lew said. "She's a prize."

"But why Audra? Why is <u>she</u> the prize? There are so many girls in California, why risk smuggling in a woman from another country?" Suzanne looked perplexed.

"From the visions I get of the lass, she's not only beau'iful, she's pure."

"I'd never seen her face until Sam showed me a photo of her." Lewis' astonished look made Suzanne smile. "It's true."

"'Ave to admit, she's been rather elusive, lately."

"I haven't gotten many hits myself. It was good to brainstorm with Linda. She grounds me, makes me feel like I'm not going crazy."

"Yeah, m'Tru is like that. But I know she'll b'glad when I'm back t'bein' m'fuddy-dud self."

"Most people don't understand what it's like to die, and come back to life. I can't say I ever felt as though I were dead…I just hung out with my dead fiancé while he scared the wits out of me. Was it like that for you?"

"Well, m'friends did all the talkin', but it was spiffy

seein' me mum and dad." He laughed. "And m'dog, Gingersnap."

Suzanne walked over to the shelf above the buffet in her dining room and picked up two crystal points. "I got these at a gem shop in Folsom. Take one. Linda says they help clarify your thoughts."

Lewis held it up, inches from his nose. "Funny," he said, squinting his eyes. "I keep seeing a wrist-ticker, it's covered in these, only they're tiny. They sparkle like diamonds, but shaped like crystals. There're a few blue ones, and two red ones. Gaudy lookin', it is."

Suzanne grabbed her phone and typed in the description on google. "This watch?"

"Yes! That's the lot."

Suzanne gasped. "I saw the same watch. A man I met at the park wore one just like it. What are the chances—"

"I thought I was goin' daft."

"What if he's—"

Suzanne dialed Sam.

S am had been roaming the streets, passing out his business card while showing Audra's photo to every Tom, Dick, and Harriet he met along the way. No luck. The angst in his throat thickened. Then his phone rang. *Suzanne.*

"A man approached me in Capital Park the other

day. I didn't get his name, but he was wearing a very expensive watch."

Sam's disappointment was audible when he said, "There's a lot of rich people in Sacramento. I don't see what—"

Suzanne cut him off. "Lewis has been having visions of the same watch. It's a shot in the dark, Sam, but we just might hit a bullseye."

"Stranger things have happened. I'll stop by in the morning. I'm going to contact a friend of mine. She's a retired forensic sketch artist. Her name's Robin Burcell —a well-known local author—you'll love her."

"We'll be here."

Sam drove home, feeling hopeful. When he pulled into his driveway, he didn't see the two men standing in the shadows. When he went inside his house, he didn't see them slash his tires.

SMOKE

"Mission accomplished," Lilly said, flicking a cigarette into a spray of sparks on the ground."

Giorgi flashed her a look of distain. "Are you trying to start a fucking fire?"

"What time is your flight?"

"Midnight." He turned to her, his eyes blazing. "Word on the street is that there's a cop looking for the girl."

"Impossible! No one knows she's here. We were extremely careful."

"There was a cop asking questions in Vienna. Rubio said he took care of him…evidently, he's mistaken. What no one bothered to tell me was he was an American—or better yet, that the fucking girl is his fucking sister!"

Lilly purred, "There is no way in hell the girl can be

linked to you." She leaned closer. "Besides, Jake has always been good about cleaning up after himself." She reached in her pocket for another cigarette. "You can always get rid of the cop."

His expression turned dark, dangerous.

Lilly eased the cigarette from the package. "I swear on my life–I didn't know."

Giorgi's laugh chilled her to the bone. He disappeared into the night like a ghost.

Lilly lit her cigarette. With each puff, she mentally kicked herself for opening her big mouth.

AUTOGRAPHS

Sam examined the damage to his tires. "Son-of-a-bitch," he seethed under his breath. He dialed AAA, and used his clout to get immediate service. He hated to pull a power play but it was crucial he get to his appointment with Suzanne and Robin on time. Robin was doing him a favor; he intended to do the customary cop thing and pick up donuts—lucky for him he allowed time for a tire change.

He checked the perimeter of his house, searching for clues. All he found were two sets of shoe prints near the back of the garage. By the looks of them, the slashers wore athletic shoes. Expensive ones. He recalled the two guys he approached on K Street. They eyed him carefully before taking his card. Anyone with a cell could google his name to find out where he lived, but why do that? Where they sending him a message? *Butt out? Stay off our turf?* Could be anything. *Could be nothing.*

. . .

At 10 a.m., Suzanne heard the doorbell ring, followed by a knock.

"Sorry, I didn't hear the bell, I wasn't sure it was working. I'm Robin, Robin Burcell. Sam Metzger said to meet him here."

"Please come in." Suzanne led the way to the kitchen. "This is Lewis Howard, from London." Lewis nodded in greeting. "Sam said you're a local author —mysteries?"

"Yes. I've published many series, and I've co-authored with Clive Cussler."

Lewis's eyes grew large. "I've read several of the books in the series, "Pirate," "The Romanov Ransom," and "The Gray Ghost." The missus gets 'em on Amazon. Fine read. Lookin' forward to the next two."

A tinge of pink colored Robin's cheeks as she smiled. "Thanks, I appreciate hearing that."

Suzanne set down four mugs for coffee. "Sam is on his way." She paused, "Someone slashed his tires last night."

Robin removed her sketch pad from her bag. "I think we can get started while we wait. Can you describe what the man looked like?"

Suzanne shrugged. "He was so good-looking, I'm not sure I have words that will do him justice."

Robin chuckled. "Do your best."

. . .

B y the time Sam arrived, Robin had sketched the shape of the man's face, his hairline, eyes, and nose. She was drawing his lips when Sam squeezed her shoulder. "Hey, woman, how've you been?"

"Busy. Working on a new novel. How about you? Heard someone slashed your tires."

"May have been someone I gave my card to last night when I was showing Audra's picture around. The temps downtown are heating up—we're the bad guys."

Robin shook her head, "I sure don't miss those days."

Sam picked up the sketch and winked at Suzanne. "By the looks of this guy, I'd say I'm lucky you picked me up at the airport."

"He may be handsome, but he gave me the creeps."

"How so?"

"Reminded me of the first time I met Dixon–gave off the same vibe."

Lew peered over Robin's shoulder at the drawing and glanced at Suzanne. "Did y'tell 'im about the watch?"

"Yes, but I didn't tell him what the watch cost. I'd never seen anything like it so I googled it while I was waiting for your plane to land—1.4 million dollars! And he was dressed casually—I can only imagine."

Sam lifted one brow. "Handsome AND rich?" He poured himself a cup of coffee and sat down. "The guy

Audra met in Vienna was good looking too. Chick bait. I'm glad you were immune, Suzanne."

His eyes met hers and melted her heart. *How can he be so strong, yet so vulnerable at the same time?* She reached across the table, patted his hand, and gave him a reassuring smile. "I must not be attracted to monsters."

Sam walked Robin to her car while Suzanne stared at the sketch she drew. Lewis had a faraway look on his face. "What's wrong?"

"Wish I had m' books for Robin to sign, that's all."

Suzanne relaxed her jaw. "Once this is over, I'll make sure you get autographed copies of the whole series."

TOO LATE

Audra barely touched her breakfast. She knew she needed nourishment if she were to escape, yet her appetite matched her willingness to take the risk. So far all he had done was chase her through the fields, wearing a flimsy dress. This morning, he arrived in the dining room wearing a black western shirt, a red bandana, black jeans, a black hat, and eel skin boots with silver spurs. He spent the whole time talking on his phone, laughing, joking, like she wasn't even in the room. But as he left, he backtracked his steps, and issued an order. "Be dressed by ten." She glared at the clock on the mantle. She had fifteen minutes to dress.

The outfit laid out on her bed made her cringe. The buckskin shift was beautifully stitched. Fringed at the bottom, beaded at the top. She slipped out of her night-gown and tossed the dress over her head. At the foot of the bed she saw a pair of moccasins to match. *No under-*

wear. Two strips of rawhide, and two bands were placed next to a brush on her nightstand.

She had finished braiding her hair when there was a knock on the door.

"Ready?" The man stood in the doorway, a gleeful expression on his ruddy face.

Audra followed him out of the house and to the barn. A beautiful Paint stood ready and waiting. "You do know how to ride, don't you?" he asked, worry lining his brow. When Audra didn't answer, he picked up the reins, and pumped them up and down, mimicking a riding motion. When she still didn't respond, anger turned his dark blue eyes dusty grey, his mouth dip down on both ends, and his nostrils flared.

She knew what she must do. Her fingertips danced along the horse's snout, her voice barely a whisper, as she cooed into the paint's ear.

The man's face brightened as he held out his cupped hands to give her a lift onto the animal's bare back. He licked his lips as his eyes traveled from her bent knee to the dark patch between her legs as he boosted her upward. Once she was mounted securely, he slapped the paint on its rear flank, and the horse took off like a bullet. Audra grabbed the paint's mane and hung on for dear life.

. . .

Sam tapped the hood of Robin's car and waved. The image she drew loomed in his mind. *Rich, handsome.* So what? There were many good-looking, rich guys in Sacramento. *He gave me the creeps.* Suzanne wasn't one to read people unless there was good reason. *Like Dixon.* A serial killer. *Who is this guy?* What does he have to do with my sister?

As he watched Robin's car pull away, he saw a green sedan drive by. He caught the passenger out of the corner of his eye, he wasn't sure, but it appeared to be one of the men he spoke to while looking for leads regarding his sister. The bandana and tattoos were a dead give-away. Why would they be following him? Unless—*they know something.*

Lilly paced her marble veranda, phone in one hand, cigarette in another. Beyond the safety of her retreat, mountains loomed in the distance. Every now and then she got the feeling she was being watched. Earlier she caught a glimpse of a light, flickering between the trees, as if the sun reflected off a lens of some sort. If there was someone out there, lying in wait, then what? And why did Giorgi blame her? She did what he asked, and as always, she was careful. *That detective has nothing to do with me.* Giorgi was no one to fuck with. If he wanted her dead, he would find a way.

She puffed on her cigarette and blew smoke at the devil. "Fuck you, Giorgi. Fuck you—and your little dog too."

She didn't need this shit anymore. She was tired of always waiting for the other shoe to drop. She came from a family of crop pickers. Grew up poor in the "lettuce bowl." She worked her way up the ladder. Went from being gang-raped to smuggling girls over the border, selling them to the brothels in Nevada, and other states. She graduated to grooming young girls for Giorgi. She made sure they were healthy before turning them over to billionaires, high-profile CEOs, or diplomats. She did what she had to do to care for her aged parents, provide college tuition for her children and private school for her granddaughter. *Time to care for yourself.* How? *Nowhere to run. Nowhere to hide.*

Lilly went inside, poured herself a glass of wine, and returned to the veranda for her evening ritual. She settled into an overstuffed chair and waited for the sun to set fire to the hills. The opulence she'd become accustomed to no longer mattered. The comfort she surrounded herself with to compensate for the things she lacked suddenly felt like shoes that blistered her feet. She lit another cigarette, took a sip of wine. *Maybe I'll move to Puerto Rico.* Once again, light flickered in the distance through the trees… and she knew…*it's too late.*

∼

RUBIO

Giorgi sipped on a glass of McCallan "Reflection" scotch. A little celebratory drink. With Lilly out of the way, he needn't worry about any more fuck-ups. True, she delivered the girl to Jake. But for chrissake, she should have alerted him immediately that a detective was snooping around. Now he would handle the matter himself, like a cat, he'd toy with the detective a little, then go in for the kill.

His legion of minions, generously paid for their loyalty, were hand-picked. Ex-military, mostly. Snipers, mercenaries…psychopaths he could count on to get the job done without questioning his motives or disrupting the flow. Human trafficking was a lucrative business, one that survived the leanest periods in history. *High profit, low risk.*

Giorgi pinched his bottom lip. His men had eyes on the detective. Lilly was right, there was no way he could be linked to the detective's sister. Still, he felt obligated to protect his clients, for they were the ones who could blow the whistle...*or at least try*. He made it a point to stay away from clients who had nothing to lose. Although Jake was single, his eighty-nine-year-old mother, who was very prominent in the political arena, was still alive. She would cut off his balls with a butter knife before she would let him sully her good name. Giorgi could relate.

His grandfather began supplying factories with slave labor during World War II. His father added commercial sex to their multi-million-dollar empire, and groomed him for succession. They preyed on the dreamers. The damaged. The desperate. He made his mark in the family empire by providing services to those pleasure seekers who were willing to pay top dollar to act out their fantasies. Millions grew into billions. He commandeered his own fledglings, like *Rubio*.

He hated to get rid of Rubio, he was his first prodigy. His father had gifted Rubio to him with the inclination Giorgi would take over the business one day, and Rubio would serve him well. Giorgi was an eager recipient; Rubio was a fast learner. Together, they learned the trade. Giorgi experienced more sex than imaginable while Rubio took notes. *Father's diplomatic immunity helped.* But lately, Rubio was more preoccupied with gambling than he was with his occupation. *Or me.*

They had grown apart physically, but the occasional times they did get together were scandalous. Rubio was one of his favorite lovers. But he had disobeyed him one too many times…forced him into becoming a cop killer. And although he wouldn't personally pull the trigger, Rubio put him in the position to make the call—muddy the waters with other cops he had on his payroll. *Not acceptable.* He hit speed dial, and listened to the ring on the other end of the phone.

"Rubio," he said, his tone soft, deadly. "Is there something you forgot to tell me?"

Audra's fingers were twisted so tight in the horse's hair, they bled. Her inner thighs were chafed from squeezing the animals middle to keep from flying off as she flew through the trees, and leapt over boulders. Hoofs pummeled the ground behind her. Adrenaline surged through her veins. She felt as though her heart exploded and lodged in her throat when the lasso circled her head and tightened around her neck. *I can't breathe.*

KEMO SABE

Tears ran down Suzanne's cheeks as she struggled to catch her breath. Lewis stood helpless, frozen, knowing that what she was experiencing was beyond her control. An image of bleeding fingers had flashed in his own mind seconds before. Fortunately, Sam intervened.

"Breathe, Suzanne, you're safe." He folded her in his arms. "Breathe, sweetheart. Shhhh, you're okay. Talk to me."

Her haunted eyes grew large. She placed her hand on her throat, her chest heaved, "I—can't—breathe," she said, her voice strained.

"Close your eyes, what do you see?"

Her hands clutched at her neck. "A rope—" Her chest heaved harder. "There's a rope around her neck."

. . .

L ewis backed himself against the wall. Visions of burning animals swarmed in his head like bees. He could hear horses braying and the thunder of gunfire. The lass moved through his vision as if she were a ghost…her smile, sweet, loving…flowers in her hand…her dress, billowing as she moved, like a little princess. The vision shifted to an American TV program he had seen as a boy. "Butch Cavendish," he whispered.

Sam turned to Lewis, "Who?"

"The Lone Ranger—before y'time, mate. Butch Cavendish was the villain."

Suzanne collapsed into a chair, her mind reeling with snippets of Audra's dilemma. When her breathing returned to normal, she nodded. "Lewis is right. As odd as it seems, I was picking up the same vibe, only I was hearing Indians chanting."

Sam slid into a chair next to Suzanne, and clicked on his phone. "Let's look on the map, see where the horse ranches are in this area."

A udra laid under a blue sky, her hands tied above her head, her legs spread, her feet bound and staked into the ground. It hurt to swallow. Tears burned her eyes, her muscles spasmed and ached. The pounding in her chest began to subside, until a shadow swallowed the sun and loomed over her body.

A sardonic laugh cut through nature's melody,

striking fear all over again. The man straddled her help-less form, arms akimbo. "Well, well. What do we have here?"

Audra swallowed her tears. She wouldn't give him the satisfaction of knowing how terrified she was of him. She knew enough psychology to know she was dealing with a sadistic monster who thrived on inflicting pain.

"Look what we got ourselves, Smoke," he said to his horse, nudging Audra's hip with his toe. "We roped ourselves a little squaw—*Pocahontas.*"

The man stepped over her body to remove a canvas bag he had tied to his saddle. Audra heard the rattle, but the sound did not compute until he dumped the contents three feet from her head. Audra's eyes were glued to the snake slithering towards her, its forked tongue navigating its course.

The man's laughter shattered her focus like breaking glass, as the snake inched closer to her face.

Audra fought waves of nausea, and the urge to pass out. The snake, about a foot from her now, decided to curl up for a nap. The man was busy on the other side of his horse, whistling an eerie tune. She slowly exhaled debating whether to move quickly, causing the snake to strike? Or pray for a miracle? She thought about the children that survived their journey to America, only to be raped, killed or tortured. Too late for miracles. Instead she prayed the temperature would drop, and the snake would wake and go in another direction.

No such luck. The man, now wearing a black mask, threw a stone, disturbing the snake. It popped its head up, and rattled its tail. *Scheisse!* Her heart beat like a washing machine filled with throw rugs on the spin cycle. A scream caught in her throat, making a squeaking noise as the snake struck inches from her right cheek. She was slipping away until a gun went off and she was suddenly covered in snake guts.

Sam made phone calls and researched leads on his laptop. Suzanne roasted a chicken, and put together a salad. Lewis excused himself from the room to ring Trudy, and have a shower.

Taking advantage of their privacy, Suzanne slipped her arms around Sam's neck, and whispered, "Hi Ho Silver," startling the both of them.

He scrunched his forehead. "Where did that come from?"

"I don't know. I merely wanted to give you a hug. The words escaped before I had a chance to think about them."

"Interesting. What does the Lone Ranger have to do with my sister?"

"My first thought is that whoever has your sister is either older...or a fan."

Sam's fingers flew across the keyboard, searching for "ranches in Northern California". The number was worrisome. "77,000. Where do we begin?"

"Perhaps you can narrow down the numbers by county."

Sam re-entered the information by county. "Better, but not great. Now all I have to do is find a way to get warrants for hundreds of ranches and farms. And that's if—"

Suzanne reached for his hand. "She's out there. She's alive, I can feel it. My heart-rate has been ebbing then soaring, as if her fear is alive within me. If your sister has the strong will you said she possesses, she'll stay alive."

"Is that you speaking? Or your spirit guides?"

"Both."

Audra's ears rang, her body shook. Her breath was ragged, labored. She thought being kidnapped was terrifying. Having a rattlesnake strike inches from your face gave the word new meaning. Urine trickled beneath her bare buttocks. She sobbed.

"Well now, lit-tle la-dy," he said. "Looks like I just saved your life. I suppose you're beholden to me now." His sadistic chuckle made her cry even harder. He undid the ties binding her feet. She was tempted to kick him in the balls, give him a reason to bash her head in with a rock, get it over with, but she was afraid she wouldn't die. He untied her hands, bound them in front of her, and yanked her to her feet. What did he mean *beholden*? He looped a rope through her wrists and fastened it to the back of his saddle. Was this what he meant by beholden? He mounted his horse and took off, dragging her behind. *I would have been better off with the rock.*

S am closed his laptop. "I'll call my friend Rhett. He owns a helicopter, and knows the area like the back of his hand. He's been taking aerial shots for many of the real estate companies around here for years."

"I'll call Sheena, see if Emmett has shown her anything unusual lately."

Lewis looked at the floor. "Y'don't need a bugger's muddle, now do ye? What will y'ave me do?"

Sam and Suzanne exchanged glances. Suzanne spoke first. "After we make our phone calls, we'll decide. Meanwhile, you're welcome to watch TV."

Lew nodded. His shoulders slumped with a sigh. "Can y'show me again 'ow to turn it on, please?"

Once more, Suzanne instructed Lew on how to use her remote and left the room. Lew sat down with his hands in his lap. He massaged his wrists. They burned.

• • •

Sheena answered Suzanne's call on the second ring. Her eyes didn't leave her son, who had stuffed his bunny into a mesh bag, looped the drawstring over the tail of his rocking horse, and scooted around the living room, dragging the bunny behind him.

CLOSE

Audra submerged herself in the jetted tub. The abrasions on her arms and legs burned in the chemically treated water. The bump on her forehead throbbed, the cut beneath her chin probably needed stitches. Her throat was raw from screaming, her heart battered her chest. She was trapped in a nightmare.

Suzanne tossed and turned in her bed. She was six years old. It was Halloween. She dressed in a Cinderella costume, and her brother Steven, dressed as the "Where's Waldo" character, ran to the door to greet trick or treaters. When they opened the door, they were shocked to see a grown-up dressed in a cowboy outfit, complete with silver pistols, and a bandana covering his mouth and nose. Suzanne froze. Steven ran to get their dad.

The man's eye's gleamed under the front porch light. Suzanne wished for a magic wand to make the cowboy disappear, *bibbity-boppity-boo*, but she knew why he was there. She *must* disappear. She stepped outside and closed the door behind her.

The woods were dark. She followed the crunching sound of his footsteps the best she could. She knew if she didn't keep up, she'd get lost. On Halloween, there would be monsters combing the woods, looking for little girls like her.

When they reached a clearing, the cowboy pointed. In the distance, she saw a beautiful castle. "I am a princess—is that my new home?"

The cowboy tossed his hat up into the air, then his bandana. A dark hood obscured his face. Suzanne was amazed by the transformation, but even more amazed by the black steed that appeared out of nowhere. She turned to see if Steven witnessed the magic, but he wasn't there. *Oh yeah, he went to get dad because*—it was too late. The man lifted her onto the horse and they sped towards the castle.

Once they arrived, Suzanne realized the castle looked much prettier from a distance. Gnarly thorn bushes clawed their way up the side of the stone wall. The drawbridge was edged in sharp metal finials. The entrance reminded her of Krampus, and his evil maw. *Krampus?* Were they were riding into the devil's lair?

The man dismounted the black steed, then grabbed Suzanne by the arm and pulled her to the ground. "I don't understand. Isn't this my castle? Why are you being so mean?"

"Run little girl. Run. When I catch you, you will be my next meal."

Suzanne didn't question his directive. She ran.

"No," Lewis cried aloud in his sleep. He covered his eyes, refusing to witness the cruelty unfolding before him. The girl, chained in heavy manacles thrashed about as rats filled the chamber. A man stepped into the cell. His boots, caught Lewis' eye, deep red, made from an unfamiliar material. His intentions drew Lew's curiosity away from the boots when he turned the lass about, pulled up her dress and raped her. Oblivious to the vermin invasion around him, the man kept pumping until the girl was but a rag doll in his mitts. When he spilled his seed, he screamed like a banshee and vanished.

His friend Jim entered the cell, dressed in coveralls, and tall rubber boots. He smashed each rat with a shovel head. He glanced at Lew, regret filling his face. "The lass will be rubbish in a couple of days, be just these rats here." He went back to work, shoveling the dead rats into a heap.

Lew grabbed the bars of the cell. "What can I do, Jim?"

Jim tapped his finger on his temple. "Use what the

good Lord gave ye, then. Y'got a bloody gift! 'E gave it to ye, use it."

Jim vanished, leaving Lew to observe the girl's limp body, lying in the dirt.

S uzanne gasped when she turned on the kitchen light and found Lew sitting at the table, his head resting on his folded arms. "Lew? Everything all right? Lew?"

Lew's body jerked upright. "Just a 'mare. Never had them before I—"

"Before you died?"

Lew swiped his face. "M'mind keeps playing tricks."

"Happens to me too. I had a dream that I was a child. A cowboy came to the door trick-or-treating, and I went with him. He took me to a castle—it was scary. He told me to run, that he was going to eat me when he caught me—it was awful."

"Strange, I was in a castle too. A man turned the lass bum over tea kettle, had 'is way with her, rats everywhere…then Jim came to clean up. 'E said I should use me gifts…a riddle if ye ask me."

"There has to be a message in here somewhere. Halloween, castles…how were the characters dressed in your dream?"

"The lass was dressed in rags, the man was big, dressed in a strange pair of boots, and a tunic." Lew disappeared into his thoughts while Suzanne put a kettle on the stove.

"We've had visions of someone dressed as a cowboy, an Indian maiden, and now medieval clothing…perhaps the man who is keeping Audra owns a costume shop."

"I feel like it's deeper than that. 'E likes a good game of cat and mouse." Suddenly, Lew's face turned to paste. His shoulders shook, he buried his face.

Suzanne rushed to his side. "What is it?"

"His boots."

"What about them?"

"I know now what they were made from."

Suzanne slid into the chair kiddy-corner from where he sat and placed her hand over his. Goosebumps covered her body. "The boots—what were they made from?"

"Skin. Human skin."

Audra heard the tumblers on the door lock clunk into place. She sat on the edge of the bed staring at the two white tablets next to a bottle of water. The note clipped to her pillow read: *Für den Schmerz.*

For the pain? Sadistic son-of-a-bitch. She swiped the pills up into her mouth and washed them down with water. She wasn't one to take medications. Her mother had taught them to use natural remedies. Lavender oil, turmeric, willow bark. But she didn't have access to those things. And if she died from a reaction to the two white tablets, so be it.

Audra pulled a blanket gingerly over her bruised, and aching body. As she drifted off to sleep, she thought about *Timmy*. A neighbor boy she knew growing up. Timmy took pleasure in tormenting his cat. He would pull the cat's fur, or drop it out of his second story bedroom window. Once injured, he would cuddle the cat, only to inflict more pain. Audra hated the boy's cruelty, and told his father. His father's words were equally cruel when he said, "It's just an animal."

Audra's captor must've been cut from the same cloth. The Metzger children were galvanized in good deeds, honesty, and kindness. The Metzger children were raised to respect living things, large and small. *The Metzger children are no longer children.* This place, this prison, headed by a monster who valued no life but his own, had no idea what she was capable of. All she needed was the right moment to strike, the right moment to reverse roles...from victim to victor. *If I survive the night.* The chemicals kicked into gear; her body sank further into the bed. The blankets swallowed her whole. Falling. Falling. Falling. *Auf Weidersehen Timmy. May you rot in hell.*

CASTLES

Sam climbed inside his friend Rhett's Bell 206B III helicopter and fastened the shoulder harness. Rhett handed Sam a headset, and started the engine. Rotor blades whirred above their heads. "Where to?" he asked.

"Let's head toward Oakland, see how many ranches are out that way."

"There's Slide Ranch between Mill Valley and Stinson Beach, that one is 137 acres, owned by the Nature Conservatory. Jerry Garcia of the Grateful Dead donated a bundle in 1970 to create a place for Bay area kids to experience nature."

Sam nodded. "It's a start…"

"You've got the N3 Cattle Ranch near Livermore. That's your largest. Seventy-nine square miles—can you imagine? San Francisco is forty-seven square miles! The guy paid sixty-eight mil for it."

Sam's interest piqued. "Who owns it?"

"William Brown bought it a year ago, why?"

"Isn't he the scientist that discovered that we all have "star" DNA?"

Rhett laughed. "No, buddy. He's a businessman from the Bay area."

"Business man. Interesting."

Sam's deadpan expression squelched Rhett's joking demeanor. "What exactly are you looking for?"

"My sister."

Suzanne and Lewis shuffled around the kitchen like two college roomies with bad hangovers. Suzanne managed toasted crumpets and coffee. Lewis preferred tea. They sat in silence, waiting for the caffeine to alert their brains it was time to wake up.

"I haven't had a night like that in a long time," Suzanne confessed. "I don't know what to make of it. Let's talk about the castles we're both seeing. There are castles in Calistoga, Pacifica, San Francisco, San Simeon…"

"They may as well be on another planet…"

"I'm sorry, you're not familiar with the area. The castles I was referring to are within 100 miles from here."

"Don't feel as though the lass is <u>that</u> far away…"

"Maybe not, but I'm not getting any hits that indicate a location."

"I'm new at this," he said, lowering his gaze. "And Jim ain't sharin' a bloody thing."

"Yeah, Jack left me in a lurch many times too." Love sparkled in Suzanne's eyes. "Eventually, I learned to swim."

"You mentioned a boy…"

"Kinda crazy, how everything happened to me. I loved Jack with all of my heart. It's been rather difficult for me to accept that he has reincarnated into—"

"What is it Lass, you've gone pale?"

"The baby, Emmett, in whom Jack has reincarnated himself, is the son of a serial killer. I sometimes wonder what he'll be like? His mother, Sheena, is a sweet girl. I pray he takes after her." Suzanne took a sip of coffee, her mind on Jack. "I can't imagine why he chose her. After all, he knew—"

"They say good conquers evil. Imagine if 'e didn't step in? Perhaps evil would've perpetuated itself… y'never know."

"How did you meet Trudy?" Lewis's face glowed with the memory. He was obviously head over heels in love.

"We were at a pub." His smile stretched lines from his face, bringing back the young man he once was. "I saw 'er sitting with another bloke—she looked bored t'tears. I never was one to scrap over a lass, but there was somethin' different 'bout 'er." He paused, letting the memory come to a simmer. "She caught me starin'…

and she smiled. Ah, she was beautiful, and I told m'self, she's the one."

"What did you do?"

"I waltzed up t'her bloody table, tapped the bloke on 'is shoulder and said, "Excuse me, lad, ye happen t'be sittin' with me future wife."

Suzanne nearly choked on her coffee. "No way! What did he do?"

"The bloke got up and blackened both me eyes…and as I'm lyin' on the floor, with me ears ringin', me face bloody as 'ell, I hear an angelic voice say, "Y'better run before me future husband gets up and drops y'dead."

"That's the most romantic story I've ever heard," Suzanne said, brushing tears from her eyes.

"It's not a sad story lass, why the tears?"

"That's the kind of love I had with Jack. When he died, my heart died too…I married the wrong man on the rebound, and gave up on love completely."

"And now? The way Sam looks at ye—well, it's the way I look at Trudy. There's more love in 'is eyes than a bucket of worms at a fishin' hole. And the way you look at 'im 'as happily-ever-after written all over it."

"Do you think if you had these visions before you met your wife, you would have pursued her?"

The smile vanished from Lewis' face. "I—no, probably not. I see the pain it causes 'er. I can only pray once the lass is found—"

"It doesn't work that way."

"Does Sam know 'ow y'feel?"

"No, not exactly. I think I'm in love with him, but—"

"Doubts aren't good in a marriage."

"No. No they're not."

Sam held the binoculars to his eyes. He wasn't sure what he was looking for. They flew over ranches speckled with cattle, neatly kept dwellings, some larger than others. After two hours of searching for anything that would give pause, Sam called it. "Let's go back."

"We can try again tomorrow," Rhett said, "head east, up toward Tahoe."

Sam sighed. "We're searching for a needle in a haystack. I have no idea where they took her. All I have are a couple of psychics trying to manifest a location. And so far, they've come up short." Sam balled his fist. Tears stung his eyes.

Rhett, patted his shoulder. "Tomorrow. Same time. And every day. Till we find her."

Audra awoke groggy, disoriented. Her head pounded, her back ached. Her stomach cramped. She squeezed her knees together. She placed a pillow over her face, and screamed.

Her frustration released, she sat up, looked around the room. Something sparkly caught her eye. She eased herself out of bed and walked toward the closet. The dress hanging there was something out of a medieval movie. A style she had seen many times at festivals. She stepped to the dressing table to find the note that read:

den Kragen tragen. Bis 4 Uhr angezogen sein.

She looked at the clock. It was 2 p.m. *Two hours to dress.* When she lifted the dress off the hanger, she gasped. Attached to the back of the dress was a metal collar with a key. Tiny spikes circled the inside of the collar. *Scheisse.*

What kind of game was this guy playing? She wished he'd just kill her and get it over with instead of playing dress-up and scaring her to death. The thought made her shiver. Maybe that's what this was all about— making her so afraid that her heart stopped. He seemed to feed on her fear one minute, and rescue her the next. Was that his fantasy? Being a hero? She ran her finger along the tiny spikes. Images of blood gushing from her punctured neck made her adrenaline kick into high gear. She fought to catch her breath. She wanted to scream, but she couldn't push enough air from her lungs to make a sound. Pinpoints of light invaded her peripheral vision; her knees became weak. *Don't do it,* she pleaded with herself. *Don't pass out.* Too late. She crumbled to the floor in a heap.

Suzanne pulled up to Sheena's house and turned off the ignition. "Are you ready for this, Lewis?"

"Never met a babe I didn't take to."

They rang the bell and waited. Sheena appeared at

the door, a worried look on her face setting the tone. "Come in, you're just in time."

Suzanne and Lewis exchanged glances. What were they walking into? When they saw Emmett, they understood.

"How long has he been—" Suzanne nodded toward the rocking horse with the sack tethered to its tail.

"That was yesterday's stint. Today he's been pulling at his neckline. I had to remove his teething bib—he kept twisting it, I was afraid he'd choke himself. Even then, he kept pulling at something, his face was turning red, and he was crying. It took over an hour to calm him down."

Suzanne smiled at the angelic boy, sleeping in his playpen. "Were there any marks on his neck?"

"Yeah, there were—tiny little red marks. I was thinking prickly heat, or roseola, but then it just disappeared, and he fell right to sleep."

"Lewis and I have been getting visions, too." Suzanne glanced at Emmett. "This has to be so frightening for him—for you."

"He's such a happy boy, most of the time. But these last couple of days, he's been hard to console. He's cutting his molars, I thought that explained his fussiness, but now I'm not so sure."

"Has he shown you any more books?"

"No, but he had a meltdown when I changed the channel on the TV this morning. It was some travel show, featuring castles around the world. When I changed it back, he moved really close to the screen, like he was in a trance." Sheena shook her head, "I just don't know what to make of it all."

"E's got the gift," Lew said. "Lad's seeing what we are."

Sheena's eyes grew large. "But I don't want him to be afraid—he's just a baby!"

Sheena's raised voice made Emmett stir. He rolled onto his back, and rubbed his eyes with his little fists. After a couple of moments, he sat up, and looked around the room. "'Uzanne, Wew," he said, smiling. He stood, and lifted his arms. "Up."

Sheena jumped to her feet and lifted Emmett into her arms. "How do you know Mr. Lew?"

Emmett laughed and clapped his hands. "Dim!"

"For the love of muffins—y'met m'friend Jim now, did ye?" Emmett reached for Lew. Lew snatched him up like a sack of potatoes, and tossed him into the air. Emmett giggled with delight, then he stared at Lewis lovingly, and wrapped his arms around his neck. He laid his head on Lew's shoulder.

Lew beamed. "Jim always wanted a lad of 'is own."

Sheena melted at the sight, tears rimming her eyes. "One day he'll have a dad who will love him as much as I do," she said.

Suzanne slipped her arm around Sheena. "You'll find a wonderful man, one day. And I believe Emmett will help."

Emmett wiggled out of Lew's arms. "Down."

The three adults observed Emmett's deliberate search for something to express his thoughts. First, he emptied his toy basket, and when that didn't pan out, he brought the TV remote to Sheena, and pointed to the screen.

"That show is over, Bud. Do you want to watch Sesame Street?"

Emmett slid off Sheena's lap, grabbing the remote from her hand in transit. He stood in front of the TV clicking through channels like a bored teenager on a Friday night. When he caught a glimpse of "Camelot" with Vanessa Redgrave and Richard Harris, he stopped. "Dat!" he cried.

Suzanne and Lewis sank into the sofa in unison. "What does it all mean?" she asked, questioning herself, more than the others.

"I'd say we're looking for a castle, right mate?"

Emmett ran to Lew and rested his hand on Lew's knee. His eyes, one brown, one green, held Lew's blue eyes steadfast. He touched Lew's neck with his tiny fingers. "Ouch," he said. "Ouchy."

"'E's going to hurt her neck?"

Emmett nodded. He ran back to his toys and piled them as high as he could. When he finished, he stood in front of the pile with his hands behind his back, his eyes closed. "Hot," he cried. "Hot!"

· · ·

Sam arrived at Suzanne's house, mid-afternoon. When he didn't see her car, he parked and made a few calls. He checked with Michele, his dispatcher. "Thought you were on vacation?" she said, sounding confused.

"I'm back in town, but I'm working a special case. Any messages?"

"Yeah, two I gave to the desk sergeant, they sounded urgent. One was weird. I could hardly understand the guy, his accent was so thick."

"What did he say?"

"He said to tell you to mind your own f'n business, only he said the real word. I can't even begin to tell you where he was from."

"Did you get a number?"

"Yes, I did, but it won't do you any good. He made the call from a burner phone."

"Anything else?"

"No, just that the call gave me the creeps."

"Why is that?"

"I heard all this crying in the background, like he had a ton of kids. Sounded like a litter of kittens at feeding time."

Hair raised on the back of Sam's neck. "Thanks, Michele. If he calls again, patch me in. I don't care what time of day or night, hear me?"

Sam dialed Andrew. "Anything?"

"Word on the street is that a new shipment came in,

but we haven't been able to get a bead on where they were taken. Anything on your sister?"

"Went scoping out the ranches from here to Oakland. Nothing suspicious. Helluva lot of places to hide a person."

"All the ranches I know of are owned by reputable people."

"There's the challenge. Know of any indiscretions? Rapes, stalking charges? Pedophiles?"

"I'll have to check the directory for specifics. There are so many fuckin' pedos in this area, it's not easy keeping up with all of them. We track the repeat offenders as closely as possible, but the ones put on probation, not so much. And with the new laws in place, we're lucky if any of them go to prison, you know that."

"Yes. I do." Sam tapped the steering wheel with his trigger finger. "The guy I'm looking for has fetishes."

Andrew scoffed, "You're kidding me, right? All these fuckers live in a fantasy world."

Sam scowled. "Right now, I need to find the one that has my sister."

"You're my first call when I hear anything, buddy. 'Til then, chin up. I put the word out. We've got eyes peeled. Let us do our job."

"Right. I'll check with you later."

Sam clicked off his phone and pounded on his steering wheel. Anger didn't accomplish a thing.

. . .

Suzanne tapped on Sam's window. She could tell he was frazzled. "Come inside. I'll fix us a meal."

Sam obeyed. Starving himself wouldn't help matters any, and any reprieve he could get from worrying, he'd take. *Weary.* That's what he felt. Desperation ravished his soul. He hadn't returned his father's calls, and he knew the anguish they were experiencing not knowing what happened to their only daughter. The daughter they doted on growing up. It would kill them to know she was in the hands of a depraved monster. Their little girl, the one they tried to protect since the day she was born. What could he tell them? *I failed?* He shook he head, trying to dislodge the thought from his brain.

Sam acknowledged Lewis with a handshake, and a nod. He couldn't bring himself to engage in small talk. His conversation with Andrew ruminated in his head amidst the message Michele relayed from the mystery caller.

His eyes followed Suzanne's every move. Every curve. The way her ponytail wagged back and forth as she busied herself with dinner. Lewis sat quietly working a crossword puzzle in the Sacramento Bee. Every now and then Lew would look to the far corner of the kitchen ceiling as if the answers were written up there.

Suzanne placed a bowl filled with fresh greens on the table, and dipped into an exaggerated curtsy, addressing Sam directly. "Did you happen to see any castles in the lands below today, m'lord?"

"I was too busy slaying dragons to notice, m'lady."

Suzanne leaned on the table, her face, inches from Sam's. "Actually, I'm serious."

His brow furrowed. "I thought you said we're looking for a ranch."

"What if this guy is into role playing?"

"That's kind of a given," he retorted. He glanced at Lew. "What am I missing?"

"Both Lewis and I had dreams about castles last night. When we went to see Sheena today, she said Emmett was fixated on a travel show about local castles. Then while we were there, he switched on "Camelot." Do you remember that movie? About King Arthur and Lady Guinevere?"

Sam rested his forehead in his hands. "Yes, but I'm getting a little confused. Are we looking for a ranch? Or a castle?" He placed his hands flat on the table and looked from Lewis to Suzanne. "It's not like someone would have both."

"Why not? Can't someone have enough land for both? Look at the Hearst castle, that place is a sprawling mecca of possibilities."

"Do you think that's where my sister was taken to—the Hearst castle? A tourist attraction teaming with people and staff?"

Suzanne lowered her gaze. Sam reached for her hand.

"I'm sorry. I'm—acting like a jerk. I know you are both trying to help, but—"

"But you don't believe us."

"It's not that I don't believe you, it's just that…"

Lewis pushed his chair away from the table and crossed his arms over his chest. "Just what, man?"

"If anyone is failing to get this right, it's me." Sam rose from his chair. "Perhaps I should go."

"Nope." Suzanne pushed him back into his seat. "We found a shack in bum-fuck-Egypt–right? We can find a castle on a ranch."

Sam lifted Suzanne hand and kissed her palm. "What would I do without you?"

"We can discuss that another time. Right now, we have to get some food into you, and then we can google all the castles nearby. Deal?"

Sam fought hard not to smile. A smile seemed inappropriate under the circumstances…yet he couldn't control the message his heart had to convey. "Deal."

Jake found Audra passed out on the floor. He glanced at the clock. Past four. Damn her for not being dressed and ready for their play-date. He had waited anxiously for her to appear in the emerald green gown. His mother had worn it to a medieval soirée years ago. Jake had rescued the dress from the pile of cast-offs sent to Goodwill.

He remembered the event like it was yesterday, even

though he was six. He remembered how his mother's braided auburn hair circled her head like a crown, held in place with jeweled pins. All eyes were on her slim figure as she floated down the stairs. Men dressed in various outfits, kings, paupers, guardsman, warriors, drooling over her beauty, and the creamy white breasts that overflowed the square neckline of the dress. She was a vision. And as one satin shoe hit the marble floor, she began issuing orders. "Get the collar. Chain him up." Jake remembered thinking his mother was referring to a dog, or one of the many animals they kept on the property. *Imagine my surprise.* His mother was referring to him.

Audra reminded him of his mother at that age. Except for the color of her hair, or at least the caramel and crimson streaks, she was a dead-ringer.

"How does it feel?" he asked Audra's limp form. "I told you one day the tides would turn, didn't I *mother*?"

Jake picked the collar up from the floor. He felt the tiny points. His hand gravitated to his neck, remembering... remembering how the men lifted his mother's skirts, bent her over a chair and ravished her while he watched, chained to the chair's wooden leg, the collar biting into his neck, tearing at his flesh.

He nudged Audra's hip. "Wake up, bitch! We have a score to settle!"

<h1 style="text-align:center">JAKEY</h1>

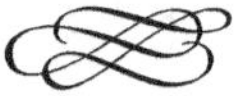

Sam, Suzanne, and Lewis hovered over Sam's laptop, scrolling through photos of castles within one hundred miles of Sacramento. Sam drummed his fingers on the table. "We don't even know if she's in the area. They could've put her on a boat, or taken her in a private plane somewhere."

"I'm no expert, but I feel like the lass is close."

"Me too," Suzanne said, kneading Sam's shoulders. "I know we can't give you an address to put into your GPS, but I think we're getting a better idea of what to search for. We know the person who has Audra lives on a ranch. The castle has me baffled, but what if it's more of an obstructed structure, like a reproduction, or miniature? Maybe it's more symbolic than a real place."

"*Maybe*? She could be locked in someone's basement for all we know!"

"You trusted me before—" Suzanne withdrew her soothing touch.

Sam turned to her, his eyes pleading. "Don't stop. Please. I'm sorry. I'm tired, snarky, and scared shitless if you want to know the truth. This is more than a job to me right now—I can't blow this. Please forgive me for being an ass."

Suzanne wrapped her arms around his stiff shoulders. "You're forgiven."

Lewis stepped away. "Time t'ring the missus."

"I think we all need a break," Sam said, closing his laptop. "We can continue this in the morning."

"It feels as though there's a lull in the storm. For now."

"We have to find her soon." Sam drew Suzanne into his arms. "I really am sorry for my behavior. I don't know what's gotten into me, taking my frustrations out on you."

"You're under an immense amount of stress. I'll let you know when you've overstepped your boundaries. Until then, kiss me."

Jake stood over Audra, his rage mixed with shame, and guilt. Deep inside, he knew she had nothing to do with his pain. He lifted her into his arms, feeling the heat from her body against his. *She's burning up.* Damn. Just his luck.

He pulled the covers back from the bed, and laid her

down gently. He felt her forehead. *NG, Jakey boy.* It was too soon for her to die. He hadn't gotten his money's worth, satiated his need to punish. *How many times are you going to kill her?* "Every chance I get until she rots in her grave."

Jake went into his medicine cabinet, shook two Amoxicillin tablets into his hand and returned to the room where Audra slept. He placed the pills next to a fresh bottle of water, settled into a chair nearby and closed his eyes. It wouldn't be much fun to pretend with someone who was sick. *A cat, with a dead mouse.* No, he needed her at her best if he were to punish her properly. *Sleep, my fair lady. Ol' Jake has a big surprise for you.*

OFFSPRING

Suzanne left Lewis on his own accord while she drove to see Grace Simms. "He's hurting."

Grace crossed one leg over the other. "That doesn't give him the right to hurt you."

"I got so used to Ben berating me, I think I became immune."

"Easy to do."

"I find myself making excuses…yet in my heart, I feel his lashing out is circumstantial, that he isn't himself."

Grace didn't interject.

Suzanne shrugged. "Or maybe Sam's stress is bringing out his true colors."

"Possibly. You did say he's a recovering alcoholic–"

"What has that got to do with anything?"

"I can't say for sure, but I imagine it's difficult for him not to anesthetize during this crisis."

"I haven't discussed it with him." Suzanne went deep within. "I won't make the same mistake twice."

"Are you falling in love with Sam?"

"I think so…but it's hard for me to allow anyone to get mixed up with this—this crazy thing I have going on. I mean—" Suzanne bit her bottom lip to stop the flow of words that validated her concerns.

"I thought he understood. After all, you helped him catch a serial killer."

"I feel like I'm letting him down. It's not like before. I don't have Jack in my head directing me. I mean he's still here, but it's different. Emmett can only communicate so much, whereas, Jack used to hijack my mind and make me see things."

"How about this guy from London? Is he any help?"

"Lewis and I are getting similar scenarios. He actually has a spirit friend who talks to him. Jim. Emmett sees Jim too. How is that for crazy?"

"Sounds pretty far-fetched, in fact I had trouble wrapping my head around the phenomenon myself at first. I had another patient who was psychic. Her warnings were very helpful. But I can relate to Sam's doubt. It's challenging to accept that another person can know things before they happen."

"So, do you think Sam and I should keep our relationship on a professional level?"

"Only you can make that decision."

"I'm not sure what will happen if we don't find his sister. It will devastate him."

"Be supportive. Help when you can. What happens is out of your hands. You didn't kidnap his sister. You're not responsible for the outcome. Her captor is."

"I hope Sam feels the same, should things go awry."

"If he loves you, he will."

Suzanne quick-stepped down the Victorian's wooden steps. When she reached the bottom step, she felt disoriented. She reached for the hand rail to steady herself.

"Are you okay, dear?"

An elderly woman parked her walker in Suzanne's path. Suzanne could see the vitality that once belonged to the woman. The words *money, power* popped into Suzanne's head. "I'm fine, Took the stairs too fast, that's all."

The woman nodded, and moved on. Suzanne went in the opposite direction. When she looked over her shoulder, the woman was *gone*.

Lewis sat frozen, staring into space. He remembered seeing his mother when he died, strangely enough…but seeing her standing in Suzanne's kitchen, fixing a spot of tea, stopped him in his knickers. "Mum?"

"'Who does that woman think she is? The queen 'erself?"

"Who Mum?"

"All those fancy gatherin's. And those poor children–the things they make them do!"

"Mum? Tell me, what woman?"

"Ye should know, Lew. Pretty is, as pretty does. That one's a fooler, she is…a bloody demon. Should've taken the child away from 'er, but nooo, she 'ad all that money."

"Mum, give me a name! I beg ye, tell me who she is!"

Lewis watched his mother evaporate before his very eyes.

Sam rang the bell and waited for Suzanne to answer. When she called, she was practically babbling.

"This is important Sam—I saw this old woman, but she disappeared. But I heard the words money and power, and then when I got home, Lewis told me his mother paid him a visit and she spoke of a woman who had power and money and—"

"Whoa—easy." Sam closed the front door behind him.

"We need t'find 'er," Lewis said, stepping into view, his voice raised a notch higher.

"How do we find out who owns land, she'd be older, prominent. Powerful."

"How prominent? How powerful? Nancy Pelosi powerful?"

"Who do you know of that stature that has committed crimes against children?"

Sam scratched his head. "The only one that comes to mind is Theresa Knorr, she's in her mid-seventies, but she's serving consecutive sentences in the women's prison in Chino. Not sure if she was rich, just know she killed two of her children, and her husband."

"This woman owns property. She's wealthy."

"Connected," Lew interjected.

"There's a retired congresswoman that came from money, but she's Asian, she doesn't fit the profile."

Suzanne threw her hands up in the air. "Who does?"

"You're saying this woman owns property, a possible castle, and hurts kids?"

"Me mum seems t'think so."

Sam shook his head. "With all due respect—"

"Dammit, Sam! We're not making this stuff up. We are both getting clues from the universe. We just need to connect the dots."

"The fucking universe needs to be a little more specific!"

Suzanne backed away. Lew stuffed his hands in his pockets, diverting his eyes from the scene unfolding before him. Sam swiped his face with his hand, as if he could erase the words he released in anger.

"I'm sorry," he said. "That was uncalled for."

"If I had a dollar for every time you've apologized lately, I'd be able to afford a trip to Paris." She folded her arms across her chest. "If you don't want to listen, then—" She lowered her gaze. "I know you're stressed, but we are not your—your—" Suddenly, she turned away, fighting her tears. A moment later, she heard the front door slam.

Sam walked a block and a half before he stopped to collect his senses. "She's right," he told himself. "I'm one huge asshole." He turned left, then right, to get his bearings. Then he headed towards the bar.

Lewis placed a hand on Suzanne's shoulder. "E's out of his wits, lass. I imagine I'd b'cheesed-off too if m'sister went missin'."

"I know he's not himself, but I don't want him thinking he can talk to me in that manner. I'm done being someone's verbal punching bag."

"Tru would've 'ad me ears boxed 'til Christmas," he said, with an affectionate pat on her arm. He checked his watch. "Time for tea. 'Ow 'bout I fix us a cup?"

Suzanne plopped into a chair and scooted herself toward the table. "He forgot to take his laptop. He'll be back."

Lewis set two cups on the table and filled them with tea. "Sugar?" he asked. Suzanne shook her head "no." "Cream?" He held up an ornate cream pitcher. Again, she nodded "no." He sipped slowly as he watched her stare at the wall. He thought about his mum, and how they would drink tea together when he was troubled. She always gave him good advice. "Who d'ye know that dresses fancy, and 'as lots of money?"

"In California, that could be anyone."

"From what me mum said, she's dishy, minted."

"Like a movie star?"

"She 'ad 'er day."

"There are several Hollywood actors that have retired in northern California…but why buy a girl?"

Lewis and Suzanne sat quietly, drinking their tea, waiting for the universe to provide the answer.

Sam stared at the glass in his hand. A double shot of Makers Mark bourbon whiskey, with a splash of water. He swirled the liquid in his glass, admiring the rich golden color. He waved the glass under his nose, inhaling the scent. But before he held the glass to his lips, he set the glass down next to the sobriety coin he had carried in his pocket for the last ten years.

He conjured the image of his first AA meeting, and how he resisted admitting he was an alcoholic. He was a cop. Cops drank. It was part of the job. Killed the pain. *That's what I need. A drink to kill the pain.*

"Drink up," the bartender said, placing a second drink in front of the other. "Your friend over there," he said nodding to Sam's left, "said this one's on him."

Sam turned to his left to see who his benefactor was, but could barely make out the man's face, sitting in the dark corner. Sam raised his glass, but he didn't drink. He plucked a twenty out of his wallet, snatched up his sobriety coin, and walked out the door.

Sam sensed the car creeping along behind him. He was still a block from Suzanne's where his gun was locked in the trunk. He opened up his phone, reversed his camera lens, and clicked a photo of the car. He wasn't surprised to see it was the same car he saw cruise by the other night.

He didn't want to incite a confrontation by turning around, and he didn't want to run. He looked for a clearing between the houses, and took a quick right, staying close to the bushes dividing the yards. He heard tires squeal. *They're pissed. Good.*

He jogged back to Suzanne's, retrieved his gun from the trunk, and went around to the back door. He peeked through the window and saw Suzanne and Lewis sitting at the kitchen table, drinking tea. He wrapped softly. Suzanne glanced at the door and rose, cautiously. Before she got to the door, she reached for something, Sam didn't see what.

"Who's there?" she called.

"It's me Suzanne—Sam."

She peeked through the window. They were practically nose to nose. He could see the turmoil of emotions in her eyes. He wanted to cry. She opened the door. He looked away. "Can I come in?"

"If you keep your apologies to yourself—"

"Promise," he said, easing past her.

"We were just having tea, would you–"

"I'm being followed."

Suzanne peeked out the window. "You must've struck a nerve."

"Yeah. Must've."

Suzanne walked past Sam, brushing against him. "We think we've narrowed it down to a few possibilities…interested in hearing what we have to say?"

Sam spun a chair around and straddled it, keeping his eye on the front door. "Shoot," he said, placing his gun on the table.

Suzanne's eyes widened, and her glance ricocheted off of Lew's. "He doesn't mean that literally."

"If I thought 'e did, I would've been shittin' me britches."

Sam exhaled. His lips tilted upwards. "I love you guys," he said.

J ake couldn't take his eyes off of Audra.

He marveled at how much she resembled his mother when she was young. *Beautiful.* Mother let him brush her hair…pour the perfumed beads into the tub. *Wash her back.* On Sundays they made pancakes, played checkers, watched movies in black and white. When he got older, they began playing dress up, spent afternoon's pretending they lived in the wild west, in a magical forest, or in medieval times. That was before the parties, before the men, before the sacrifices, and the bonfires in the woods…when she referred to herself as a virgin…when she was a good mother, and didn't thrive on other people's pain. Before she went to Hollywood and became *a monster*. She told him once, "What you see, is what you'll be." *You're so right mother. Look at me now.*

They hadn't spoken in years. His mother resided in a private care facility that catered to celebrities. She still attended star-studded functions, but always with the help of one of her well-paid aides. She no longer approved of his insatiable appetite for the depravity she introduced him to. She preferred to stay in her ivory tower, where she could deny the past, and pass judgement on the present. She cleansed her soul with charity contributions, setting up foundations for the underprivileged, while supporting her only son's twisted life-style.

JACKPOT

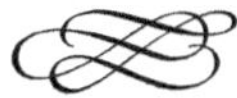

Rubio decided it was time to disappear. His last phone call with Giorgi made his flesh crawl. He knew that tone. *Deadly.* He had witnessed first-hand what Giorgi was capable of. Experienced his wrath once or twice himself. The most disturbing was when he bashed in the head of a fourteen-year-old Israeli boy who couldn't get a hard-on on command. When Giorgi wanted sex, he expected his partner to be ready, willing, and able. He said it was for the boy's own good. His new owner may not be as generous.

Rubio was born ready for sex, provided he didn't over indulge in drugs or alcohol. However, he recalled what happened one night after delivering a dozen prepubescent girls to a sheikh in Bahrain. Giorgi was ecstatic over the gold bars he received as payment, and pulled him into a seedy Pub, for a celebratory drink. After two beers, Giorgi became school-girl-giddy, animated, and giggly. This was not the Giorgi he was used to, and found this side fun, and entertaining. Two beers led to three, then four, and Giorgi grabbed his hand, placed it on his erection and gave Rubio a come-hither look that took him by surprise. Rubio dodged his advances claiming Bahrain was not the safest place to get drunk or horny. "Let's go back to the hotel," he remembered saying.

"You're a bore!" Giorgi spat at Rubio, making his heart race. He was used to Giorgi's Jekyll and Hyde personality, but he rarely showed that side of himself outside of a controlled environment. Public intoxication laws were stringent in Bahrain, Rubio didn't want to end up in prison.

Giorgi sulked during their ten-minute ride to the hotel. Once they were in the elevator, Giorgi slammed Rubio against the wall, and kissed him hard. "I want you," he said, "I want you to fuck me—*bad*." Rubio came away with a fat lip, but Giorgi didn't stop there, determined to have his way.

When they entered the hotel room, Giorgi kicked the door closed behind him and began ripping at Rubio's clothes.

"Take it easy," Rubio said, shielding himself with a pillow. Giorgi's crazed-filled eyes turned pitch black. He slugged Rubio in the jaw.

"Don't talk back, bitch," he seethed in *that voice*, ripping the pillow out of Rubio's hands. Rubio relented, knowing Giorgi bested him in size and strength. Giorgi's sardonic smile was one of victory. He undressed as if his clothes were flammable, and his erection was a torch. "Take off your clothes," he demanded.

Rubio obeyed. He had dressed down to his underwear when Giorgi noticed Rubio was limp. He grabbed at the nylon briefs and pulled them down, furious with what he saw. He pushed Rubio onto the bed, began rubbing, stroking, sucking…using encouraging words on the flaccid member. "Come on, baby, you know you want to feel my tight ass around you." It was no use.

"Must've been the beer," Rubio lied.

Giorgi didn't speak. He hit Rubio so hard across the face, Rubio saw stars. When he tried to get up, Giorgi hit him again. And again. And again.

Later, when Rubio's friends asked if he had pissed off a Russian prize fighter. Rubio laughed and said, "No. Just some drunk." Those who saw Giorgi's bruised and swollen knuckles put two and two together. *Giorgi never apologized.*

Rubio dumped his top dresser drawer on the bed. He picked out a couple of his favorite T-shirts, seven pair of underwear, and four pair of socks. He opened the closet, ripped three pairs of jeans off of hangers, two dress shirts, and a jacket. He took one pair of leather boots, one pair of dress shoes, and his favorite Pumas, and tossed them next to the items he planned to take. He folded, rolled, and packed his suitcase as if he were headed on a business trip instead of escaping with his life.

One quick stop to his favorite casino. The ten-thousand crispy euros in his pocket made him feel lucky despite the hit he was sure Giorgi had out on him for not telling him about the cop. He wouldn't dare shoot him in his own casino.

First, a drink. Loosen his inhibitions, get his mind off of things. He passed the roulette tables, and a bank of 100€ slots. *What the hell.* He slipped a bill from the ruby clip he bought last week when he won the ten-thousand euros. He slid the bill in the machine and pulled the lever. The barrels spun, around and around until one fleur-de-lis settled in place. Then a second stopped next to it. Then a third. Rubio raised his eyes to the prize—JACKPOT 4,500,485.09. Butterflies swam in his stomach as the fourth and final fleur-de-lis settled in place. Flashing lights blinded him, bells shrieked like a fire alarm. Whoop. Whoop. People gathered like flies to the chaos. The numbers were no longer visible. All he saw was WINNER, *der SIEGER* flash in its place. Three attendants rushed to his side, urging on-lookers to step back. The attendants opened the machine, turned off the sirens, and began doing their inspection. Rubio's face flushed with all the attention he was getting. He could hardly believe his luck.

It took nearly an hour for the machine to be cleared. Once the inspectors were finished, Rubio expected to receive a check, but that wasn't true, because of the amount, they must contact the Glücksspielkommissar.

Rubio's elation was waning fast. "I'll be at the bar," he said, pointing.

Immediately when he sat down, he became a magnet for women wanting a rich man to fulfill their dreams. The bartender picked up on his dilemma and hurried over. Rubio scowled. "Where's Franz?" He knew he could trust Franz.

"Covid." The bartender smirked. "What you drink?"

Rubio was cautious when eating and drinking out. Giorgi was notorious for hiring unscrupulous bartenders who slipped things into a "prospect's" drink. It made Rubio's job easier, but he worried about the same happening to him. *Not tonight.* Tonight, he won four-and-a-half million fucking euros. Besides, he only ordered beer on tap. "Stiegl," he said, drumming his fingertips on the inlaid wood. A couple of women hovered nearby, hoping to catch Rubio's eye. He pretended to focus on the KENO numbers on the screen above the bar. The bartender set his beer on the bar. "On the house," he said, grinning. Rubio raised his glass. "*Zum Gewinner!*" The bartender nodded, and disappeared.

Rubio guzzled down half of his beer. *Winning makes a guy thirsty.* He took a few more gulps and drained the glass. He scanned the area for the bartender. He was gone. *Shit. Guess it's not my lucky day after all.*

Two men helped Rubio off his stool. He could barely stand. His stomach cramped, he was nauseous, his head light, detached. He felt cold, as if his heart couldn't pump blood to his extremities. He couldn't catch his breath. He heard the sirens outside the casino. He knew what was coming. It wasn't the gaming commissioner. It wasn't good. *Giorgi-Porgi, puddin' pie, spiked my beer and made me die.* The oxygen mask covered his blue tinged lips. He closed his eyes. *Breathe.* Nothing came out.

D.O.A.

Giorgi got the text at 11:02 a.m. Rubio was pronounced dead at the hospital. *Heart failure due to fentanyl.* Giorgi slipped into a terry robe. Water in the pool below shimmered in the morning sun. A swim would do him good. Relieve his stress. He still had a mess to clean up. The cop was still searching for his sister. *Rubio, Rubio. I thought I taught you better than that.*

"Salvadore!" Giorgi's tone sounded chipper. "What's going on with the hemorrhoid I asked you to lance?" A woman standing near the elevator scowled, and turned her back to Giorgi while he listened to excuses on the other end of the line.

"I see," he said. "I may just have to take care of the matter myself." The woman gasped. When the elevator door opened, the woman beelined for the stairs.

· · ·

Sam climbed into Rhett's helicopter, and fastened his belt. "Let's head towards Tahoe. We're looking for a ranch with a stone structure that looks like a castle."

Rhett raised his brow. "I've been photographing property around here a lot of years, Sam…nothing like that is coming to mind."

"My sources are telling me they see castles."

"There's a few around…Vikingsholm in Lake Tahoe is one, there's a couple in the bay area…Hearst Castle is another…"

Something didn't feel right. Both properties were state parks. Sam couldn't imagine his sister being held captive in such a public place. "Any you know of that aren't public?"

"No, but that's not to say there aren't any Tudor homes around."

Rhett fired up the engine. Sam watched the dust on the ground swirl below him. *Where are you, Audra? Where?* Soon they were a thousand feet up, and climbing.

Suzanne dressed in a pair of faded jeans, and a navy tank top. The temperature had reached an unseasonable high, which called for layering. If needed, she kept a sweatshirt jacket in the car. She slipped into her Nikes and descended the stairs.

Lewis was sitting at the kitchen table, reading a book he picked from her bookcase. He marked his place when she entered the room, and lifted his gaze. "I feel a little guilty seein' the sights with the lass still out there somewhere."

"We aren't going to do her any good sitting around moping." Suzanne opened the refrigerator and gathered ingredients for a picnic lunch. "Fresh air will do us both some good…and if we're lucky, our spirit guides will tell us exactly what we need to know."

Lew scratched his head. "Spirit guides, y'say—is that what they call 'em?"

"Linda gave me the low-down on spirit guides when I met her. They are heavenly beings that watch over us, help us navigate our path." Suzanne tore open a package of sliced turkey, and placed a few slices on two pieces of bread. "Mayo okay with you?"

Lewis chuckled. "Lass! If y'didn't know—we put may-o on everythin'!" He closed the book with a clap. "A spot of mustard would b'nice, too."

Suzanne finished the sandwiches, packed an apple for each of them, a bag of chips to share, and two bottles of water. "Let's go," she said, holding the door open for Lew. "Tell me if you get tired. I wouldn't want to be the one to tell your wife I ran you ragged. I promised her I would make sure you took it easy."

"Tru worries 'erself. I feel fine."

"I thought we'd head to the Preston Castle in Ione. It was a boy's reformatory at one time. People say it's haunted. There's a ranch nearby…are you ready for this? It's called *Neverland,* I wonder if it was named after Michael Jackson's place?"

"Maybe." He closed his eyes. "Could be we're steerin' the cart up hill."

"I feel drawn to the castle, and you're right, we may not find Audra there, but we may get closer to the truth."

Suzanne parked the car in the visitor's lot and turned off the ignition. The castle loomed ahead of them. "Gives me the willies. How about you?"

"Them poor children," he said, sadness erasing any hint of amusement from his face. "Y'neglected t'tell me 'ow they died."

"I'm not sure—what are you getting?"

"It's more what I'm feelin'," he said rubbing his arms to ward off trepidation. "Like m'bones are broken." He clamped his hands over his ears. "They're screamin', I can 'ear 'em."

Suzanne started the engine, and put the car in reverse. "I'm sorry I brought you here," she said, tears filling her eyes.

Five miles down the road, Suzanne pulled over. "Are you all right?" she asked, swiping tears from her cheeks.

"It stopped." His head bounced her way. "Did y'feel it too?"

"I felt your pain."

"What kind of world are we livin' in? They beat 'em, starved 'em, neglected 'em when they was sick…bloody monsters, they was."

Suzanne bent forward, resting her forehead on the steering wheel. "I didn't pick up on anything that had to do with Audra, did you?"

"No. But I'm feelin' whoever has 'er experienced pain as a child."

Suzanne closed her eyes. Stone walls surrounded her. Rats crawled beneath her feet. She was frightened, cold. Her lips quivered as she pleaded for her life…a sinister laugh echoed in the dark, dank prison; his words poison to her ears…*how does it feel? How do YOU like it—mother?*

J ake reached his breaking point. The girl was bought to fulfill his fantasies, work out his animosity toward his mother. Twenty-four hours had passed since he found her lying on the floor. He felt her forehead. *Burning up.* Fuck. He sat her up, her head lolled to one side. He opened her mouth and forced a pill down her throat, following up with a water chaser. She didn't choke. *Thank God for small favors.*

He eased her back down. No sense wasting more time watching her sleep. He had animals to tend to, he hadn't eaten…*she'll come around when she's ready*, he surmised. *Something mother would say.*

Jake locked the door behind him. On his way

outside, he stopped in the kitchen, and grabbed a box of cereal from the pantry. He hopped into his golf cart, and headed for the stone structure situated near the edge of his property.

His mother had the tower built for his seventh birthday. One of her rich "boyfriends" financed the endeavor. The guy was a sick fuck with more money than grains of sugar in a ten-pound bag. It seemed everything he touched turned to gold. The guy's parents had adopted him when he was in middle-school, left him millions when they died. Jake's mother confided that the guy landed an acting gig and made bank, winning an award for best supporting actor. As his fortune grew, so did his quest for excitement. That's where mom came in.

She was willing to role play—he was willing to pay. *Little did he know who he was playing with.* The man "accidentally" fell from the top of the turret to his death before the project was complete. Jake always wondered whose idea it was to dig a 200-foot hole in the center of the turret. His mother told police she assumed he was digging a well. When she turned on the waterworks, devastated over the tragedy, the police also fell…*fell for her lies.*

The only thing his mother ever said to him was, "Jake, you could have waited until after I married the bastard."

A year later, she married Mitchell, who added his contribution by expanding the structure. The additions included two more turrets, a bailey large enough for his mother to host events during summer months, a barbican to add strength to the structure, a drawbridge that opened over the seasonal creek running through the property, and a porticus, the metal gate that kept intruders at bay.

When it was finished, the miniature design rivaled medieval castles worldwide, and Mitchell's untimely death left his mother filthy rich.

From the beginning, the castle had been one of his mother's best kept secrets. *Her own personal torture chamber*. Few people knew the castle existed, and the ones who did, didn't dare tell for fear of being connected to the unmentionable occurrences that took place there. In winter months when deciduous trees dropped their leaves, the structure was barely visible from the air. Come March, overgrown trees and shrubbery hid the structure from sight.

Jake flashed on her next husband. *Now, there was a piece of work…the man was ten years younger, a narcissist, and very cruel.* If anyone had an ill effect on his mother, it was Gerald. Gerald fucked anything with two legs, *including her son,* and was the only one who made her cry. She took roles doing explicit love scenes to make him jealous, instead, he increased his sexual activities.

Jake was twelve when Gerald died an unfortunate death. His mother was in Europe on a film shoot. Gerald took advantage of her absence and made sexual advances toward Jake. Jake didn't want to play "horsey." A fight ensued. Jake picked up a shovel. When the police arrived and saw the condition Jake was in, they deemed the incident self-defense. Jake wasn't charged, but he was put into foster care until his mother returned to the states. When she arrived, she acted mortified, glad Gerald was dead. To think someone violated her baby boy...the performance, her best yet. *Hypocrite.* She'd been buying children from Giorgi and abusing them for years. Her and her rich friends...*Now, it's her turn to pay.*

First, he needed the girl to recover, be a worthy adversary. He paid handsomely for her, spending his mother's blood money to finance his escapade. *Why not? She taught me well. Use, abuse, hide the bodies...*

G iorgi stripped out of his swim trunks, poured himself a drink, and clicked on the TV. He wasn't expecting to see his face plastered across the screen. He picked up his phone.

"Chris, my man. Have a jet ready for me at—" he paused, checked the time on his phone, "six-thirty."

He ended the call and made another. "Put Antonio on," he demanded. He waited a few seconds before issuing his second order. "Get rid of the problem—now —do you hear me? I don't care what you have to do— do it." Giorgi hung up, mumbling under his breath, "Fuck."

. . .

Sam pulled onto Suzanne's street, when he noticed her car wasn't in the drive. He kept going, heading for home. He wanted to shower, shave, change his clothes. He felt like a rumpled mess. Inside and out.

Rhett flew him up to Tahoe, around the lake, and into Reno. They made several sweeps over Emerald Bay State Park, Vikingsholm Castle, and the Rubicon Trail. Nothing. *Where are you?* He asked himself repeatedly. One clue. *Just give me one clue.* He wasn't even sure Audra was in Sacramento. The more he thought about it, the sillier the notion became. Of all the places in the world, what are the chances she'd land in his backyard. *Suzanne has never been wrong.* Was it enough to trust her now? *You have no choice.* Trusting people wasn't one of Sam's virtues. Meeting Suzanne allowed him to get in touch with emotions he didn't realize he possessed. If there were anyone in the world he should trust, it was she…and yet…he was a cop. A detective. It was in his DNA not to trust. He needed to try harder to understand her gift and the sacrifice she was making to help him. *If only the girl wasn't my sister.*

Steaming water trickled down his body, his eyes and mouth shut tight against the spray hitting his face. He blinked water from his thick lashes. Let the air out of his lungs. He scrubbed away the ache in his limbs, the pain in his soul. Thirty-six messages from his dad waited in his voicemail. He didn't have the courage to listen. He failed them. *Failed them all.*

He turned off the water. He couldn't drown his sorrow. He tried. The water turned cold. He stepped out of the shower. Face the music. He toweled his body, and put on his favorite sweat pants. He wandered around the house, procrastinating, prolonging the inevitable. He finally picked up the phone.

"Hallo, Papa." Sam sank into a chair adjacent to the living room window. He watched the car crawling up the street, toward his house. He didn't have to think twice, he hit the floor just before a spray of bullets sent glass raining down on him.

His father's voice, barely audible in the distance, scolded. "Sam! *Was ist das für ein Geräusch?*"

Sam reached for the phone that flew from his hand when he dove for cover. "Dad, that noise was—a disturbance outside—I'll call you back."

Sam ended the call and dialed 911.

"What's your emergency?" the dispatcher asked.

"I'd like to report a drive-by shooting…"

Giorgio hurried up the steps of the Cessna Citation X+. First stop, MIA, *appropriate*, then from Miami to VIE. By the time Metzger's death hit the airwaves, he'd be in Vienna's finest hotel sipping champagne from an Austrian crystal flute. The resemblance in the drawing of the wanted man he saw on TV was too close for comfort. What gave Giorgi leeway was his clothes. The man on TV didn't seem the type to afford a

Tom Ford T-shirt or Stuart Hughes suits. He used the on-line check-out, pre-ordered a cab to the airport, and didn't plan on being seen in public for the rest of the duration. Once he was home, he could breathe easy. No one knew who he was, except for Lilly, and she was no longer a problem. His minions, knew him as Cody Smith. Most of his clients knew him as "John." No last name necessary.

It was Giorgi's job to know everything about his clients, not the other way around. Most of the time, he handled deliveries from afar...*Jake's purchase required a personal touch.* Jake's mother, Adrianne, was Giorgi's father's client for many years.

In that time, only once was there any suspicion of wrong-doing. Giorgi, only twelve years old, helped his father, Tito, with a pick up in Croatia. It was right before the country won its independence in 1995. *That* job proved to be trouble. Giorgi befriended a boy in the town square, named Filip. He gave him chocolate, and a Rubik's cube. Then, he lured the boy into an ally where one of Tito's men was waiting.

Filip was brought to the US with dozens of other misplaced orphans, who were sold to Jake's mother, Adrianne. When the boy was taken to the castle with the rest of the kids, Adrianne did a head count, and a quick critique to choose the best for herself. Filip was overlooked.

Filip, unhappy with his fate, made a run for it. He got as far as a truck stop six miles from Adrianne's ranch. He told a highway patrolman he escaped the ranch...the highway patrolman filed a "found juvenile" report and went in search for an interpreter to translate the boy's story.

When the highway patrolman dispatched a patrol car to the ranch, Adrianne denied ever seeing the boy, which was half-truth. The policeman filed a report, only stating he had interviewed Adrianne, and found nothing suspicious to corroborate the boy's story. Somehow, the story leaked to the press, and the reporters took liberty turning the film star's situation into a smear campaign. Adrianne threatened to sue for defamation of character, and the matter was dropped.

Giorgi knew they couldn't connect him to the cop's sister's disappearance, and yet, there he was, or at least his likeness, on national TV. *Fucking Rubio.* It was all his fault.

Sam swept up the glass, and waited for one of his guys to deliver a sheet of plywood from Home Depot. He expected the hitmen to return. He'd be waiting.

Robbie Platz pulled his pick-up into Sam's driveway forty minutes later. Sam opened the garage, and the two men slid the plywood off the bed, and into the house. Twenty minutes later, the hole was temporarily patched.

Sam escorted Robbie to his truck, gun in hand.

Robbie departed safely, and Sam returned to the house. He dialed his father.

"Sorry, Papa."

"What is going on, Samson? Where are you? Where is Audra?"

"I'm back home, Papa. I don't know where Audra is. I went to Vienna, met with Britta, the police…"

"It's not like her not to call."

"I know Papa. I'm doing my best to find her."

"I know you are son. What can your mother and I do to help?"

"Be there in case she finds her way home. If I find anything out, I will call you. Give Mom a hug for me." Sam hung up the phone. It rang in his hand.

"Suzanne." He poured a glass of water from the tap, and straddled a kitchen chair. "What's up?"

"Anything new?" she asked.

"Someone shot out my front window. Luckily they missed." He sounded glib. Inside, his stomach churned.

"You're kidding!"

"Wish I was. You were right—I hit a nerve—I just don't know whose."

"Lewis and I both believe the person who has Audra is rich."

"No shit."

"More sarcasm? Let me guess, the next two words out of your mouth will be I'm sorry."

"You ARE psychic!"

The click on the other end of the phone hit Sam like a

slap in the face. He redialed her number. The call went to voicemail.

"Suzanne—okay, I'm not sorry. I'm being an ass, there's no excuse. I promise not to apologize until I can assure you that I'm finished being an ass, because I don't know when that's going to be. It could be a week, a month, a year—who knows? All I ask is that you don't take it personally. I'm frustrated, pissed, a little fucked up in the head right now, and you are the only person I know who understands what its like to feel so fucking helpless. Don't come here, it's not safe. I'll call you tomorrow. Forgive me. Please."

Suzanne listened to the message. Tears filled her eyes. She wanted to believe Sam was different, that he was the one. Stress changed people, brought out the worst. *Lord knows you're not perfect.* "Give it time," Grace's words of wisdom rambled in the mix. Her therapist was right. *Focus on the things you can control.* It wasn't her place to "fix" Sam, or control his behavior. It was her job to make sure she didn't get swept away with the undertow.

Lewis made himself comfortable in front of the television. The shows were much different from home. Intense. Dramatic. Americans lacked humor. He changed the channel. He was getting quite good at navigating his way through the myriad of stations. He stopped between each channel to get a gist of the story before moving on to another. He landed on a classic movie channel, the plot thin, but a particular actress caught his eye. Beautiful. She swooped down the stairway, revealing long shapely legs, and a heavy bosom through filmy material flowing behind her. The man waiting at the bottom of the stairs was mesmerized as well. Until…he removed a pistol from his breast pocket, took aim, and put a hole in her heart before she reached the last step.

Lewis watched in horror as the woman transformed into a wolf, howling, and thrashing about…but as the animal took its last breath, it transformed back into the beauty again. The man checked her pulse, brushed her hair back from her eyes, and lifted her into is arms.

Suzanne startled him. "Isn't that what's-her-name?"

"The wolf or the actress?"

"She used to be quite popular. She's got to be in her eighties."

"I don't fancy 'er. She's beautiful, but wicked."

"Wicked?"

"Twisted."

Suzanne watched the credit scroll down the screen. "Adrianne Darr." She googled the name in her phone. A list of movie posters filled the screen. Suzanne advanced to Wikipedia. "Says here she's originally from this area. She lived in Hollywood for many years before returning to her roots. She bought a 27,000-acre ranch in Northern California, where she lives with her son, Jacob Levitz."

"A litt-le over 42 square miles. That's a kingdom."

"There has to be county records."

"Indeed."

"Why do you think she's wicked?"

"Did ye not see 'er turn into a she-wolf?"

"I thought you meant the guy was a wolf. She wasn't a wolf. He shot her because she cheated on him."

"No, Lass! She turned into a bloody werewolf after he shot 'er, and she turned back t'human again."

"Lewis, I've seen this movie several times. That's not what happened."

"Then I'must be flippin' m'lid."

"No, no. Let's think about this…there must be a reason you saw her as a wolf."

"Bugger if I know."

"Wolves, castles, cowboys…what's do they have in common?" Suzanne refreshed her phone. It was all right there. "Adrianne Darr… "Pistols and Petticoats," Medieval Warriors," "Queen Wolf," "Felicia and the Fairy Princess," "Mother, May I," a story of a woman obsessed with her son…"

Suzanne googled the name again. This time adding a current date. "Well, forget Adrianne Darr. She was last seen being wheeled on stage to speak in her hometown in Burbank, California."

"What 'bout 'er son?"

"Jacob Levitz…" Suzanne plugged the name into her search engine. Jacob Levitz was a common name. She retyped his name with actress Adrianne Darr. One listing came up. She turned the phone toward Lewis, and sighed. "It's an obituary."

"Do ye 'ave a PRO 'ere?" Suzanne's brow furrowed. "A place where they keep records…we call it the PRO in London."

"Public records office."

"We can check 'is death and 'is Mum's property."

"Who needs psychic powers when you can do old fashion detective work?"

"'Ave ye heard from Sam?"

"No, not yet." Her shoulders dropped. "I'm sure he's busy."

Lewis nodded, flashed her a sympathetic smile. "Sherlock 'olmes in the mornin' tis, then."

"Yes. Tomorrow's another day."

Audra tossed and turned in her feverish state. She was ten. Mama, Papa, and Samson were in a festive mood. It was dark…the streets, filled with families celebrating All Saints Day. A Ferris wheel in the distance terrified her. She broke away from her family and hid in the stairway leading to the church basement. She could hear her name being called, but she refused to answer, and cupped her hands over her ears. All around her, "Au-draaa, Auuud-raaa!" Perspiration beaded her forehead. She felt as though a stick had lodged in her throat. She drew her arms tight across her knees and hugged them to her chest. *If I'm very still, they won't find me.* She didn't want to ride the Ferris wheel. She didn't want to fall to her death.

She listened to her name being called for several minutes before she felt the hand on her head. *Sam.* "Audra, you don't have to hide," he said. "I won't let anything happen to you." She crouched closer to the stone wall. *Liar.*

S am parked a few houses down from Suzanne's, his eyes glued to her bedroom window. He slouched down each time a car went by. Whoever wanted to scare him, or wanted him dead, had driven by her house… had followed him here. There was no guarantee she wouldn't be their next target.

D.O.A.

Suzanne greeted the sun. She couldn't sleep. An elusive butterfly. A word on the tip of her tongue. A detail she couldn't grasp. She had an inkling of something important just outside her reach. She revisited her memories at the Preston Castle…*horrible what happened to the children there.* The energy thick, disturbing. *Neverland Park. Nothing alarming.* What then?

Her encounter with Sam? She would have to dig deep to understand how she felt about that. He was already rooted in her soul. Their love must be nourished properly or the possibility of love would die. She worried about his safety. She had the dreadful feeling someone wanted Sam dead.

A golden ray fell across her lap and stretched across the kitchen floor. She wished she could summon him to her side. Together they would begin the day. Figure it all out. Instead, she heard Lewis' soft shuffle enter the room.

"Yer up early lass, couldn't sleep?"

"Nope. Something's bugging me, I can't quite figure it out. How about you? Did you sleep well?"

"Like a wee babe–except for the movies playin' in m'mind. "'Aven't been in so long…"

"That's it!" Suzanne grabbed her phone. She typed Adrianne Darr images into Google. The photos that popped up on her screen ranged from the early seventies to the early two-thousands. "Look at her, Lew! Who does she remind you of?"

Lew took the phone from Suzanne and studied the images. His jaw dropped. "Bugger the Pope—why didn't I see this last night? The earlier photos are a spit 'n image of the lass."

"I'm calling Sam." The phone rang in her hand. "Sam? I–"

"I need to speak with you in person. Can I come by?"

The knock on the door came two minutes later. Sam appeared with a tray of coffee, and a bag of pastries. "I couldn't find scones at this hour, Lew, hope you're okay with Danish and doughnuts."

"I'm fancyin' the looks of that jelly roll," he said smiling.

Suzanne remained guarded. Sam kept his distance, physically, at least. His eyes followed her through the kitchen as she gathered plates and napkins. He noticed the dark shadows beneath her eyes. He probably had a set to match. *Neither one of us has slept.*

"I want to show you something," she said, thrusting her phone in his face.

Sam squinted at the photos. "Who–"

"Adrianne Darr. She acted in cowboy movies, medieval movies, themes Lewis and I have been seeing...*and* she owns 27,000 acres in Northern California."

Sam's eyes widened. Hope washed over his scruffy face. "I would have never—"

"Lew suggested we go to the public records office for answers. Adrianne had a son, Jacob Levine. According to Google, he died in 2015."

Sam checked his watch. "Their office doesn't open until nine. Let me see what I can find out...meanwhile, I need to move you both to a safe place."

Suzanne tilted her head. "Something you want to share?"

"A couple of goons shot out my picture window last night. They've been following me ever since I showed Audra's photo around town. They know I come here. It's not safe for you to stay here."

Suzanne's pitch lowered a notch, as if another entity was speaking through her, "They're protecting their interests, Sam—they're sex traffickers."

"All I know is I have to find my sister."

· · ·

Jake rose early. He had dismissed his staff, two weeks off with pay, the customary time it took for him to exhaust his playmates and dispose of them. During that time, he tended to his menagerie of animals. He didn't worry about his house guest. A micro-tracking device inserted under her left shoulder blade, a place she couldn't easily reach, kept her from escaping. The electrified fence installed around the perimeter of the property served to keep his animals and his guests in check. Surveillance cameras were installed throughout the 42 square miles.

All it took was one child to escape before all precautions were taken to make sure it never happened again. His dear, sweet mother saw to it that the property remained a safe haven for her devil-worshiping, and extravagant hunting parties she hosted back in the day.

When Adrianne turned seventy, she had a stroke, and required more care than her lifestyle on the ranch allowed. She moved to L.A., where she planned to remain until her death, leaving Jake to carry on in her absence. His idea of a good time wasn't inclusive. He put his own obituary in the paper. The only people he had regular contact with were three orphaned staff members, and Giorgi Von Graff, his supplier.

His mother's attorney paid all the bills, including the food, feed and essentials ordered by his housekeeper, and delivered weekly. In the years he had been flying solo, Giorgi mixed it up, sending him different ages, sexes, and races. Jake had improved his hunting skills, come to grips with his feminine side, and learned to appreciate the sinful depravities his mother and her companions indulged in regularly. The only time he entertained was when Giorgi came to town. Giorgi provided the invites, background checks, and anonymity contracts.

Jake didn't consider by the time he reached his mother's age, the money used to fund his excursions would be gone. He didn't plan that far ahead. Resentment coursed through his veins. Being denied a normal life, he cursed his existence…*and the girl lying in the other room*…the girl who looked like his mother before she destroyed his life. *The virgin.*

ROLEPLAY

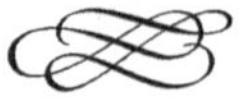

Sam, Suzanne, and Lewis bellied up to the counter at the recorder's office. "Last name Darr, D-A-R-R, first name Adrianne," Sam said.

A curly haired woman with a toothy smile replied, "Isn't that the name of that actress? Geez, is she still alive?"

"That's what we're here to find out."

"Well, if she owned property in Sacramento County, I should have it." The woman refreshed her screen, typed in her passcode, and Adrianne Darr's name. "Nothing here. Are you sure that's her real name?"

"Try Adrianne Levitz," Suzanne said.

The woman typed away. "Hm, nothing under Adrianne Levitz either."

Sam released a heavy sigh. "There has to be a way we can cross check the counties..." Sam produced his badge.

The woman glanced from one face to another, "You can find so much online these days, have you tried searching the internet? I would think with your *credentials*, you'd have access to whatever you need."

"Thanks for your time," Sam said, his smile glib. The woman's pursed lips said a lot about her willingness to help. Flashing his badge may have been overkill. He was out of his district. His title held little weight in Sacramento. *Wedding crasher.*

Sam drove down the hill to Folsom. "Early Toast" was calling his name. The host seated the three-some by the window furthest from the door at Sam's request. He would be able to keep an eye on the parking lot. So far, he hadn't noticed anyone following him since they blasted out his window the night before.

He opened his laptop. "Order what you want... everything is great. The orange juice is fresh squeezed." He busied himself logging into a program he used to access driver's licenses. He typed in Adrianne Darr. Nothing.

Suzanne and Lewis exchanged glances. Lewis leaned forward, his expression blank. "Do ye have angels nearby?"

Sam scanned his surroundings. "None that I know of."

"Ye should look harder, Jim says."

Sam raised an eyebrow. "Angels? I don't get it."

"I don't either." Lew lowered his gaze and opened the menu. "Don't suppose they serve bangers and mash…"

Suzanne interjected. "There's a town called Angel's Camp—it's quite a distance from here—hour and a half's drive."

Sam's fingers flew across the keyboard. "There's a lot of open land out there, it's worth checking out." He clicked on the plus icon to enlarge the map, and angled the screen toward Suzanne and Lewis. "see anything?"

Suzanne moved closer to the screen. "I see a lot of acreage—but nothing is standing out."

Sam moved the screen around and resumed his search. "She must go by another name. There are no DMV records for Adrianne Darr. What was the son's name?"

The waitress brought coffee. Suzanne took a sip. "Levitz, Jacob." They paused their conversation to give the waitress their full attention. Suzanne ordered a veggie omelet and orange juice, Sam held up two fingers, Lewis ordered poached eggs, a bran muffin, and juice.

"She must've filed marriage certificates," Suzanne said, holding her mug with two hands. The warmth felt good. *Cold.*

"Which one is Darr's son?" Sam asked, sharing the screen.

"Google his name with hers. You should see the obituary, but there weren't any photos."

Sam leaned back, clasping his hands over his head. "You're right. No photo. Without a photo, I'm stuck. There's fifty-seven Jacob Levitz's listed on the DMV site." He continued typing. "Twelve are either dead or driving on an expired license, eighteen are due to renew this year, twenty-seven renewed in the last two years." He slapped his hands on the table. The silverware bounced and clattered. "Damn."

"What about Darr's agent?" Suzanne asked. "He must know her real name."

Sam input the info into Google search. "Oliver Higgins. Died October 12, 2018." Sam slid his laptop to one side.

The waitress set a plate before him, then Suzanne, and Lew. She smiled at Sam. "Be back with toast. Ketchup? Hot sauce?"

"More coffee, please," Suzanne told the waitress. She then placed her hand on Sam's. "What about fellow actors?"

Sam scrolled through articles, photos, and movie clips. All of the movies Adrianne starred in pre-dated the eighties. Few had co-stars younger than her, which meant very few were still alive, and those that were, may not remember. He kept scrolling. "Well, I'll be damned."

Lewis and Suzanne froze, mid-bite. Suzanne slid into Sam's side of the booth. "Good news?"

Suzanne read aloud. "Boy accuses actress Adrianne Darr of holding him prisoner on her Calaveras County ranch." Her eyes rose to the heavens. "Thank you, Jim." She smiled at Lew. "Angels Camp is in Calaveras County."

Jake set Audra's breakfast tray on the dresser. He could see from where he stood that there was little change. He clamped his hand over her forehead. *Hot.* Her skin was clammy, her hair wet. He rolled her to one side, and felt the heat from her back. The antibiotic wasn't working. Dark shadows circled her long lashes, her cheek bones protruded from her face. Her lips, cracked and dry, had not uttered a word in days.

Unnerved, Jake lifted one lid, then the other. The girl's pupils were dilated. Her condition seemed grave, but Jake refused to be alarmed just yet. *Not your first rodeo.* He had witnessed his mother in this condition many times. He knew what to do.

Audra dreamt she was seven. Christmas day. *My sled.* Sam insisted she ride with him down the hill to make sure it was safe. She refused. She wanted to ride solo. The snow was *icy.* She flew down the hill unaware that the bottom had been bathed in sunlight all after-noon. *Hot?* The snow had turned into a slushy pond. She lost control, plunging in *arsch* first. The water was cold. *So cold.*

WATER

Sam slid behind the wheel, Suzanne took the passenger side, Lew took the backseat. "Calaveras County Sheriff's department promised to get back to me. The dispatcher vaguely recalls rumors of the ranch being haunted, satanic rituals, animal sacrifices, but nothing about pedophilia."

"But they gave you an address, right?"

"I need a warrant to step one foot on the place."

Suzanne raised her brow. "You'd think they'd be eager to help."

Sam pulled onto the freeway heading east. "You'd think. Got the feeling I stirred a hornet's nest." Sam peered into the rearview-mirror at Lew. He looked peaked. "You okay, Lew?"

"We'd better shake a leg. The lass rode 'er sled into the pond."

Lew's words kicked Sam in the gut. The memory

flashed through his brain with lightning speed. "Did you see something, Lew?"

"Ol' Jim's nickin' m'thoughts. That's what 'e said."

Sam glanced intermittently into the rear-view mirror, reliving the memory as he spoke. "St. Nicholas brought Audra a sled for Christmas when she was seven. I took her to Camp King Oberusel so she could try it out. I wanted to ride with her on the first run, but she insisted she wasn't a *säugling*. A baby. And due to *my* immaturity, I let her go."

Suzanne's curiosity piqued, "Was it steep? Did she get hurt?"

Sam shook his head. "No, she made it down the hill just fine…however, the sun had melted the snow at the bottom of the hill, and she landed in a substantial puddle." He chuckled wistfully. "She was soaked." He glanced at Suzanne. "We never thought to bring a change of clothes, and the heater in the car sucked. She shivered all the way home."

"D'ya know t'meaning of it all?" Lewis asked.

"Not sure," Sam said. "All I know is that my parents weren't happy. Audra came down with pneumonia and almost died."

J ake dunked Audra repeatedly under water as if he were dredging chicken in an egg wash. Vivid recollections of past experiences numbed his brain.

The first time his mother took Adrenochrome, she

had a reaction. Despite her concerns, friends encouraged her to indulge. It didn't take much convincing. Jake begged her not to do it, but in hindsight, she probably took it in spite of him. It was her way of getting back at him for ruining her perfect body. For aging her prematurely, for his need to be breastfed, or lifted out his urine-soaked bed. He learned at an early age to be seen and not heard. By the time he was ten, he served his purpose convincing the children his mother purchased to cooperate in the "games." He kept them from revolting by sneaking food and water into the cages while his mother fucked three or four guys in the bedroom, in the name of the Prince of Darkness.

When Jake turned thirteen, he was initiated into the coven. His proof of allegiance to Satan was to kill his only friend. His dog, Patches. A dog that wandered onto the property, suffering from mange. Jake hid Patches in the castle, nursed him back to health. Instead of decapitating the dog, like he was supposed to, he put Patches in a pillow case, and stashed him in the back of a grocery delivery truck, in hopes the dog would find a good home.

Jake grew up in a secret garden, denouncing God, defiling His creations, and serving the woman who detested his very existence. Was Karma in play? He desired to seek revenge through this virgin—purchased for an obscene amount of money—money that could have sustained him for five years.

He dunked Audra once more, pulling her up by the

hair before she drowned. He wanted a replica of his mother…and that's exactly what he got. In his mind, he had performed this same ritual on his mother many times. How easy it would be to lose sight of his goal. *Drown the bitch, right here, right now.* No. He had other plans. He wanted her to taste the fear his mother had instilled for most of his life. He wanted her to scream, shake until <u>her</u> bladder let loose, until fear squeezed the air from <u>her</u> lungs, and made <u>her</u> heart feel as though it were about to explode. And once he caught her, he would fuck her until her eyes rolled to the back of her head, humiliate her until she cried for mercy. And THEN he would kill her. *Die,* something he wanted to do every day of his miserable life.

BABYTALK

Sheena phoned her pediatrician. "Emmett's fever went from 104 to 100 in a matter of minutes, should I be concerned?" Sheena listened, her eyes on her toddler, snuggled in a chair with his favorite blanket, a stuffed horse, named "Brownie," a book about a jumping frog named Joe, and a T-shirt with a skull, a guy named Kurt bought her when they attended the Calaveras County fair her freshman year in college. She thought it odd that he dug it out of a bag of clothes she packed for Hospice a week ago. "No, I didn't give him anything. He doesn't seem to have another tooth coming in…uh, huh, uh, huh. Okay." Sheena hung up the phone.

"Well, buddy, Dr. Colasanti said if you're not better by tomorrow to bring you by for a visit. What do you think?" Sheena felt Emmett's forehead. "You feel a lot cooler, baby. Let's take your temp." Sheena held a digital thermometer to her son's forehead. The thermometer vibrated. "99.1," she said. "That was a fast recovery," she said, kneeling by his side. "What's going on?" she asked, more out of curiosity than concern.

Emmett threw the horse and frog off the chair. He twisted the T-shirt, and grunted, pulling it until his face turned red.

Sheena sat back on her heels, watching her son traverse through emotions he wasn't equipped to handle. Frustration, and fear reflected in his heterochromatic eyes made her heart break. "C'mere, Buddy," she said, lifting him into her arms. She held him close and whispered, "Mommy loves you."

J ake carried Audra back into the bedroom, where he towel-dried her hair, pulled one of his mother's flannel gowns over her head, lifted her into bed, and covered her in a down comforter. "I'll give you one more day," he warned, "then…well, as mama once told me, 'you'll just have to buck up bucko.'"

"O fficer Tom Jensen, Calaveras Sheriff's department calling for Sam Metzger," the voice announced over the car speaker, when Sam picked up.

"Speaking," he said.

"I understand you're trying to obtain information on Darr Ranch."

"It's detective Sam Metzger—I have reason to believe a woman is being held captive on the Darr ranch."

"Ohhh. Really? And what makes you think that?"

"I have my sources. I was told I'll need a warrant. I'm on my way to the courthouse as we speak."

"You're wasting your time. Mrs. Darr no longer lives on the ranch."

"And her son?"

The officer cleared his throat. "Well, detective, I believe Jacob died a few years back…"

"I wasn't able to find records of his death."

"The place hasn't been occupied in—"

"What can you tell me about the boy that claimed to have escaped from the ranch?"

"Geeeez, that was years ago. Seems the kid was a runaway. There was no evidence to substantiate his accusations."

"Do you happen to know Adrianne Darr's real name?"

"Hm, that's not her real name? I wasn't aware of that. Always knew the place as the Darr Ranch."

"What do you know about a castle on the property?"

"Where are you getting your information from?"

"Are you saying there is no castle?"

"I'm saying I haven't been out there in years. Been no reason to."

"How about an address? I can check for myself."

"De-tec-tive, why would you want to waste taxpayers money? I told you, there's nothing out there."

"With all due respect, I'd like to see for myself. Address, please?"

"Really, detective, I—"

"Officer Jensen, is there a problem?"

"Maybe you better stop by the station before you head to the courthouse. After all, you <u>are</u> out of your jurisdiction."

J ake turned on the monitor and left the room where Audra slept. She felt cooler to the touch, but her temp rose two points from the time he retrieved her from her ice bath. He was hungry. Soup sounded good. The girl could use nourishment as well.

When Jake's phone rang, it startled him. He dropped the spoon he was stirring with into the soup. Hot broth scalded his skin. "Mother fucker!" He threw the phone across the room, shattering the device into tiny pieces. Officer Jensen's call went unanswered.

LULLABY

"I'm here to see Officer Jensen," Sam said, reaching into his pocket and producing his badge. The woman behind the desk squinted, withdrew a pair of reading glasses from the edge of the pencil holder, and took another look.

"Well," she said, country slow, "Ya just missed him."

"How can I reach him? It's important."

The woman made a clicking sound with her tongue, and called over her shoulder to a man sitting at the back of the room. "Leonard? C'mere, would'ja?"

Leonard eased his way up to the desk. "Can I help you?"

"I spoke with Officer Jensen earlier regarding the Darr ranch. I need an address." Sam spun his badge around to face Leonard.

"Something happen that I'm not aware of —*detective?*"

"We have reason to believe a missing girl may be held captive there."

"I doubt it. That place is a fortress…been abandoned for years…ever since Ms. Darr went into a home. Poor dear, first her son, then her health…"

"Funny, I can't seem to find any information on Jacob's death, there are no records pertaining to Ms. Darr's property, no DMV records…" Sam pierced Leonard's good ol' boy persona with his cold stare. "Seems like Ms. Darr has something to hide."

Leonard blinked a few times, collecting himself. "You know how it is with those Hollywood celebrity types…they do their best to protect their privacy."

"I only want to take a look, my lead may be nothing…but I do have an obligation to the tax-payers to serve and protect their best interest, and right now a young girl is missing."

Leonard side-stepped to a computer, clicked a few keys, and hit enter. "I don't see any recent missing person reports," he said, his features twisted into a stink face. "When was the report filed?"

"Two weeks ago, in Vienna Austria."

"What the hell she do—swim here?"

"She was smuggled here by a human trafficker."

Leonard shifted his weight. "You don't say?"

"I don't expect you to keep up on international trade, I just want an address so I can collect my paycheck with a clear conscience."

"It's customary to forward information to the

different counties. Sounds like this is personal, you being from Goldorado County, and all," he said, taunting Sam for a rise.

"Personal?" Sam sneered. "Very."

Leonard lowered his gaze to the computer, his finger's poised on the keys. "What's the girl's name?"

"Audra," Sam said, his tone sharp, tempered steel. "Audra *Metzger*."

Audra's breath echoed in her ears. The metronome in her chest beat at the lowest point of the spectrum. In her mind, her eyes were open, her cheeks inflated with air, her lips sealed tight. *Go to the light*, the voice inside her head urged. However, her soul differed. She heard her Oma's sweet voice recharging her spirit with "*Guten Abend, gut Nacht*," a lullaby she sang when Audra was a little girl: "*Guten Abend, gute Nacht, mit Rosen bedacht, mit Näglein besteckt, schlupf unter die Deck: Morgen früh, wenn Gott will, wirst du wieder geweckt, morgen früh, wenn Gott will, wirst du wieder geweckt.*" Tomorrow morn, if God wills, you'll awake once again. *Tomorrow morn, if God wills, you'll awake once again.*

When the fist pounding and handle jiggling stopped, Jake grabbed his shotgun and charged out the door. "What the fuck are you doing here? How did you get in?"

Officer Jensen leaned against the cruiser, a toothpick hanging from his thin lips. "Thought you outa know some detective from Goldorado County is about to pay you a visit."

"You don't know how to use a phone?"

"Called you three times. You didn't pick up."

"Must've been indisposed."

Officer Jensen spit the toothpick from his mouth. "That's what he's coming to talk to you about. Seems he's got his tighty-whities in a bunch over some missing girl."

Jake's eyes narrowed. "I have no idea what you're talking about. Now get the hell off my property before I—"

"Before you what, Jake? Call the cops?" Jensen's cocky smirk disappeared, he stood erect, and took one step forward. "Well, well, what do we have here?"

Jake raised the barrel of the gun, his head swiveled to the right, catching a glimpse of the girl hanging on to the front door handle before she collapsed in the doorway. He turned back, cocked the lever on the shotgun, and blasted Officer Jensen to the ground.

Jake swept the girl up by the arms. He dragged her to the bedroom, hoisted her onto the bed, removed a pair of hand-cuffs from the nightstand, and latched her to the bedpost. He didn't have time to chase after her, *at least not now.*

He grunted, lifting Jensen's limp body into the cruiser. He slid behind the wheel and sped across his property heading northeast towards the castle. He reached in his pocket for his trusty fob. *Shit*. He jumped back into the vehicle and sped back to the house. He left the cruiser running as he sprinted into the house, grabbed the fob, and sped off again. If Jensen wasn't yanking his chain, the detective could arrive at any minute. He needed time to get back and hide the girl.

He clicked one button on the fob to open the drawbridge, the second opened the portcullis. Once in, a lever, hidden behind one of the stones opened a trap door leading to an underground garage. There, Jake swapped the cruiser for a golf cart, jumped in and raced for home.

When he entered the house, he heard the buzzer go off for the perimeter alarm. *Show time*.

Sam received more information from the local grocer than he did from the police department. Seems everyone in town knew where the Darr ranch was. *Everyone but the police.*

The trio wound down Highway 16, through Angels's Camp, and picked up 108. The Darr Ranch covered both Calaveras and Tuolumne Counties. Their instructions were to look for a rusty windmill past New Melones Lake and make a left. Take the narrow-unmarked road to the end and take a right. After that, good luck. "Darr ranch has better security than Ione prison," claimed an elderly gentleman with a bushy beard. Sam's curiosity was piqued.

Lew opened his window and stuck his head out. "Ol' Jim is doing a jig. 'E says life is a stage, not t'fall for any bunk."

"Sounds like Jim and Jack missed their calling…they should've been detectives."

Lew chuckled. "'E means well."

Suzanne chimed in, "Jim's right. I get the feeling our presence is expected. Time to hide the bodies, is what Jack would say."

"Leave the police work up to me," Sam said, his voice laced with sarcasm. "I'm a professional."

At the end of the dirt road, Sam turned right. They bumped along until they stumbled upon a thirty-foot chain-link gate, attached to thirty-foot fencing trimmed in razor wire. Sam picked up a stick and poked the fence. As expected, a strong electrical current zapped the stick into a cinder. Sam pressed the button on the call box to the right of the gate. After a moment. he heard a voice.

"Ola'."

"My name is Detective Sam Metzger. I'd like to come in and speak with you."

"*No Inglés.*

"*Ven a hablar.*"

"What do you want? I'm just the housekeeper."

"I want to come in and speak to you. It won't take long, I promise."

Sam heard the gate buzz, and pushed the handle. Suzanne and Lewis stood by the car waiting for Sam's signal to advance, but he held up his hand to halt. He unlatched his holster, then the safety clip, when he heard, "Bring your friends. Leave the gun on the hood of your vehicle."

Sam obliged. He figured he was being watched, and had planned ahead. He waved to Lewis and Suzanne, who were also prepared with bullet proof vests beneath their clothing. Just in case. It was highly unusual to involve civilians in police work, but he needed them to help find his sister.

The sprawling residence in the distance belonged in the Hollywood Hills. The dry fountain centered in the circular drive rivaled those in Europe, with its rearing white marble equine figure, eyes wide, flaring nostrils, open jaw. Sam remembered his teachings about the Four Horseman of the Apocalypse. The white horse represented the *anti-Christ*.

Suzanne shivered. "I don't like this place," she whispered. She peered over her shoulder at Lew, who had slowed his pace. "You all right, Lew?"

"Been better," he huffed.

The girl tucked away in one of the secret soundproof chambers his mother had built for her escapades gave Jake time to don a pair of glasses, and remove his front partial. He had darkened his greying hair with the spray color his mother used on set in her hay-day, switched his bloody Tommy Bahama shirt for a Led Zeppelin tee, his Guess jeans for a pair of paint stained board shorts, and jammed a feather duster in his back pocket. *Ready.*

He paced back and forth in front of his surveillance monitor. The detective appeared to be in good shape. He could almost smell the woman's fear. The man who lagged behind reminded him of the drunks that staggered around the house during one of his mother's soirees. Actors, producers, directors, politicians...clergymen...influential men and women who got their jollies worshipping Satan, participating in orgies, defiling children, then returning to their high-profile positions and their sainthood on Monday, making decisions for the masses, making cash donations to one cause or another. The do-gooders of the world. *Mother.*

Jake opened the front door, confronting the detective with his abrasive demand. "Show me your badge."

Sam produced his badge. "May we come in?" He nodded toward Lewis. "My friend here could use a glass of water. He went through open-heart surgery recently."

Jake laughed. "Gee, shall I make lunch too?"

Suzanne stepped forward and smiled. "Just the water—please."

"Wait here."

Sam pressed tape strips on the inner and outer door handles, flipped the film side over each strip, and stuck them back in his pocket. Jake returned with the water.

"Okay, state your business. I have this big-ass house to clean before six tonight. I'm meeting friends at Olive Garden. The five-dollar meal deal ends at nine, and I have a long drive."

"Where is the owner?"

Jake rolled his eyes. "I'm hired by an agency. They don't tell me shit." He placed his hands on his hips. "Anything else?"

"I'd like to come in and look around."

"Correct me if I'm wrong, but every cop show I've watched on TV indicates you need a warrant."

"Only if you have something to hide."

"Did you not hear me? I'm busy! I've already spent too much time. I could've had one of the bathrooms cleaned!"

"A girl is missing."

"And you think she's here?" He laughed. "And how do you suppose she got in?"

"I could review the surveillance tapes…"

"And I could lose my job. Get a warrant." Jake pushed the door closed; Sam stopped it with his foot. Jake flung it open. "What?"

"I'll be back," Sam said, his eyes, lethal. "And I will kill anyone who hurts her."

Jakes pupils dilated. Sam took one step back as the door slammed. He did an about face. "What do you think?"

Suzanne and Lewis spoke in unison. "She's in there."

S uzanne's brain buzzed with images, fragments of Audra's face, and a room she had seen years ago in a movie with Jodie Foster. *Panic Room.* But this one was different…this one was made for–*kittens.*

Lewis's head began to spin. He bent down and put his head between his knees. "I feel sick."

"Is it your heart?" Suzanne leaned over the front seat. "Tell us what to do. Do you need a hospital?"

"It's me stomach. I dunno. Came on so quick."

Sam put the car in reverse. "I'm taking you two back to the house."

"You need us," Suzanne protested.

"I need a swat team!"

"She's in a safe room." Suzanne closed her eyes, then opened them. "In the back of the house. There's no door."

"How do I get in?"

"It'll come to me." Suzanne squeezed her eyes shut. The bumpy road made it difficult to concentrate. "I can see the room—"

"I need more!" Sam snapped.

Suzanne clicked her seatbelt, and faced forward. She swallowed her anger, and focused on Audra. "Call the FBI."

"I have no proof."

"You will when those fingerprints match Jacob Levitz's."

"If."

She whipped her head to face him, her eyes flashing. "You can either be a pessimist, or an optimist—you can't be both."

Sam checked the rear-view mirror. Lewis glared back. "You're right." Sam stopped the car. He selected a number on his phone and hit send. A man's voice responded with a greeting on the other end. "Andrew–Sam. I need your help."

Andrew buzzed Sam, Suzanne, and Lewis into his office. "It's the best I could do," Sam said, handing Andrew the prints.

Andrew led the trio through a maze of cubicles into a brightly lit lab. "We just need something to match the prints to our data base. If he has publicly announced his demise, and is posing as someone else, we may have enough…but I'm not going to blow smoke, buddy, it's highly unlikely the FBI will step in."

Sam raked his salt and pepper hair with his fingers. "What about the lack of cooperation from the local P.D.?"

"She's there," Suzanne piped in. "Lew and I both felt it."

Andrew gave Suzanne the once over. "I'm sorry, I didn't catch your name."

"My name isn't important. A young woman's life is at stake. She doesn't have much time. And now that her captor knows we know, there's no telling what he'll do."

"The place is the devil's playground." Lewis said, "There's children everywhere," he added. "Dead children."

Andrew squinted at Lew. "How do you know that?"

"Jim told me."

Andrew clapped his hands together. "And where is this Jim? I would love to know where he gets his information."

Lew shuffled his feet. His desperation vented Suzanne's way. "This wanker isn't going to help us."

Suzanne tapped Sam's shoulder. "Lew's right, we're wasting precious time. Let's go."

"I'm sorry I got you involved in this mess, Lew."

"Ye didn't put the visions in m'head now, did ye lass?"

"It's difficult getting the police to believe you. I encountered the same resistance when Sam and I worked together before." She sighed in resignation. "Sam is very good at his job. I sometimes feel I am more of a hindrance than help, but if we keep working together, we may eventually synchronize."

"If I was wearin' 'is shoes, I'd be bonkers. The lass isn't well. She needs t'be found soon, or she'll die."

• • •

S am peered over Andrew's shoulder. The technician processed three partial prints of the tape. The computer program scanned through millions of prints, searching for a match. The program stopped, prompting a name, address, and DMV photo. "Here we go," Andrew said, hitting the print option. He hit continue, and waited for the printer to spit out the first profile. He briefly studied the document and handed it to Sam.

THOMAS WAYNE JENSEN

DL: B7726693

DB: 06-24-81

ADDRESS: 15224 Peach Blossom Rd.

Angels Camp, Ca. 95732

ORGAN DONOR X

S am pointed at the screen. "That's the officer who wouldn't cooperate."

"Okay, I'll admit something stinks, but is it enough?" Just then, the program stopped again, prompting another name.

JACOB LEE LEVITZ

DL: N/A

DB: 09-23-62

ADDRESS: 666 LEVIATHAN WAY

ANGELS CAMP, CA. 95732

. . .

"Check out the address!" Andrew scooted his chair to the side.

Sam moved closer. "The sign of the devil, and the gatekeeper of hell."

Andrew scrolled down. "These finger prints were obtained from a mortgage company. Jacob's name was entered on the title to the property twelve years ago, but —" He scrolled down further. "The property was taken over by a firm, Mammon and Asmodeus. Now that's creepy."

Sam shrugged. "Sounds Greek to me."

"You don't know your bible, buddy. There are seven demon brothers, seven sins. Lucifer, pride, Mammon, greed, Leviathan, envy, Satan, wrath, Asmodeus, lust, Beelzebub, gluttony, Belphegor, sloth. They used three of the names right here, I'm sure somewhere they've used them all."

Sam raised his brow. "Why make it so obvious?"

"That's their way. In our face. I went to a Catholic school. I know this shit."

Sam nodded. "Do we have enough to get a warrant?"

"I can do even better…"

Tears poured down Suzanne's cheeks. Terror ripped at her soul. She could almost feel his hot breath in her ear. "How do _you_ like it?" he said.

Suzanne looked down; blood droplets bloomed on the front of her blouse. She couldn't move her feet. Shackles burned her wrists…the stampede in her chest reached her ears, the top of her head throbbed, ready to burst. The car door slammed, and she screamed.

Lewis grabbed her shoulders. "Calm down lass, be still."

Sam held her face in his hands. "Suzanne, it's not real. Breathe."

She looked haunted. "Oh, it's real…Very real."

"Our experience didn't go as planned," Jake said, as he positioned Audra's body on the altar. He held her feet in place with a thick leather strap, shackled her wrists to heavy gauged iron chains above her head. "I wanted to play… just like we used to…only I wanted to scare <u>you</u> this time. You always got to be the villain. I always got locked inside the castle, while you watched them do things to me from your throne. You watched them hunt me down– rape me–you heard my screams–and you did *nothing*."

Jake stripped naked and donned one of the red satin robes he pulled off a wooden rack bolted to the wall. He laid an assortment of daggers near Audra's feet. He smoothed damp hair back from her feverish forehead. "We could've had fun…why did you have to get sick?" He kissed the tip of her nose. "Do you remember when I had chicken pox? That's the only time you showed any concern...any compassion. I always envied the children you brought here. At least you put an end to their misery."

Audra couldn't find her way through her mental haze certain she had entered the gates of hell. Her flesh burned. Her bones felt broken. When she opened her mouth to scream beetles scurried down her chin, tickled her neck, marched between her bare breasts down to her belly. She couldn't see them, but she knew where they were headed...they would climb inside her, lay their eggs. The image triggered *Belvedere Gardens*; she was five. Sam picked a flower and placed it in her hair. She was so happy, so proud of her flower, she was a princess. Suddenly, dark clouds gathered overhead, the wind blew wicked and fierce. A beetle escaped from the flower and perched on her cheek. Paralyzed with fear, she screamed for Sam, but he was gone.

OPEN SESAME!

Andrew gave the signal. Thirty men dressed in S.W.A.T. gear spread out. Two men installed a cut-off switch, disarming a large section of the electric fence. Using heavy-duty bolt cutters, they removed a chain link panel. The other twenty-eight men checked weapons, and set up surveillance equipment. Once inside the property, the men scattered, taking positions around the perimeter of the house. Several engaged drone equipment to scan the property for a heat source.

Sam kept his phone open to receive Suzanne and Lewis' assessment. "The castle is hidden toward the back of the property," Lew said. Sam gave a directive to Andrew, who in turn dispatched men accordingly.

Sam and Andrew approached the front door to the house and found it unlocked. The two men split up; guns drawn. "Clear," Sam announced into the mic attached to his headset. "Going upstairs,"

Andrew went from room to room, finding each one empty. Sam inspected a statue of a horned figurine with angel's wings, strategically placed on a crescent shaped table between two rooms. He found a button on the bottom of the base, and pressed it, aware that he may have opened Pandora's Box.

Inside the room to his left, a panel slid open, revealing a stairway. He cocked his Glock 17, and proceeded with caution. When he reached the fifth stair, he saw the contents of the room below. A bed, an end table with a ballerina lamp, and a wall decked with chains, shackles. A printed poster, one would expect to see in a pediatrician's office, depicting growth measurements hung on one wall.

Next to the poster, Sam saw a metal cart with a tray. He stepped in for closer inspection...scalpels, rubber tubing, a tooth extractor, and an assortment of wire speculums for keeping one's eyes open. He revisited the bed. The sheets were rumpled, making Sam believe his sister had been in the room, perhaps when they paid Jake a visit earlier. He smoothed the sheet, imagining Audra's life essence on his fingertips.

"Metzger!" Andrew shouted, "Come up here."

Sam left his apprehension in the room and jogged upstairs to meet Andrew.

"Couple of things I want you to see," he said, leading Sam down a long hallway. "Let's go in here first."

Sam whistled low as they walked into an elaborate

looking conference room. "Geezus." His stomach churned as he spied the artwork on the wall. Children being violated by adult figures wearing animal heads, men dressed as bunnies, sodomizing toddlers, scenes of torture, and blasphemy. Crosses hung upside down. On a credenza at the far end of the room was a painting of thirteen adults, dressed in red robes. Sam zeroed in on a petite figure, a woman, with a small naked boy kneeling at her feet, a metal collar attached to a chain, around his neck.

Andrew came up behind him. "I'm not a profiler, but I've read about these cases. A child who has been a victim of so-called satanic ritual abuse forms an attachment to the abuser when it's someone they rely on for their survival, like a family member, a neighbor, clergymen, or any trusted adult." Andrew pointed to the petite figure in the photo. "In this case, Jake's mother. I'd say this guy most likely has suffered displacement, and is acting out the evil that has been done to him under the guise of Satanism or some other cult."

Sam shook his head, sickened by the thought. "You said there is something else you want me to see?"

Andrew patted Sam on the back. "Yeah, c'mon." He escorted Sam to a room the size of a master bath filled with monitors. Each monitor, assigned to a particular area, revealed activity. The men saw the S.W.A.T. team in action. Sam wondered how many of these rooms there were. Andrew pointed to a wall made of stone. "Do you see what I see?"

· · ·

Suzanne left Lewis alone in the car. She walked over to the missing fence panel. She closed her eyes summoning Audra's face. Her mind's eye produced a woman who could've passed for Audra's double. One woman's soul, tormented, the other's soul void of redemption.

Suddenly, a sharp pain pierced the bottom of Suzanne's foot. Blood filled her mind's eye. She heard chanting, the voice summoning the beast. Fear clutched her heart in a tight squeeze. Lights danced in her periphery. She collapsed on the ground.

Lewis sat in the backseat of the car feeling useless. "Bugger me, Jim," he whispered. "You said find the lass. Now what—sit on me arse while the police grope in the dark? Give a chap a lift, ol' friend. Where is she?"

The hair on Lewis's arms stood up. Visions swam in his head. Castles, demons, daggers, and blood.

Sam and Andrew radioed the team. They directed the drone operator to where they had seen the castle on the monitor. Their drone operator zoomed in on an area toward the back of the property. Mindful of cameras and traps, the duo took off running. Dogs, barking in the distance, sounded stationary, as if they were penned. After about a mile, they caught a glimpse of the castle, nestled between sequoias, shrubs, ferns, and berry bushes. The lush greenery muffled their foot-fall as they ran toward the structure. But what they hadn't figured out was how to get in.

Lewis helped Suzanne to her feet. He grabbed a bottle of water from the car, uncapped it, and brought it to her lips. "Slow and easy, lass."

Suzanne bent over, her hands on her knees. "This is the part that sucks. I can feel her pain, and I can't do a damn thing to help her."

"Take another sip, we'll figure it out."

Suzanne snapped at him, "You got any brilliant ideas? I sure don't." She stood erect, swiping her hands through her hair, her tone softer. "Now who's getting testy?"

"Don't ye start apologizin' now. Audra's in the castle. I see her, she's lying on a stone slab, shackled. He's performin' some kind of a ritual."

"We can't go in there," she said. "The S.W.A.T. team has direct orders to—"

"Y'got yer phone. Call Sam, tell him I see a foot-bridge on the north side of the buildin'. Jim says every-thin' is hidden in plain sight."

Sam led Andrew and his team to the north side of the castle. There, they found the footbridge, just as Lew described. Once inside, they examined the stone blocks for buttons and levers. After a thorough search, they found one that opened a stone panel leading to a stairway. The men split up, filing down dank narrow hallways. Sam and Andrew took the stairs leading to an underground garage where they found a police cruiser with Officer Jenksen's dead body inside. Beyond that, an iron grate blocked the entryway to what looked like a tunnel.

"Hold the light," Andrew commanded, extracting a small case from his vest pocket. He chose two picks, stuck them inside the lock, working his magic. When he heard the locking mechanism click, he twisted the shaft releasing it from the body. He discarded the lock, and unlatched the grate. They followed the tunnel at a quick pace, checking the walls for inconsistencies. The tunnel veered to the right, taking them into the heart of the castle. Sam followed Andrew, tapping on the walls. After fifty feet they heard a hollow *thud*.

Audra opened her eyes in disbelief. *I must be dead.* She saw the devil hovering over her naked body, anointing her with her own blood. His eyes, burning hot coals made her think of paintings she saw at the Belvedere castle depicting chaos, pillars of fire, demons swarming sinners, devouring their souls. Here, there was only one demon. Perhaps the rest were on holiday? Or maybe her sins were unworthy. She had never felt the need to go to church, which was always a strike against her when arguments ensued with her parents regarding her independence. "I'm a good girl," she murmured. She never imagined she'd end up in hell. Yet, *here I am.*

"You were never a good girl, Mother." Jake said flatly. "Look at what you created? The devil's spawn." His laughter echoed inside the chamber. "And now you get to feel <u>my</u> wrath."

Jake ran the tip of the dagger between her breasts. "I remember begging you—begging you to play with me, begging you to love me, begging you to make them stop. Do you remember what you told me?" He yanked Audra's hair, forcing her to face him. "You told me pain tempers a soul. You said if I learned to enjoy the experience, that one day I would enjoy inflicting pain on others. Well, you got your wish. Now it's *your* turn."

"I am NOT your mother," Audra cried. "I could never be so cruel," she sobbed.

"Cruel? Is that what you call what you and your friends did to me? To all those children?" Jake shook his head, his tone adamant. "Torture, mother. I'd call it *torture.*"

S uzanne's eyes scanned the room as the observer. Audra, chained as Lew had said, was conscious, and pleading for her life. The man stood over her, a dagger poised in his grip. Behind him, a rack of red satin robes, hanging from hooks. To the left of the table, she saw a stone wall, shifting her sight to the right, *a door*. She imagined Sam on the other side. *So close.*

Sam ran his hand along the vertical seam, feeling for anything that would serve as a latch, or lever. Nothing. He pounded on each stone block until he heard a thud. He lit the area with a flashlight, discovering one corner of the stone was worn. Slipping his fingertips beneath the worn area, he discovered a lip, and pulled. The stone cover opened, revealing a pin pad.

Andrew peered over Sam's shoulder. "Appears to be a mechanical keypad. Step back." Andrew produced a gadget the size of a flip phone and held it over the keypad. "19-1-20-1-14, there we go." The door opened. "Works on an alphabetical sequence."

"What did you spell?"

"Satan."

Jake whipped around, facing Sam and Andrew, their guns drawn. He moved closer to Audra, placing the dagger at her throat. "Stay back, or I'll kill her!"

Andrew stayed back. Sam stepped forward, dropping his gun to his side. "You don't want to do that Jake. Your mother would be so disappointed."

"You know nothing about my <u>mother</u>."

Sam swept the room with his open hand. "You spend a lot of time down here, Jacob? Mom set you up with your own little torture chamber? Is that why you faked your death?"

"<u>She</u> was the devil, not me!"

"Prove it," Sam said. "Put the knife down. Move away from the girl."

Jake pressed the dagger further into Audra's flesh, drawing blood. Sam raised his gun, and shot one round, grazing Jake's ear. "The next one will hit between your eyes."

Jake dropped the knife, and crumbled to the floor. Sam grabbed a robe from the hook, covered Audra, unlatched her shackles, and gathered her into his arms. Andrew handcuffed Jake, and read him his rights.

The S.W.A.T. team left their posts and gathered by the front of the castle. Audra was put on a stretcher, and taken to the ambulance waiting by the house. Sam dialed Suzanne. "She's safe. Audra's safe."

Suzanne heard relief in Sam's voice, through a strain of tears. Her own eyes shed tears as she hugged Lewis. "She's on her way to the hospital. Sam will call us later."

Lewis threw his hat in the air. "Did ye hear, Jim?" he cried to the heavens. "The lass is safe!"

Andrew eased Jake into a squad car, and slid in beside him. "You don't seem like the type of guy to get your hands dirty, Jake, who got the girl for you?"

"I don't know what you're talking about. The girl found me. I didn't find her."

"That's not true. The girl was kidnapped from Vienna, and brought all the way here, just for you."

"How do you know that?"

"A little birdie told me. And they put a hit out on my buddy." Andrew touched Jakes injured ear. "This is nothing. Wait 'til the boys in prison find out what you are—they are going to have one helluva good time with you, Jakey boy." Andrew sighed. "That is unless you want to share a name with me."

"Ask my mother."

"It would be so much easier coming from you."

"I only know him as Giorgi."

"Giorgi. That's a start."

ANGELS

Audra peeked under the bandage between her breasts. No stitches. She laid her head against the pillow, when she heard a knock on the door.

Suzanne entered, along with Lewis, carrying a vase filled with a colorful bouquet. "I hope you don't mind our visit. Lewis is headed back to London tonight, and he wanted to meet you before he left."

"Jim didn't tell me how beau'iful ye were, lass. I'm chuffed it all worked out."

"We're all happy you're going to be okay. Sam said they're treating you for pneumonia, and a bladder infection, but you'll be fine in a week or two."

"My brother told me how you both were instrumental in finding me." A smile brightened her face. "Thank you both."

"You're welcome. I can't help but wonder if there were—"

"Others? Yes." Audra's eyes welled with tears. "I don't know what happened to them. I was taken off the boat separately."

"Your brother is an excellent detective. He will do what he can. After all, he found you, didn't he?"

Sam arrived on cue. He kissed Suzanne on the cheek, shook Lew's hand and went to Audra's side. *"Wie geht es meiner kleinen Prinzessin?"*

"Your little princess isn't so little anymore."

Sam leaned forward and kissed her nose. "You will always be my little princess." He patted her knee. "I called mom and dad. They are relieved to say the least. I also called Britta, she was a big help. She told me about the guy you met on the train."

"Rubio."

"Yes. I'm looking into these traffickers further."

"There are others, Sam. Children. Little children."

"Yes. Andrew is working on that." He turned to Suzanne and Lewis. "I have my friends here to help as well...we'll find them."

Lew's smile faded. "Find the angels, ye'll find the children."

∾

GIORGI

Giorgi drove to his favorite flat in Salzburg, overlooking Hellbrunn Schlöss, a pleasure palace with trick fountains built in 1612 for prince-archbishop Markus Sittikus. Georgi's father had taken him to the palace when he was a child. He pointed out how humans indulged in different forms of pleasure. "Wet T-shirt" contests of yesteryear. A fornication playground. He said Master architect Santino Solari was brilliant, commending him for mixing fun and lust under the pretense of rest and relaxation. It was all there…man's appetite for all that is forbidden under God's rule, and yet Solari was commissioned to build the Salzburg Cathedral. His father claimed he was not ashamed of his profession, after all, it was not he who originated the idea.

He thought about how good it felt to be alone. Being in the U.S. gave him *agita,* and he'd been home a few hours when he heard Jake was arrested. His minions took him out before he had a chance to talk. At least that's what they claimed. The detective, the girl's brother had eluded them, but he had to trust they didn't fuck-up with Jake, and since there had been no sign of trouble, he felt assured the job was done. None the less, it never hurt to lay low.

Giorgi removed his kidskin boots and Alpaca socks. He unbuttoned the top two buttons of his Loro Piana Vicuña polo about to pull it over his head, when he heard a knock on the door. *No one knows I'm here.* He sat quietly on the edge of the bed, commending himself for remembering to latch the security chain. However, his penthouse suite was only accessible with a keycard. He got up and peeked through the fish-eye lens. *What is he doing here?*

Policeman Irlich von Steuben stood outside Giorgi's hotel room, anticipating the browbeating he would receive for daring to invade Giorgi's privacy, and worse, breaking protocol. Von Steuben knocked again, sensing the suspect's surprise, and anger, at the intrusion even before he opened the door. He was correct in his assumption.

"What the fuck do you want? How did you find me? How dare—"

Sam stepped into view. "Don't blame him, he was merely following orders." Sam gestured to the group of

FBI agents blocking each end of the corridor. Sam smiled, like a shark, about to take a bite of something tasty. "I'm Detective Samson Metzger, the brother of the girl you had Rubio kidnap for Jacob Levitz. It will be my pleasure to see these men take you into custody." He paused for effect, "Oh, and by the way, we found the kids that were taken to...*Los Angeles.*"

Giorgi's face paled. "I have no idea what you are talking about. There must be some mistake."

"No mistake." Sam nodded to the agents. "One thing the devil can never seem to grasp...the world is filled with angels..."

That morning, the L.A. Times reported:

INTERNATIONAL SEX TRAFFICKING RING EXPOSED—47 CHILDREN RESCUED

Three Arrests Include Hollywood Actress, Her Son, and Austrian Kingpin!

Following tips from Sacramento's Police Department, the FBI infiltrated a human trafficking ring selling children ages 2-17 for sex.

The sting began with the rescue of a young woman abducted in Vienna and sold to 89-year-old-actress Adrianne Darr's son, Jacob Levitz, for sex.

Ms. Darr has been implicated in past procurements and subsequent murders of sex trafficking victims. Levitz's arrest led the L.A. police department to assist agents in rescuing 47 children from a warehouse near L.A.'s garment district at 3 a.m. yesterday.

Officials also arrested the head of the multi-billion-dollar operation, Giorgi Von Graff, in Salzburg.

Detective Samson Metzger, of the Goldorado Sheriff's Department claimed the tip that lead them to Los Angeles, the "City of Angels," was truly divine.

RETURN

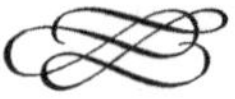

Trudy greeted Lewis with open arms. "I knew y'd come back t'me, Luv."

"Can't say I'm not chuffed t'be back." He held her tight, kissing the top of her head. "One day, I'd like t'go back t'America…see the sights…together."

"Did y'get rid of yer demons?"

"For now. We got the bloody thugs that took the girl, but I can't say the visions won't 'appen again. Suzanne said dyin' changes a bloke. I believe she's right."

Trudy patted his chest. "At least it didn't change what's in 'ere."

"If anythin'," Lew said, "m' heart grew bigger."

"Oh dear, I almost forgot." Trudy rushed out of the room and returned with a heavy box. "This arrived for ye yesterday."

Lew sliced the box open with a butter knife and hurried to examine the contents. Joy washed over his face. "For the love of muffins," he said, pulling six books written by Clive Cussler and Robin Burcell out of the box. *All signed by the author.*

Sheena peeked in on Emmett. *What a day,* she thought. Emmett's fever returned to normal out of the blue. He was sleeping soundly, which he hadn't in weeks. His tiny hands rested beneath his cheek, his features relaxed. "Sleep, my little angel," she whispered.

AMEN

Morning drizzle disappeared revealing blue skies, and sunshine. "This is it," Sam said, leading Suzanne to an iron gate. Sam handed two tickets to the young lady at the door, and ushered Suzanne to the counter to pick up headphones for tours of the lower and upper floors of the Palace.

The couple strolled through the halls admiring frescoes painted by Carlo Innocenzo Carlone, Marcantonio Chiarini, and Gaetano Fanti, just as Audra had months earlier. Sam slipped his hand in Suzanne's, "This is where the Austrian State Treaty was signed in 1955, by Leopold Figi."

"I want to see, "The Kiss," Suzanne said, her lips finding his for a brief connection.

"The Klimt exhibit is in upper Belvedere. We can go there now if you like," he said, his eyes focused on her mouth.

"It's all so beautiful, I can only imagine growing up with all this culture at your fingertips."

"Wait until you see the gardens. We can get a good look from the balconies on the second floor, but you must experience the scent, and the beautiful arrangements with a cappuccino or a picnic lunch."

"Sounds like heaven," she said, leaning closer. "I feel like I'm dreaming."

Sam wrapped his arm around her and drew her close. "I aim to please."

When the couple finished their tour, they stepped outside into the afternoon sun, cappuccinos in hand.

"This is our favorite spot," he said, nodding toward a rose garden, filled with colors fit for Monet.

Their scent perfumed the air, and Suzanne breathed deeply to capture their essence. "I could stay here forever," she said, taking a seat on a bench nearby. "I can see why this would be such a special memory for you and your family."

As if Suzanne's words manifested Audra, and the Metzgers, the couple saw them heading toward them. Sam greeted them with quick hugs, and the excitement of one about to show off a new car. "Mama, Papa, this is Suzanne."

The Metzger's extended their hands to shake Suzanne's, but Audra intercepted by rushing in for a hug. "I'm so happy to see you!" Suzanne returned the hug enthusiastically.

Suddenly, clouds gathered overhead, the sky bruised

with dark masses, swirling with thunder and lighting. Suzanne held Audra tighter. Over the girl's shoulder, Suzanne could see the reason for the sudden change. Giorgi Von Graff, strutted toward them, a black crow perched on his shoulder. His eyes, glowing hot coals, his smile, a maw of razor-sharp teeth.

Closer.

Sam sheltered his parents under both arms. The wind blew in gusts so powerful the roses were stripped bare.

Closer.

Fear bubbled in Suzanne's throat, thwarting her effort to scream.

Closer.

She tried with all her might.

Closer.

She could feel the heat from Giorgi's body.

Closer.

Inches away.

Perspiration trickled down her brow. She clutched Audra tighter, opened her mouth wide, and pushed the air from her lungs. Finally, the sound escaped with a loud shrill.

"Suzanne!" Sam shook her shoulders. "Suzanne, wake up, it's not real."

Suzanne gasped for air. "I saw him, I saw Giorgi!"

"Giorgi's in prison, he's not going to hurt you, or anyone else again."

Sam lifted her chin, his lips brushed her eyelids, her

nose, and settled on her mouth. "It's over, sweetheart. Everyone is safe."

"I had a dream…it was beautiful. We were at the Belvedere Palace, we saw all the magnificent artwork, you were showing me the gardens, we were drinking cappuccino, your parents and Audra showed up…and then…he was standing there, like the devil."

"He's evil all right," Sam said, snuggling Suzanne into his arms, "but I assure you, *he's just a man.*"

The End

ABOUT THE AUTHOR

Dänna Wilberg has written, produced, and directed multiple award-winning short films, produced and hosted TV programs in Sacramento for over a decade, and was one of the first writers to be inducted into the "A Place Called Sacramento" Hall of Fame.

Her published romantic-suspense trilogy, "The Red

Chair," "The Grey Door," and "The Black Dress," featuring young psychotherapist, Grace Simms, poses the question: What do we *really* know about another person?

Her current work, "Borrowed Time, Book 2: Missing," is the continuation of Wilberg's paranormal-suspense series, featuring "intuitive" Suzanne Cash, Detective Samson Metzger, and villains you will love to hate. The author weaves true-to-life scenarios into her story telling, and gives her muse free rein to steer her in the right direction.

Aside from writing, Ms. Wilberg loves spending time with family, spoiling her grandchildren, traveling the world, volunteering for non-profits, and singing Karaoke. She believes the universe is a mystical, magical realm of which she is blessed to be a part.

ALSO BY DÄNNA WILBERG

NOVELS

Borrowed Time Book 1 - Broken Promises

Borrowed Time Book 2 - Missing

The Red Chair

The Grey Door

The Black Dress

ANTHOLOGIES

Malice in Dallas, 2022

The Second Corona Book of Horror Stories 2018

Capitol Crimes 2017

Our Dance With Words 2015

Capitol Crimes 2008

Look for Borrowed Time Book 3 - Mind Games (2023)

COMING NEXT!

COMING 2023

Borrowed Time Book 3 - MIND GAMES

Gen-X suicides are on the rise. But why? When Suzanne Cash witnesses the aftermath of a young woman who takes her life by jumping out of a window in Paris, she is horrified. But soon, she realizes similar tragedies are filling the headlines. This young woman is not the first, and Suzanne's psychic senses switch to high alert.

Are these young victims really fed up with life? Or is there something more sinister going on? Are they out of their minds? Or is a puppet master calling the shots?

If you wish to pursue more information on this subject, the following are good resources to get you started. The more you know...

"The phenomenon of satanic ritual abuse has become popular in the last thirty years because denial is the first stage of trauma; as the sexual assault of children has been more widely acknowledged and reported by the news media, members of Western society have become traumatised by these disclosures. The reaction to this has been a generalised attempt to relegate this behaviour to outsiders, evil forces and criminal conspiracies, rather than to admit that the perpetrators are likely to be our neighbours, colleagues or relatives." — From: **"Signs of the Devil: The Social Creation of Satanic Ritual Abuse" by Morandir Armson;** https://www.academia.edu/

According to the Report from the UNODC, (United

Nations Office on Drugs and Crime) "the most common form of human trafficking (79%) is sexual exploitation. The victims of sexual exploitation are predominantly women and girls…"

…"Worldwide, almost 20% of all trafficking victims are children…"

https://www.unodc.org/unodc/en/human-trafficking/human-trafficking.html